Slowing Down Amelia

Dana Harp

Dedication

To every girl who ever wanted to grow up a little too quickly.

Contents

Prologue

1999

I might actually die.

My aunt literally just told me she was deserting me forever.

Okay, maybe not literally.

OKAY, maybe she didn't even say forever. And technically, sure, she wasn't even my aunt. But Hadley was my mom's best friend and had been in my life for as long as I could remember so as far as I was concerned, Hadley was my aunt. Mom used to tell me their friendship origin story like it was a fairytale, my favorite bedtime story.

But now? Now it felt like a mean joke. Why become my aunt, pseudo big sister, best friend, if she was going to do this? She was my go-to for everything, the things too embarrassing for my mom, the secrets too stupid to say out loud.

Like I was about to tell my mom about my middle school drama? Yeah, absolutely not.

What now? Who was supposed to fill the hole she was about to create?

"Amelia?" Hadley's cerulean eyes grew as she evaluated my reaction – or lack thereof.

The pepperoni pizza in the center of the table steamed like it was trying too hard, like it still thought it was the highlight of the night when, really, it was just sitting there, completely irrelevant.

I focused on the steam, ignoring everyone. I was not ready to look at Hadley, who was patiently waiting for me to process what she had said. Uncle Josh, who sat across from me, looked like he'd seen a ghost, and his long-time fiancé Stephanie looked like she wanted to fix something, but there was nothing to fix.

Usually, pizza nights meant laughing too loud, fighting over the last slice, and tricking mom into letting me get a refill of Coke. Tonight? Everything felt wrong.

Mom's hand landed on top of mine, giving it a gentle squeeze, grounding me back to reality, whether I wanted it or not. I swallowed hard. "Sorry, what?"

I'd heard her, we all had. But I didn't believe her.

"I said, sweetheart, I'm moving."

"But you love your condo." I sank slowly in my seat and pushed my plate away.

"I do love my condo, but I've been working with a realtor, and I found a place right in the town where my mom grew up..." She glanced across the table to Josh and gulped. He was my mom's brother, my uncle, but one of Hadley's best friends. She dipped her head and rubbed the crook of her neck but didn't say anything else.

"But you realize Montana is like an eight-hour flight, right?" My uncle croaked.

I stared at him, his mouth left parted.

I turned my body toward Hadley. "Is that how far it is? That's *literally* across the country." When I looked around the table, nobody seemed to respond to me. It's like the entire pizzeria fell silent. Tears welled beneath my meadow green eyes as my breath hitched in my throat. "Why is nobody saying anything?"

Stephanie broke the silence. "Hadley's mom grew up in Montana, sweetie. I'm sure she's told you about it before."

I nodded. I knew her mom had died when Hadley was my age and that she never really knew much about her besides that she grew up in Montana, loved horses, and was a great mother to Hadley for thirteen years before cancer took her away.

"Stephanie is right, sweetheart. Listen, I love living here near all of you. You guys are the family I was able to find during a time in my life when I so desperately needed to know I was not alone."

Hadley reached for my cheek, brushing away a tear like it was something simple. Like it wasn't proof that she was ruining everything. Her brows knit together, and for a heartbeat, her face crumbled. A shadow of sadness passed through her eyes, but she blinked it away quickly, smoothing her expression – probably hoping I hadn't noticed. I had. I wanted to swat her hand away, but instead, my fingers curled into hers, holding on even when I wanted to let go.

Soon enough, I'd have to let go.

"But what happens once you leave? You won't need us anymore."

"Miss Meels, that's outrageous. I will forever need all of you. Moving to a different state does nothing to change our love. We are family for life. We can talk on the phone whenever you want, or send emails... Heck, maybe you can even teach me that AOL messenger you girls seem to always be using."

"You're too old for IM, Aunt Hadley." I sniffled out a sad laugh.

"Ouch, I see how it is," she smiled. "Well, we'll figure it out. Once I'm settled in, I expect all of you to visit. And I'll come back and visit, too. It'll be okay, I promise." She said this last part while looking at my uncle, though her hand continued to hold tight to mine.

"I'm proud of you, Hadley," my mom finally said, dabbing a rogue tear with the edge of her white napkin. "This place will not be the same without you, but you're right... we'll figure it out. This is huge for you."

For her, maybe. For me? This was devastating. No more riding my bike down the road to her house. No more having her be the voice of reason when Mom or Dad started to act particularly overbearing. No more shopping trips or ice cream sundae movie nights.

I looked around the table, expecting to see widespread worry but, as far as I could tell, everyone was back to normal. Stephanie was leaning needily against my uncle, taking baby bird bites of her pizza. Hadley was reaching for her second slice, laughing at whatever story Josh was telling. My mom, who usually picked the pepperoni off her slices, was eating hers fully loaded. That was different. Maybe she needed the greasy comfort.

Come to think of it, my uncle would normally be three slices in by now. And while he certainly seemed normal, deep in his story, eager to make everyone laugh, his slice sat untouched.

I still couldn't understand how they'd move on so fast from Hadley's epic mic drop moment. Like this wasn't the worst day of my life. Like Hadley wasn't about to disappear from my life forever. For some reason, I was the only one who seemed to really care.

One Year Later

2000

"Can Chloe sleep over tonight?" I grabbed a handful of the trail mix from the bowl next to my mom before dropping onto the sofa, mindlessly playing with the lace hem of my tank top.

"As long as it's okay with her mom." She folded a corner in her Danielle Steel novel, lifting her reading glasses into her glossy red curls, and focused on me.

I squinted as hard as I could, trying to read the title on the cover but she was fast, it was already tucked between her thigh and the side of the sage green armchair. "Can I read that when you're done?" I attempted to nod casually toward her leg, already knowing the answer. It was the same as the last three books she read.

"You're fourteen, Meels, try again in a few years." She smirked. "So, Chloe's mom? Should I give her a call?"

"You can if you want, but she'll be fine with it. Mr. Zhang gets back from his business trip today and things usually get pretty... loud, ya know? I think Chloe and her mom would *both* like to sleep here."

"Things are that bad, huh?"

"Based on how many times Chloe tells me how lucky I am that my parents live apart? Yeah, I'd say so." I shrugged. "Which is weird, because I know I shouldn't be happy my parents are divorced but," I tossed more of the mix into my mouth, not waiting to swallow before I continued. "You guys have had different houses for as long as I can remember and you get along really well. Sometimes *too* well. Like better than all my other friends' parents do. You're even kinda flirty. It's actually very gross."

"You know, your dad was the Jonathan Taylor Thomas of our day. Total heartthrob."

"Ew, Mom." I rolled over on the sofa and covered my eyes, not wanting to watch her theatrical swoon.

"Good looks *and* a good job? Hard not to flirt with a catch like that."

"I'm literally getting sick. You know you're single, right? Why are you so gross?" I made a show of dry heaving over the side of the gold and olive plaid sofa.

Once Mom stopped laughing, she continued her sentiment. "It's a good thing that your dad and I get along, though, and you're right we've done things this way since you were a toddler. Not all kids are that lucky. We just learned we worked better as friends. It sounds like the Zhangs are going through a rough patch in their marriage, but it's a shame that it's happening in a way that's affecting Chloe."

"So I can tell Chloe she can spend the night? She really doesn't want to be there when her dad gets home."

"Of course, she's always welcome. Just make sure her mom knows where she'll be."

"Thanks, Mom." I stood up but lingered instead of rushing off, like I normally would.

"Is everything else okay? You're normally eager to call Chloe or do whatever it is you do on that AOL messenger."

"I message people, Mom. It's literally in the name."

I quickly offered a saccharine smile before she chastised my sass. Deciding how to change topics, I fiddled with the ends of my hair for a moment before shoving the pile behind my shoulders. I had inherited my mom's impossible-to-tame voluminous curls, except while mine were a light copper, I swore hers were the exact shade of a slice of pepperoni. It was way cooler.

"Anyway, I wanted to ask you about Aunt Hadley."

"Aunt Hadley? Well that's random. You usually find us old folks to be *such a drag*."

"Nobody says that, Mom. I just remembered hearing you say something to Dad about how she found that riding ring her mom used to work at. I wanted to know how that went. I haven't gotten to talk to her in a few weeks." I walked over, grabbing the entire bowl of trail mix this time, and sank against the arm of the couch, stretching my legs out across the cushions.

"Why the sudden interest? You don't want to let Chloe know she can come spend the night before her dad gets home?"

"I may have told her an hour ago... only because I know you're the best mom ever, so *of course* you'd let her come over. You'd never let her suffer in a house of horrors."

"Mhm." She pursed her lips and rolled her eyes.

I scrunched my face up and closed one eye, waiting to see if I'd get yelled at for such a bold assumption. When she smiled, I relaxed and continued with my plan. "So Aunt Hadley found the horse ring?"

"Yes, she finally found the riding ring where her mom spent her childhood. Hadley tried to find the uncle, too, or I guess it would be her great uncle, but unfortunately, he passed away. He would have been ninety years old, so it's not like he died a spring chicken."

I nodded along, popping mini pretzels and m&ms into my mouth. "It would've been impressive if he was still riding horses at ninety," I laughed, immediately realizing I sounded a little too invested.

"Right. She did find out that this great uncle of hers had kids, though, so that was exciting. Those kids now have grandkids, believe it or not. So Hadley has really been processing this whole family thing. She went from having no family left to all of these new people and to be honest, they never knew she existed either, so it's been a lot for them, too."

"Wow, that *is* a lot. I mean *we're* her family, too... She remembers that, right?" I dug around in the trail mix bowl, diverting my attention.

"Of course, honey. We always said, sometimes the family you choose is the best family you can have. It's just been an experience for her."

"Right. Duh." I smiled. I went into this conversation planning to lay some groundwork, so when I brought up my big summer idea later, my mom wouldn't think it was coming out of nowhere. But now that we're talking, I was remembering just how much I'd been missing Hadley. She used to call us almost daily and now I was lucky if we talked once a week. There were times when something dramatic happened at school on a Tuesday, but by Saturday, when I finally got ahold of her, it felt like an outdated update that wasn't worth mentioning.

I still hadn't told Hadley about Jessica, a sophomore girl who lived two doors down, calling me a little baby when I asked if Chloe and I could swim at her house. Jessica used to be nice to me. We played together all the time growing up. But ever since she started high school, she's treated me like a pile of red ants, avoiding me at all costs. She said she'd never be caught dead hanging out with a loser little kid like me and made a comment about how I probably still wore Limited Too one-piece swimsuits. She wasn't wrong... but I still went home and cried. To myself. Because Hadley hadn't picked up when I called.

I shook my head. Forget Jessica and her stupid tiny bikinis. I was supposed to be laying groundwork! I looked back at mom, who was unfazed by my momentary distraction.

"So what else?"

My mom tilted her head, squinting at nothing. "Oh! She was able to meet one of the granddaughters recently. She's the only one who still lives in Montana. I think her name is Teresa."

"I still can't believe she actually moved to *Montana*."

"Why? Because there's no Starbucks?" She teased.

"Yeah." I drew out the word like it was the world's greatest offense. Because it was. "I really don't know how she's surviving out in the middle of nowhere. I hope she doesn't turn into a weird cat lady."

"That's a little dramatic, Meels. Even for you."

"Still made you laugh. I'm glad she met some family. I know how excited she was to move."

"Yeah, she spent years talking herself into it. It's been weird, though, without her here, hasn't it?"

"Yeah, I miss her." I frowned and chewed on the inside of my cheek.

Deciding I showed enough interest for now, and afraid I'd become actually upset, I changed the topic. "Anyway, I think *Dawson's Creek* is starting soon."

"Ah, so that's what this was. I'm a stand-in until your favorite show starts and until Chloe gets here? I feel honored."

"As you should," I giggled as I jumped off the couch and returned the now empty bowl to my mom. Oops. With a flippant wave I ran to my bedroom, eager to log on to AOL. I had just enough time to fill Chloe in before I'd head back downstairs to the den to watch tv and plot.

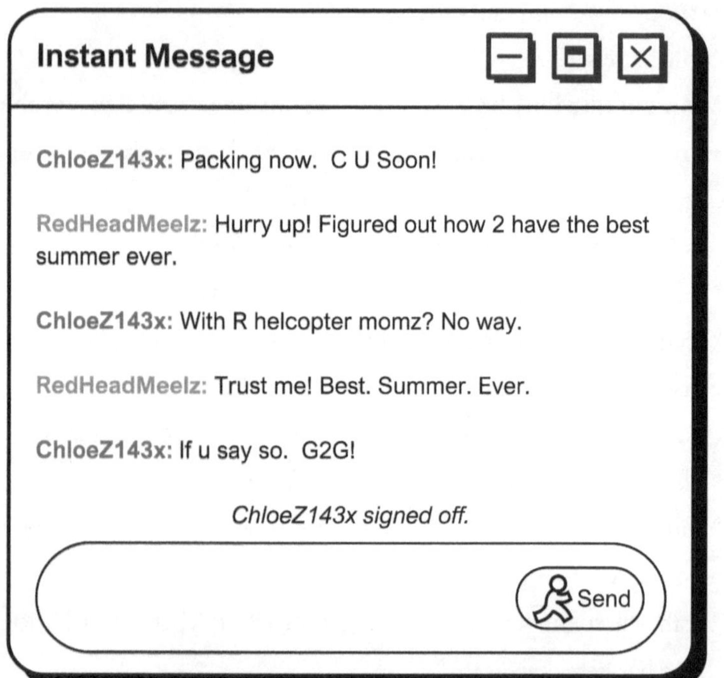

Amelia's Big Idea

"You wanna do what?" Chloe shrieked.

"Shh!" I threw my pillow at Chloe's face. "Are you trying to wake my mom up?"

"Sorry, you just sound insane. That's your big idea?" Chloe lowered her voice, but her dark brown eyes stayed wide. "Do you not remember what happened, like, literally a week ago?"

"Here, Chlo, have some Skittles. I don't have any chill pills so these will have to do." I giggled, tossing some rainbow-colored candy at my always nervous friend.

"I'm serious! We couldn't get an Auntie Anne's pretzel without our moms hovering at Orange Julius. They didn't even pretend to hide."

"That's even more reason why we need to do this, Chlo! We can't start high school with our biggest adventure being that time our moms let us shop in Victoria's Secret but only for sweatpants, *not* the underwear."

I watched Chloe look down at her bright pink sweatpants with Love Pink lettered down the side of her left leg. "I mean they *are* comfy sweatpants, but you have a point."

"I know I have a point! This is our big summer before high school. We need to have some fun, some *experiences* before ninth grade or we'll end up as loser fresh*meat* instead of cool fresh*men*." After what Jessica said – and that time Frank Plimpton called me a big-boobed baby in gym class because I cried when the volleyball hit my face – I was determined to grow up. I didn't want anyone to think of me as a child. I could be a fun teenager, just like the rest of them. I just had to figure out how.

And this summer was the perfect opportunity to revamp myself and start high school cooler than Jessica.

I traded my bag of gummy worms with Chloe's Twizzlers as we stared at each other; my eyes filled with hope, hers with hesitation. "Fine, you win," Chloe sighed. "I'll listen. Tell me exactly how you see this working out."

We spent the next hour hatching a plan to convince our moms to let us spend the summer in Montana with my aunt.

"My aunt promised me last year she'd talk to my mom and work it out, so we should definitely get her on our side. She's also, like, a decade younger than our moms so she's pretty chill. It's going to be so easy to go out and find parties and things to do. I can't see her even caring what we're up to. She has blind trust in her sweet, sweet Meels."

"If only she knew." Chloe giggled.

We liked to think we were wild childs, but neither of us had gone to a party that hadn't involved roller skates, Rita's Ice, or the community pool in Chloe's development. I'd definitely been grounded before, but only for "forgetting" to do my homework or being too sassy for my parents' liking. Chloe's parents were super strict, but she was way too afraid of disappointing them to ever do anything wrong.

Chloe dropped the last gummy worm into her mouth, twisted her silky black hair into a ballerina bun, and grabbed the Sally Hansen Purple Power nail polish from my desk before she sat back down on the floor, her back against the bed.

I was doing my best to paint my toes with the Peek-a-Blue color though, despite my best efforts, I was getting paint all over my cuticles. I wiggled the toes on my painted foot and laughed. "I mean, I am pretty innocent... but that could all change." I grinned at my friend before returning my focus to the art project that was my left foot.

"You're impossible."

I shrugged; a smile stuck to my face. I knew better than to share all of my summer ideas with Chloe. And I had a lot. Right now, I just needed to get my best friend on board so we could convince our moms. That's going to be a battle in itself. School was ending soon, and we needed to get this plan in place soon so it really could be the best summer ever.

"Okay, so even if your aunt convinces your mom... who's convincing *my* mom? And my dad!"

"That's just it, Chloe."

"What's just it?"

"You said your parents have been fighting a lot and it's been hard at home. Don't get me wrong, I'm by no means trying to use that to our benefit. It's really crappy and I'm so sorry for it. Truly."

"Okay..."

"But... it is what it is. And wouldn't you rather let them figure out their situation without you being subjected to the constant fighting? I mean it's kinda win-win."

"Except for the part about my parents fighting, right?"

"Right. Like I said, I really didn't mean to make it sound like I'm using your situation to our benefit. I wish you weren't going through any of it, and I hope they work it out."

"Or not. I just hope they figure whatever it is out. Together or separate. I just want the fighting to stop." Chloe deflated and slouched lower against the bed. "Maybe you're right. Maybe if I gave them nothing but space, they'd be able to work out their drama without worrying about what I might hear or see."

"Exactly!"

"Okay, fine. You win again, Meels. But I'm not asking my parents without you next to me and definitely not until you get your aunt and parents on board."

"That's fair. Yay!" I squealed and clapped my hands like a toddler trying chocolate for the first time.

It was Chloe's turn to throw the pillow. "Now who's being too loud!"

"Whoops." I whispered. "Ohmigod, I'm just *so* excited. You just wait. This is definitely going to work, and we'll end up the coolest kids in our grade. Who else will have spent their summer across the country *without* their parental units, doing *whatevs* they want!"

"That's probably not going to be us either, Meels." Chloe laughed. "It would be fun to get away, though." I could tell she was starting to let herself suck into my infectious energy. She was never concerned with what other kids thought about her and never cared about becoming popular. I wished I was more like her, but more so I wanted to be like my parents. High school sweethearts, naturally popular, attractive.

Chloe leaned her head against mine and sighed. "What do you think we'd do first?"

We spent the next two hours giggling, our ideas getting wilder and sillier the more tired we grew. Eventually, somewhere between throwing our own house party and wondering if Montana had beaches for a bonfire sleepover, we drifted asleep in my queen-sized bed, feeling hopeful that maybe this plan would actually work. We'd find out tomorrow.

Feeling Out of Touch

The next morning, the sun blasted through my two windows, forcing us awake hours earlier than normal for a Saturday. We stood in front of my full-length mirror, debating the best way to bring up our, okay my, Montana plan while fixing our appearance. Chloe only needed the first thirty seconds of our talk to run her fingers through her straight midnight locks. I, on the other hand, spent the whole fifteen minutes trying to comb through my bedhead only to give up and throw my wild curls into a pony to deal with later.

Once I decided we had prepped enough, despite Chloe's reservations, I tugged her hand, causing us to practically tumble out of my bedroom and into the hallway. We started whispering back and forth as we entered the kitchen where my mom was humming along to "That Don't Impress Me Much" on the radio while she flipped pancakes.

She turned around when she heard us giggling. "What's so funny, you two?"

"Nothing, Mom!" I smiled and took a seat at our shiny wooden Ethan Allen table. "Breakfast smells delicious."

"Yeah, Ms. Sanger... super delicious."

My mom chuckled. She always tried to break Chloe's ridiculous manners, but it never worked. "Call me Meghan, honey, but thank you.

They have chocolate chips and should be ready in a minute. There's bacon already on the table under that napkin and strawberries in that bowl." She pointed at the blue ceramic bowl on the kitchen table. "I'll bring these over in a minute."

We continued to whisper once my mom turned around and started pouring the last of the batter onto the griddle. "Just trust me. I made sure to ask about my aunt yesterday before you got here so it won't be weird that I'm bringing it up again this morning."

"If you say so." Chloe shrugged. "What's your plan if she says no right away?"

"I'll just play into how much I miss my aunt now that she's gone. If it doesn't work on my mom, it'll *definitely* work on Hadley."

"That's awful, Amelia." Chloe shoved me in the arm.

I plucked a strawberry from the bowl and smiled. "It's only awful if it's a lie but I *do* miss my aunt."

I really did.

Right as Chloe was about to respond, my mom walked over with a plate stacked high with chocolate chip pancakes. "Okay, you two, now I know something is up. You girls are never this quiet. No hot gossip you wanna share louder than a whisper?"

"Nobody says hot gossip, Mom." I rolled my eyes but smiled and grabbed two pancakes along with the bottle of Mrs. Butter-worth's syrup. "There's nothing to dish, anyway. We were only whispering so we wouldn't interrupt your Shania Twain concert."

"Ha. Ha."

"I think you have a beautiful voice." Chloe smiled as she delicately spread butter across her pancakes.

"Always the charmer."

"She's just being polite, Mom." I showed Mom my cheesiest smile.

"Amelia Marie, why are you being mean to your sweet, old mom?"

"So you admit you're old?"

My mom laughed at the lighthearted skit we often played out. "Just eat your pancakes, sassy girl." She waved her fork at me like a magic wand.

"Your mom's so cool," Chloe whispered not all that quietly.

"I heard that," My mom wiggled her eyebrows and grinned. "I knew I was the cat's meow."

"Mom!"

"I'm just kidding, Meels. I knew *that one* was out of touch."

I cleared my throat, realizing this was my chance. "Speaking of out of touch…"

"Is that what we were speaking about?" She cocked her head.

"It is."

Out of the corner of my eye, I noticed Chloe, who was starting to sweat, shove an oversized portion of pancake in her mouth. "Ohmigod, Chlo, don't choke. I swear I wasn't going to make you talk."

Chloe's cheeks matched the strawberries on her plate. She covered her mouth with her left hand as she tried to quickly finish chewing. She looked like a squirrel on display. I swear the faster she tried to chew, the longer it seemed to take. She ended up coughing out, "too much pancake."

I felt bad about how hard it made me laugh.

Still laughing, I redirected. "Anyway, I was about to say how out of touch I've been feeling with Aunt Hadley."

"Oh?" my mom set her fork down. "That's not what I was expecting you to say. Is that why you were asking how she was doing yesterday? Are you missing her?"

I glanced at my best friend before responding, giving myself a second to take a deep breath. "Yeah, I'm definitely missing her. I know she calls when she can, but it's still not the same. I miss the way she used to just be here to hang out or... I don't know. I guess I just miss having her around." I swallowed back the unexpected emotion with a gulp of milk.

"I see. I miss her, too."

"Yeah, so I was, or well, we were... me and Chloe—"

"Chloe and I," my mom corrected.

Don't roll your eyes. "Chloe and I," I said slowly. "Were thinking about how the summer is starting in a few weeks and how it could be the perfect opportunity to spend more time with Aunt Hadley."

"Oh. I don't know, honey. We can certainly ask her."

"Ohmigod, really?" I shrieked. "See I told you it would be no biggie," I rambled to Chloe before I victoriously swirled my forkful of pancakes through the syrup river on my plate.

"Yes, really. But it might be too short of notice for Hadley to organize a trip here. I'm not sure how her work schedule is and what kind of commitments she might have in Montana to think about." My mom stood up, empty plate in hand, and walked to the sink. "She'll be so happy to know you want her here, though."

Chlo and I looked at each other and held a panicked conversation with our eyes. Chloe shrugged and shook her head, but I was definitely not ready to give up so quickly. "Well, actually, I was thinking what if me and – I mean, Chloe and I, go visit her? Then she wouldn't have to mess with her work schedule. It'll be summer so we won't have anything going on and with Chloe's parents being in their situation, it would be a nice break for her, too."

"Hang on. Let me get this straight." My mom leaned against the sink. We sat on the edges of our seats and held hands nervously under the table. "You want to make a trip to Montana?"

We nodded in unison.

She rubbed her forehead with the tips of her fingers, eyes scanning the kitchen like she was mentally juggling a dozen responsibilities. Then she looked at me, thoughtful. "I could maybe get a few days off from work... I'd have to see if I can get coverage, but it's not out of the realm of possibilities. I'm not sure how much spare change I have lying around for a hotel, though I doubt Hadley would ever let us stay anywhere that isn't her house..." Her voice trailed off as a small smile tugged at the corner of her mouth. "Hmm. Okay, let me see how much comp time I can get from work and then we can see what Chloe's mom thinks." She leaned forward, eyes brighter now. "Sound like a plan?"

"Uhh, well... it sounds like *a* plan, but it wasn't e-xact-ly what we were thinking..." I grimaced, suddenly realizing that of course my mom would want to see Hadley, too.

"Okay, spell this out for me, Meels. You clearly have something specific thought up in that beautiful brain of yours, so spit it out. What am I missing?"

I gulped. Here goes nothing. "We were thinking we could go without you. Don't get me wrong, we love your company. This breakfast, for example, has been just the best. And all of our trips to the mall when you and Mrs. Zhang are three feet behind us? Love that. But we're going to be freshmen and school's only going to get harder and this might be our last summer to really enjoy our time and be kids. But not like little kids, grown kids. Grown, responsible kids who are totally capable of spending the summer with super-responsible Aunt Hadley."

Shocking me entirely, my mom belly laughed. "Are you done?"

I bit my lip and stared, confused. "Yes..."

"Okay, so you're not suggesting we go on a family vacation, then. You're suggesting two fourteen-year-olds fly across the country all by themselves and spend the summer without any parental supervision?"

"I mean, we'd be with Aunt Hadley the whole time. She's as much an adult as you are, Mom."

"Yes, she certainly is. She just doesn't have kids, let alone teenagers. There's a lot to think about here, Meels. We don't even know if she'd be interested. It's a huge responsibility."

"She promised me I could visit and you agreed." I whined. Chloe sank uncomfortably in her seat and started to pick invisible lint off her Paul Frank monkey print pajama pants.

"Okay, let's calm down, little miss. You're not asking to go spend the day alone at Colt State Park. You're asking to get onto an airplane and travel many states away and then spend weeks away from home. You've never even been to sleepaway camp and selfishly, I've never been away from you for more than three days at a time, either. This isn't so simple."

"Will you just think about it mom? Please?" I pressed my hands together in a dramatic prayer pose and jutted out my lower lip in an exaggerated pout.

She blew out a slow breath and clapped her hands over mine. "Yes. I'll talk to your dad and your aunt and we'll weigh the pros and cons and discuss the gravity of what this would look like and mean. Does that sound reasonable?"

"Yes!" I yipped, erupting our hands into the air. "That's totally fair, thank you so much mom. I know you're going to see just how great of an idea this is. Plus Aunt Hadley definitely misses me, I just know it. She'd love to have me for the summer... and Chloe, too!"

"Speaking of Chloe. I'm almost certain I know this answer, but does your mom have any idea about this big plan you two concocted?"

With a soft laugh, Chloe shook her head. "No, Ms. uhm, Meghan. She has no idea and I'm not even sure how to ask her, but Meels and I were talking last night about how it might not be a bad idea to give her and my dad a few weeks by themselves, to work out whatever it is they need to work out."

"Ah. Yes, all the messy adult stuff. Amelia told me a tiny bit of what's going on and I'm sorry you're getting stuck in the middle of it. This might not be Montana, but you're always welcome to hang out here. My only rule is that one of your parents has to know you're here and be okay with it."

Chloe looked genuinely light. "Thank you. Breakfast was really delicious. I usually just have Cap'n Crunch and sometimes I don't even use milk."

"Nothing wrong with cereal," my mom winked. "Now, while I clean this mess up, why don't you girls go chillax or whatever it is you planned to do after ambushing me first thing in the morning."

"I'm going to let *chillax* slide since you're being so open to this idea," I grinned. "There's a *7th Heaven* marathon starting soon, so we'll be in the den if you need us! I'm so excited!"

I doubted cool high school girls watched *7th Heaven*, but it was just Chloe and me, and we loved the cheesy plotlines. For me, the overdramatized family drama was hilarious – so over-the-top. Nobody acted like that in real life. But for Chloe, I think it was something else entirely. She didn't laugh the way I did. She watched like she was studying it, like she was trying to understand what it might feel like to have a family that talked things out. Apologized when they messed up. Said things out loud instead of tiptoeing around each other. I never asked her about it directly, but I noticed in the way she leaned in during the emotional scenes.

I didn't say any of that out loud, though.

"Zero promises, girls. Truthfully, I'm not sure the weight of this has even sunk in."

"I know." I wrapped my mom in a tight hug. "It's still exciting to think about. I bet Aunt Hadley will love the idea, you'll see."

Not wanting to give my mom a chance to rebut, I grabbed Chloe's hand and hurried out of the room. "Don't forget," I exclaimed from the hallway. "We'll be right in the den if you need us!"

"Yeah, yeah."

Happy Pizza

"Mom! There's someone at the door!" I shouted, not breaking eye contact with the television. We were hours deep into a *7th Heaven* marathon and had just started the episode in season three where one of Mary's teammates handed her natural energy pills to help her get back into basketball after knee surgery – right when the doorbell interrupted us.

I wondered if I'd ever need energy pills. My mom relied on coffee to stay energized and let me get Frappuccino when we passed a Starbucks, but I never thought of it as a form of energy. I guessed it had caffeine, but I liked it because it made me feel sophisticated. Like I was part of some grown-up club, even if mine came with whipped cream and extra caramel drizzle.

"Can you see who it is? I'll be down in a minute."

"Sure, Mom!" Chloe and I got up and walked down the hallway toward the front door. The tv in the den stayed on and the rest of the episode, where the dangerous and damaging side effects of the energy pills are explored, aired to an empty room.

I looked through the peephole, spotting a familiar face and two Domino's pizza boxes, and quickly swung the door wide open. "Dad! What're you doing here? You know it's not your weekend, right?"

"Yes, Meels. Can't a dad stop by with pepperoni pizza and garlic breadsticks for his favorite daughter and favorite daughter's best friend?"

"I'm your only daughter," I squinted suspiciously.

"Ah, semantics. Are you hungry for some 'za? Your mom knew I was bringing food, so I doubt you have any other options." He chuckled.

"Hi, Mr. Sanger." Chloe blushed and waved at my blonde-haired dad, staying out of his way as he carried the white and blue cardboard boxes to the kitchen.

"Hi, honey. How's it going? How's your pops holding up?"

"Well, he's home and I'm here, so..."

"Hm, I'm now remembering the list of topics I was supposed to not bring up. My bad, C-lo."

"Dad." I grabbed his shoulders and squared myself in front of him. "'Za? C-lo? You know you're just as embarrassing as mom, right?"

"I can't possibly be *as* embarrassing as your mother. I've heard some of the slang she's tried to use."

"You're getting close," I said, rolling my eyes. "Mom! Dad's here and he brought Dominos!"

I turned back to him and let him know we were going to wash up before sitting down to eat.

We hurried down the narrow hall to the small half bathroom, not bothering to take turns. Sharing the water, I whispered, "They must've talked. Why else would he randomly show up? I just can't figure out if the pizza is to celebrate or to soften the blow..."

"I have no idea. I just can't get over how nice your parents are. I mean they're both pretty cringy but they're still cool, Meels. And no offense, but also, they're like, super attractive. I mean, your mom looks like a pin-up magazine version of the little mermaid, and your dad is like—"

"Ew, please stop." I wrinkled my nose. "Whatever you were about to say, don't. I get it, everyone tells me he's not ugly, but I don't need the details."

"Not ugly is putting it mildly. I don't even think I can sit across from him, it makes me very uncomfortable. He looks like the Abercrombie and Fitch models that are plastered on the windows at the mall."

"Well, you've ruined that store for me, thankyouverymuch."

Chloe let out a raspberry for a laugh. "I'm not wrong and whatever, you should be grateful, you got the best from both of their genes. You look like a Victoria's Secret Angel and I look like a fourteen-year-old pancake. Literally you could be my babysitter," she laughed again.

"Ohmigod, that's so funny. It's not true, plus you're like four inches taller than me, but it was still funny. Okay, okay. I think we've wasted enough water... let's go find out if this is happy pizza or sad pizza."

"So..." I drew out my words as I reached for a slice of pepperoni. I studied my parents' faces. "You guys look happy, right? You're happy? Should *I* be happy? Chlo, do they seem happy to you?"

"I think you should probably just chill and give them a chance to respond." Chloe widened her eyes at me before she smiled politely across the table. "Also, thank you for the pizza, Mr. and Mrs. Sanger."

"You're welcome," my mom winked.

"If only those manners rubbed off on our daughter, right, Megs?" He elbowed my mom playfully before he sprinkled crushed red pepper over his slice.

"That'll be the day."

"Dad!" I whined. "I have manners. I'm just trying to figure out why you're here."

"Wow, I'm really feeling the love," he grinned.

"Sorry. I am excited that you're here *and* that you brought pizza. I'm just anxious to hear what you and mom talked about."

"How do you know we even talked," he teased.

"Ohmigod, please just tell us. This is child abuse. Tell them, Chloe," I demanded. "Tell them this is torture."

"We *would* really like to know if you guys had the chance to talk," Chloe mumbled uncomfortably while she folded and unfolded the edges of her napkin.

"Okay, okay. Andrew, we better tell the girls," my mom laughed as she blotted the grease off her pizza with a napkin. "For Chloe's sake."

"You're right." he waved his crust in the air before he took a large bite. "Go ahead, Megs."

"Alright, girls. We talked to Aunt Hadley about your idea for this summer and she thinks it could be a lot of fun."

"OHMIGOD, REALLY?!" I jumped out of my seat and did a happy dance, pulling on Chloe's arm until she joined me. She wasn't much for sporadic dancing, but looked equally elated standing next to me with her hands covering her wide smile.

"Now, hang on a minute, Amelia Marie. Before you shatter our eardrums, listen to the entire thought, please."

"Sorry, Mom, go ahead." I bit my bottom lip, but it did nothing to stop the smile that stretched from ear to ear. My heart pounded so loudly I could barely hear her. This could be it. A fresh start. A chance to become unforgettable.

"Your Aunt Hadley is on board with having you girls visit her this summer but your father and I are still adjusting to the idea. You've never spent time away from both of us at the same time and this wouldn't be like you're an hour away. You'd be on the other side of the country and there's no fast way for us to get to you if there were to be an emergency. Aunt Hadley and her boyfriend would be the only adults you'd know and honestly we've yet to even meet Marcus. But," my mom sighed, "Hadley is incredibly responsible and we do trust her. Though taking care of teenagers is a whole different beast so we need to have a few more conversations about it. But as it stands, we're thinking that yes, it would be okay for you to go spend some time with your aunt. Where she lives in Montana is a safe area and she assured us a few times that she's settled into her home enough and that it wouldn't be an imposition. So, it's not a golden one hundred percent yet, but there is a very high chance that we can make this work. Okay?" Her eyebrows rose and the corners of her mouth tilted up. "You can react now."

"Wait," my dad interjected before I had the chance to say anything. "Before you freak out, hang on." He pulled my mom's hand and dragged her from the kitchen table, guiding her out of the room and into the hallway.

"Okay," he shouted. "We're a safe distance away. Have at it." He draped his arm around my mom's shoulder as they listened to Chloe and me absolutely freak out over the possibility of going to Montana for the summer.

But beneath my squeals and flailing arms, a small part of my stomach flipped with nerves. What if I got there and still wasn't enough? What if I tried to be the cool version of myself, and nobody invited me to hang out. What if I spent the summer on my aunt's couch with her cat, doing exactly what I would've done here – only a million miles away from my mom? I shook the thought off as quickly as it came. This was my chance, and I was determined to take it.

"Are you sure this is a good idea?" I heard my mom whisper once she thought we were distracted. "You realize I'm going to spend the entire summer crying and freaking out, right?"

"It'll be okay, Megs. She's growing up, and who better to watch over her than Hadley."

"I know you're right, this just seems insane. They're barely fourteen."

"They'll be in middle-of-nowhere Montana, not the Las Vegas strip, Meghan. I think it'll be fine. And lucky for us there's a wild new invention called the telephone."

My mom elbowed him in the gut which caused him to bend in half before she giggled and returned to the kitchen. "Now, there's still the elephant in the room that you girls are probably ignoring..."

"My parents?" Chloe's smile immediately fell.

"That's the one. When I called your mom earlier she was not against the idea. She's not fully on board either, but we're going to get together tomorrow to talk it out. It may not be a bad idea for your parents to have some time to themselves to work out some of the issues they're needing to work out. In the meantime, your mom and dad *are* on board with you spending another night here, so a double slumber party is in the books for you girls. We'll head to J.D. Shuckers tomorrow for lunch with your parents to talk out the potential summer plans and then you can head home with them from there. Sound okay?”

Chloe jumped up and ran into my mom’s arms. “Thank you, thank you, thank you.”

“Oh, you’re welcome, sweetheart. No promises, though, okay?”

“I know. Just thank you for trying and also for always being so nice to me.” Chloe melted into my mom’s embrace, absorbing a love I knew she desperately wanted and needed. It reminded me how lucky I was that my cringey parents were functional.

“Always.” She squeezed Chloe a little tighter. “Okay, girls, go do whatever you two do, but stay out of trouble.”

“Thanks, mom! Thanks, dad!” I threw some air kisses left and right before I captured my best friend’s hand and we all but stumbled up the stairs to my bedroom ready to plan our summer adventure.

Sensory Overload

"This is crazy," I marveled. "One week ago we were in Mr. Santiago's math class and now we're on our way to the airport!" I turned toward Chloe in the backseat of my mom's Chevy Malibu and lowered my voice. "I'm a little nervous, but mainly excited. What about you?"

"I think I'm going to throw up."

"What's that honey? Are you okay?"

"I'm okay, Ms. Sanger," Chloe rushed to confirm. "I'm just really nervous about flying. How much longer until we get there? I think I just need to get on the plane. You know, like ripping off a Band-Aid?"

My mom tittered. "I know what you mean, honey. We have about twenty more minutes until we get there but I hate to break it to you, there won't exactly be any Band-Aid ripping."

"Oh. Um, what do you mean?" Chloe bit the inside of her cheek and anxiously reached for my hand.

"I'm sorry, sweetheart, with how much your dad travels for work, I figured he filled you in on what to expect."

"He's just been busy." Chloe lied, not wanting to admit he'd been avoiding home on purpose lately.

"I'm sure," my mom nodded. "First you'll drop off your suitcases at baggage check, so you'll only need your backpacks. After that, you'll head to security. That's as far as I can go, but I'll walk you there. Once you're through, you'll officially be inside the airport."

"*Then* we get on our plane?" Chloe's voice wavered.

"Well," she blew out her air and switched on the left-hand blinker as she approached a traffic light. She took a moment to find Chloe's eyes in the rearview mirror. "You'll find the gate where your airplane will be, but there may still be another thirty to forty-five minutes until the attendant starts calling for you to board." She clucked her tongue like she did whenever she was trying to think of what to say. "But," she sang, "if you girls end up with extra time, the airport has not one, but two Starbucks stands!"

"Two Starbucks?! Crisis averted, Chlo!" I whooped.

Chloe nodded with an apprehensive smile.

"You'll be fine, sweetie." My mom turned up the dial on the radio and we listened to "Say My Name." Normally, she'd turn songs like this off, or at least try to turn them into background noise, but today she let it slide, probably noticing Chloe's nervous energy. She always knew exactly how to calm her down without making a big deal of it.

Chloe was a quiet worrier, and it had taken my mom a while to figure out how to support a kind of reservation I never exuded. But after eight years of knowing Chloe, she seemed to have mastered it.

I, on the other hand, was almost obnoxiously like my parents – naturally outgoing. I never worried about what might go wrong and loved jumping into things. I usually spoke my mind, too, which, okay, *has* gotten me grounded a few times.

But! My tenacity was also how I got my first (and only) boyfriend. I convinced Bryce in March that we were the perfect match and it was so great. Well, mainly great. We held hands in the hallway every day and we pressed our bodies really tight together whenever we hugged goodbye. I broke up with him, though, because he never had anything to say that wasn't about wrestling practice and honestly it got gross holding his abnormally sweaty palms. It was probably how he won so many of his wrestling matches. Nobody wanted to touch his sweaty skin.

Anyway, I really needed to figure out what else was involved in being someone's girlfriend. That was the whole point of this summer adventure – new experiences. All the same, at least I had someone I could refer to as "my ex," even if it was a two-week-long eighth grade relationship. Chloe, meanwhile, was too shy to even talk to the guys in our grade, let alone try to hold their hand. It would be fun this summer to try to break her out of her shell. I decided to make a secret goal: get Chloe to kiss someone before we leave Montana. Don't tell her.

I looked over at my best friend and could see her starting to relax. I knew this was why my mom let us listen to Destiny's Child. I faced Chloe, smiled, and started singing. It only took a second until she joined in and we belted the lyrics while we danced against our seatbelts.

"Ohmigod, Chlo, I love this song!" I exclaimed as the song changed and "No Scrubs" filled the air.

My mom rolled down the windows with a laugh. "Have at it girls, we'll be there in a minute, so now's your chance."

I looked at Chloe with a twinkle in my eye. "A scrub is a guy that can't get no love from me..."

Chloe laughed, throwing her hands out the window as she sang, "Hangin' out the passenger side of his best friend's ride—"

"Trying to holla at me!" We sang, hands clasped together, into each other's faces about loser men we had no business singing about. We completely forgot we were on our way to the airport, that was until my mom turned the volume down and pulled into a parking lot.

I peered out my window just as an airplane descended, rattling the car. "Is that plane crashing?" I shrieked.

"No, sweetie, it's landing. We're at the airport, remember?" She laughed.

"Yeah, but that was headed, like, right for the building."

Chloe looked like she was about to cry.

"I promise it's not. The runways are just past the building. It might've seemed like that plane was headed toward the airport, but I promise it was on the right path. It's just an optical illusion."

"Okay, but if it *was* crashing, I was totally right to freak out," I muttered, rubbing my palms on my shorts. I wasn't used to worrying, and I didn't like the feeling.

We got out of the car and collected our luggage just as another airplane boomed overhead. Chloe startled and dropped her backpack on the asphalt. "Oh god, you're right. They're like an inch above our head. Are we sure they're not going to hit?"

My mom picked up Chloe's backpack and slung it over her shoulder, opposite her beige monogram stamped Dooney & Burke handbag. My mom believed that you only need a few nice things to offset an otherwise thrifty wardrobe, which was why her designer handbag rested against an outfit crafted from Sears' spring discount rack.

It's also how I convinced my mom to buy me a few new outfits for this trip. Most of my wardrobe came from Boscov's, but last week I got to pick out a couple things from American Eagle and Aeropostale. She drew the line at Hollister, deciding it was ridiculously priced and even more ridiculously lit. *How are we supposed to see anything in here with the lights all dimmed?* And *Who keeps spraying cologne?* she had complained. It was so embarrassing.

I didn't care about the lighting; I just wanted the clothes. Jessica practically lived in Hollister. So did all her friends. And even though she made fun of me after school, I still wanted to dress like her. Maybe then I wouldn't be the girl she teased – maybe she'd remember how much fun we used to have before she started high school and joined the cheer team.

I rubbed my hands anxiously against my new AE low-rise jean shorts. They had frayed edges and a worn-in look that was super on trend. When my dad saw them he rolled his eyes and jokingly asked why we paid for used clothing.

I took a deep breath in, mentally reminded myself what was on the other side of this airport, and forced my nerves into an enthusiastic smile. "I don't know about you, Chloe, but I'm ready to get inside."

"Um..." Chloe gripped the handle of her suitcase but her feet stayed planted.

I flipped my backpack onto my shoulders and looped my arm through hers. "Best summer ever," I whispered in her ear.

"Best summer ever," she quietly repeated, her voice shaky but growing steadier. "Okay, let's go." She said, this time with more confidence.

"Yay!" As I eyed the massive airport, I forgot all about my nerves, excited again for our adventure.

"Okay, girls, let's go. I'll stay with you for as long as I can. Eventually we'll part ways but that shouldn't be a big deal since you're such *grown* independent ladies." She ribbed.

"That's us!" I grinned and pulled Chloe in tighter against me. We walked with linked arms across the parking lot and through the airport doors labeled Delta Air.

Once inside we paused to take in the scene. Everyone seemed to be in a rush. They also seemed to know exactly where they were headed. Chloe and me? We looked at my mom like baby deer caught in headlights.

"Look around, girls. This is the start of your amazing summer adventure. Take it in." My mom smiled at Chloe and winked at me.

I sucked in a lungful of airport air and blew it loudly. "Ohmigod, we're really doing it."

"You're really doing it." My mom laughed. "Follow me. Let's drop off your suitcases so you only have your backpacks to worry about."

We followed my mom obediently, arms looped and eyes wide. I'm not sure what Chloe was noticing, but I was in definite sensory overload. There were staticky announcements coming through a loudspeaker that clashed with the otherwise ambient music, people who rushed to and fro somewhat rudely with suitcases of all sizes and shapes, and large screens hanging from the ceilings that displayed flight times like the T.V. guide channel listed upcoming shows. I was completely overwhelmed, a little bit nervous, and definitely excited.

When I glanced at Chloe, I was surprised to see her laughing. When I cocked my head, she leaned into me and whispered, "Should we have worn matching tracksuits?" Her head tilted to a couple to the left of us that we'd soon be approaching. They were wearing identical royal blue velour tracksuits with white pinstripes down the side. The woman's jacket was unzipped and displayed a form fitted white tank top, while her partner's was zipped three quarters of the way up and displayed nothing but his hairy chest.

"Oh, gross." I stuck my finger into my mouth and faked a gag.

We laughed so hard we walked right into the back of my mom.

"Whoops, sorry, Mom. We were distracted taking in the scene."

“So I heard.” She laughed.

We started giggling again. This was going to be so much fun.

40,000 Feet Up

An hour or so later we were sitting in row twelve, seats A and B. Chloe by the window and me in the aisle. When we first boarded, I was nervous we'd be on the side with three seats, but luckily my parents had thought of everything. I would have been terrified to sit next to a stranger for ten hours. We spent too many hours learning about stranger danger to be literally stuck with one.

Chloe, already buckled in tightly, sucked on her blended mocha Frappuccino while she looked out the small, rounded window and watched the baggage handlers cart luggage toward the airplane. A few minutes later a flight attendant, in a bright blue twinset sweater with a maroon, beige, and blue checked scarf around her neck, handed us tiny packets of pretzels and salted peanuts. She asked us if this was our first flight and when we nodded, she told us her name was Kendra and pointed to the button above us that we could press if we needed anything during the flight. She promised we could even press it if we started to feel nervous.

We held hands as the airplane roared to life, the power from the engines causing our drinks to vibrate. We watched with bated breath as the ground fell away, and the plane tilted upward. Before we knew it, only clouds filled the window. It was incredible.

"Ohmigod, Amelia. How is this real life?" Chloe was astonished.

"This is crazy!" I marveled.

I picked up my caramel Frappuccino and slurped from the straw before unzipping my backpack to grab the book I packed. I opted for *Ella Enchanted* since my mom confiscated my copy of *Go Ask Alice*, claiming the themes were too grown-up for me. I'd only made it through the first 20 pages. When I reached for my mom-approved book, I noticed a card attached to a shiny package. When I pulled it out, I realized it was a shoppe box of Gertrude Hawk peanut butter smidgens – my favorite!

"Look, Chlo! Chocolate!"

"Ooh, smidgens. I love these little guys. My mom only ever buys them around Christmas when they're shaped like mini Santas."

"Those are cute. It looks like these are little seashells. My mom literally thinks of everything, I swear." I ripped open the bag and handed a chocolate to Chloe before I opened the accompanying envelope.

Amelia,

We hope you have the time of your life with Aunt Hadley and Chloe this summer. We can't wait to hear about all of your adventures. Please make sure to make Hadley's life easier, not harder.

Love always, Mom & Dad

P.S. we don't love you a smidgen, we love you a lot! (are you cringing?)

I all but snorted when I read their joke. I really would miss them. I thought about showing it to Chloe but stopped myself. Her dad hadn't even made it home from his business trip in time to say goodbye this morning. I didn't want to rub my parents' humor in her face.

"I saw you got a gift too, right?" I said instead, tucking the note into my backpack. "It looked like your mom handed you something before we left."

"Oh. It was just a math workbook so I can stay sharp ahead of AP placement testing. Eyeroll."

"Oh, gross."

Chloe nodded her agreement and returned to the crossword puzzle she had been working on. I shoved the chocolates into my backpack for later and opened my book, settling into my seat to relax.

A half hour later, Kendra stopped by to check on us. We let her know we were okay and that it wasn't as scary as expected. Though the thought that we had nine more hours to go felt pretty daunting. She told us we'd get a boxed lunch halfway through, but if we needed any drinks in the meantime to just hit the button. "Actually," she smiled. "I'll be right back."

"I wonder what that was about?" I asked Chloe, who shrugged in response.

Kendra appeared a few minutes later with her arms full. She leaned forward and handed us both a blanket, a small pillow, and a sugar cookie in a paper wrapper. "These are some of the freebies our first class guests get to enjoy. We had a few extras, so I thought I'd sneak them back here." She winked at us, bringing her pointer finger to her mouth to indicate it was our little secret.

With the blankets and pillows in hand, we were able to really get comfortable. She had also shown us the button on the side of our armrest that reclined our seats. Tucked in, Chloe's pillow against the plane, and mine against her shoulder, we fell asleep within minutes.

I woke up to our inevitable, pending death.

The plane shook like the Scrambler ride on the boardwalk from vacation last year. I looked around, horrified, and tried to remember if I told my mom I loved her before we walked away.

Wait.

Was I the only one losing it? Why was nobody alarmed? We were literally turning into scrambled eggs. I held my breath and quickly reached overhead to press the attendant button before I wrapped my arms protectively around myself, mimicking the seatbelt I had already pulled tighter across my waist.

A moment later Kendra walked over, seemingly calm, and asked me if I needed anything.

"Um, why is nobody freaking out? Is this one of those scenarios where you're, like, trained to ignore the fact that we're dying? Like the band that kept playing on the Titanic while the ship sank?"

Kendra knelt in the aisle, placing her hand on my knee, and smiled. "Oh darling, we are not dying. I promise."

"I can feel it!" I knew I was spiraling. Like the plane.

"That feeling is something we call turbulence, and it's actually quite normal. Usually it's from the weather, or a jet stream, which more or less means a band of strong wind. The uneven movements in the air cause the airplane to shake or jolt a bit. It can admittedly be jarring if you're not prepared. I'm so sorry you got scared, darling, but I promise we are very safe."

"Promise?"

"Yes. In fact, unlike the musicians on the Titanic, if conditions do get bad, which is extremely rare, we were trained to sit down and buckle up, just like the passengers. I would never be walking around freely like this if we were in danger."

"Okay, that makes sense. I'm glad they don't make you walk around and hand out pretzels and orange juice while we're crashing." I smiled.

"Me, too." Kendra laughed. "I see your friend is still asleep. That's good," she smiled. "We'll be serving lunch in about thirty minutes. If you want to let her sleep, we can always pick a meal for her. There's going to be three choices. A turkey sandwich platter, a cup of chicken salad with pita bread chips, or alfredo noodles with a side salad. They all come with another drink and a pudding cup."

"Yum, those all sound good!"

"Great. I'll let you think about what you both will want, and I'll be back soon. If you feel nervous again, you know how to reach me."

With that she sauntered off and I giggled at myself, feeling silly for having freaked out.

Baggage Claim Reunion

It didn't take us long to find Hadley, despite the crowd, since she took it upon herself to make a welcome sign out of neon green poster board. Large sharpie letters spelled out "Amelia & Chloe, Time to Party like it's 1999!"

Classic Hadley.

Chloe tapped my arm and pointed toward my aunt, giggling.

"Yeah, I see her," I laughed. "How could I not?"

Hadley was practically bouncing, waving the sign like we had just returned home from war. A lump rose in my throat out of nowhere. I hadn't realized how much I missed her until right now.

"Let's go, Chlo," I said, already halfway into a speed-walk. "Before she starts whistling for us." I tried to sound chill, but my legs had other plans. We were practically jogging now, my heartbeat thudding with anticipation. I just needed to reach Hadley. To wrap my arms around her and feel whole again.

Hadley dropped the lime poster board as we approached, leaving room for me to jump into her arms. She was tall and slender like Chloe, but I didn't care, I trusted she had enough muscle in her thin arms to catch me. Luckily, I was right. She spun me around before setting me back on my feet and collecting Chloe into the hug.

"Girls!" She clapped her hands together. "I'm so happy you made it safely. I cannot wait to hear all about the flight."

"It was crazy, Aunt Hadley. I thought we were dying at one point."

"Wait, really?" Chloe stuttered.

"Well, no... it turned out to be normal turbulence." I shrugged with a chuckle.

Hadley laughed and shook her head.

We made our way over to the carousel and waited for our suitcases to appear. While we stood there, Hadley let us know that next we'd call my mom from the payphone to let her know we landed safely. She went on to explain it was a 40-minute drive to her house and didn't want to make my mom wait any longer than she already had.

"I think that one's Chloe's." I bounced on my toes & pointed to a turquoise suitcase that was rounding the corner. Hadley leaned in and grabbed it off the conveyor belt just in time.

"Meels, there's yours!" Chloe pointed at the pink and purple suitcase headed our way. It was easy to spot in the sea of black luggage. I grabbed it but nearly fell backward from how hard I tugged to get it off the belt.

"Whoa. That was a close one." I laughed, steadying myself. "We only had one suitcase each, Hadley, so we're good to go! I can't wait to see your house."

"I'm glad you're excited. We can grab take out on the way, since honestly, I don't have anything prepared for dinner and not many places deliver to me. But before we figure that out, let's swing by the payphones so your mom can stop pacing holes in the floor."

"Sounds good." *Sorta.* What did she mean by there aren't places that deliver? How far out in the middle of nowhere did she live? Hopefully there's civilization or it's going to be really hard to follow through on a lot of my secret plans for this summer… Ugh. I should've known when my mom told me Hadley didn't have a Starbucks in her town that this wouldn't be like home. I hope this whole adventure wasn't pointless.

"Amelia?"

Hadley was staring at me; I must've zoned out. "Sorry. Um, jet lag," I offered lamely. That's a thing, right?

"You feel jet lagged already?"

I laughed and shrugged.

"Right. Well, let's call your mom and then we can grab milkshakes for the drive. You know, to help battle your jet lag." Hadley laughed as she picked up the shiny black pay phone receiver and started dialing.

"Hey, Meghan. Yep. All is good. I have the girls right here with me, luggage and all. Yep. You got it, one sec." Hadley turned toward me with a smile and wiggled the receiver.

I grabbed the phone and said hello. Why was she crying? "I'll miss you too, mom. I will, I promise. Mom," I whined. "Hadley has a phone at her house. It's not like we're never going to talk again. Okay. I will, hang on." I turned to Chloe. "My mom says hi and is reminding us to call your mom. She said she'll give her a call now, though, so we can wait until we get to Hadley's."

When Chloe nodded at me, I gave my attention back to my mom's voice. "We're going to go now, Mom. Aunt Hadley said we're going to pick up dinner on the way home. I can't wait to see where we're going to be spending the summer. I will. Okay. *Okay.* Love you, bye!"

I hung the phone up and grabbed the handle of my rolling suitcase. Chloe was already holding hers, standing beside me. We both looked to Hadley for direction. "There's a Roy Rogers near the exit," she said. "Let's grab shakes before heading to short term parking."

Who the heck was Roy Rogers?

Hadley's House

"Your house is so cute, Aunt Hadley."

Chloe and I sat on a walnut bench that tucked into a rustic barnwood table in the buttercup yellow painted kitchen. There was a set of black appliances along the left side and back walls, including the gas stove where Hadley currently stood, waiting for it to slowly warm a kettle of water for peppermint tea, something she liked to drink, apparently even in the summer.

"Thanks, sweetheart. Feel free to make the spare bedroom your own. I'm sorry it's pretty bare right now but maybe you girls can help me decorate it while you're here."

"That sounds like so much fun!" I loved when my dad let me decorate my bedroom when he moved into his new condo last year. He wasn't all that excited when he saw the bright pink paint sample I grabbed, but three coats later, I had the brightest room in the place.

"Are you sure you don't want to split up and use both empty bedrooms? I know I have a bunch of bookshelves in one, but there's still a bed and plenty of closet space. I hate for you two to feel cramped and forced to share a bed."

Chloe and I looked at each other and smiled. It was a no brainer.

"We definitely want to share a room. We actually assumed we'd be together since we're used to sharing a bed whenever we have sleepovers. The only difference is at home we share a queen bed, so the king bed is an upgrade." I laughed.

But as soon as the words left my mouth, something shifted.

I'd been dying to get out of Rhode Island. Out of my house, away from my parents, ready to spend the summer reinventing myself before high school started. I wanted new memories, new stories, new photos to hang in my locker. Four weeks in Montana hadn't felt like enough when our moms booked the flights.

Now, standing here, it somehow felt too long.

The homesick feeling crept in so fast I didn't know what to do with it. I missed my mom in a why-can't-I-hear-her-voice-right-now way. Sure, she was embarrassing, and I loved giving her sass like it was my job, but wasn't that just the mother-daughter deal? Underneath all of that, she was the most caring, thoughtful person on the planet – who was currently on the other side of the planet.

I reminded myself why I needed this. I'd listed it off enough times in my head: freedom, independence, proof I wasn't some clingy little kid.

Still, I was grateful Chloe was sharing the room with me. Being with her felt like a little piece of home. We always shared bedrooms.

And, like Mom reminded me twenty times, there's a phone in Hadley's kitchen that I can *always* use. I'd tried to argue for the importance of getting a cell phone – *what if there was an emergency and we weren't by her kitchen?* – but the stupid landline was all I got.

"Yeah, I agree." Chloe grinned, interrupting my silent spiral. "It's going to be so much fun to spend the summer in the same room."

"Well, it's settled, then." Hadley lifted the kettle off the stove when it started to whistle. She added two packets of peppermint tea into the rolling water to steep. "Are you girls sure you don't want any tea?"

"No, thanks. The milkshake earlier was surprisingly delicious for Ray— whoever, but it's definitely too hot to even think about hot tea."

"How have you never heard of Roy Rogers?" She laughed. "Tomorrow we'll take a walk into town and I'll show you around. Believe it or not, there's a Roy Rogers there, too, right at the end of town. It's one of the only restaurants you can walk to from main street, besides Pancake Patty's and Grandpa Mac's."

"Grandpa Mac's?" My face fell forward. Just how honkytonk of a town was this? "Is every restaurant named after someone?"

"Huh." Hadley smirked. "I never really thought about that. Grandpa Mac's is a cute little restaurant that built a menu based on different macaroni & cheese dishes. It's much better than you'd think. And I know what you're thinking. Where are you going to get your Frappuccino when the closest Starbucks is three towns over."

"Three?" I shrieked.

"Yes, three. You know, growing up I hated coffee, and I never had special foods and drinks. You should feel lucky you even know what a Frappuccino is."

"Yeah, yeah. You sound like my dad."

"Ouch." She clutched her chest like I'd shot an arrow through it. "Brutal."

I smirked, but didn't apologize.

"Anyway," She continued, saying the word slowly. "I was going to say there's a place downtown called Java Joe's. I guess you're right about the way these places are named. It's so obvious now." Hadley snorted with amusement and shook her head. "Most of the high school kids hang out at Joe's, so maybe you'll meet some kids your age. They have a lot of fun menu items and are always trying out new drink concoctions. I'm sure it'll fill the fancy lil' coffee hole in your heart."

Hadley was laying it on thick, but with a smile. She poured her peppermint tea into a Lewis & Clark coffee mug and slid into the bench opposite us. It was pretty cool that her kitchen table didn't have chairs. It felt very western.

"I'm sure I'll survive. So what should we do tonight?" An unexpected yawn trailed my question.

"Well, I figured I would give you girls time to unpack and settle into your new space. I'll get going on reheating the Chinese we picked up earlier and then maybe we'll throw on a movie and relax. Little Foot is hiding around here someplace, I'm sure she'll make an appearance when she smells the reheated food. We can hit the ground running tomorrow, but sooner than later that jet lag will *actually* kick in."

"A movie night sounds fun, Aunt Hadley." I nodded, feeling the exhaustion settled behind my eyes. "We'll be back out when dinner is ready."

Chloe and I scooched off the bench and walked down the hallway past a bathroom and the first spare bedroom, stopping in front of the third door, which led to the room we'd be staying in. The fourth door, at the end of the hall, belonged to Hadley's room, which she included in our tour earlier and was absolutely beautiful. Unlike our room's empty beige walls, Hadley's were painted a sage green and there was a stunning framed print of a brown pinto horse standing in front of a wooden barn with a snowy background centered above her king-sized bed, which was covered in what looked like the fluffiest white comforter I'd ever seen. Her dark wooden furniture was decorated with picture frames and candles and the oatmeal-colored carpeting kept the room feeling warm. She had her own bathroom and a huge walk-in closet. There was even space for Little Foot to have an intricate three-level cat tower, complete with a sisal rope scratching post, hanging cat toys, and a carpeted hut at the top. My aunt definitely knew how to pick a room!

I was excited to help decorate the room that Chloe and I would be staying in. The walls were bland right now, but the room was a decent size. We had a king bed with pine wood nightstands on either side, and a matching set of long and tall dressers against the left wall. On the right wall was the door to the closet, which wasn't quite as big as Hadley's but still big enough to take a step in, then move slightly to the left or right. Next to the closet was a white three-shelf bookshelf that was half full, with a small blue vase with fake flowers, two candles, and a white alabaster horse figurine filling in the gaps. I was excited to see a small television sitting on top of the bookshelf. I had tried to convince my mom to put a tv in my room back home but she said it would rot my brain.

I took a deep breath in, exhaling through my mouth, before I dropped backward onto the blue striped comforter. Wow, this bed is comfy. Chloe was quick to join me and we laid side by side and stared up at the ceiling.

"We made it, Chlo."

"Are you sure we're not dreaming? There's no way this is real."

I turned my head to face my best friend and smiled. "I would pinch you but then you'd pinch me back and it'll be a whole thing. So let's skip that." I giggled.

"I hate being pinched. Good call. I'm actually exhausted and this bed is insanely soft. I feel like it's hugging me." Chloe said as she yawned.

"It really does feel like that. I was going to suggest we unpack but let's just lay here until Hadley calls us for dinner. We can unpack later."

Chloe nodded before resting her head against mine. It only took a minute until we were both sound asleep.

"Sorry we fell asleep last night, Hadley. I don't even remember closing my eyes."

"Yeah, me neither. When I woke up, I swore I was being swaddled by a cloud."

Hadley chuckled softly. "I'm glad you girls like the bed. I picked out new mattresses when I first moved in. The brand, uh, Tempur-Pedic, is all about the science of sleep, but honestly when I laid on the mattress in the showroom, I was like who cares about science, sign me up. Three, please!"

"You should tell my mom." I smiled cheekily.

We slept right through dinner so I was more than starving this morning and excited for Pancake Patty's to be our first stop. We were currently walking into town, which was only a few blocks from Hadley's house. For as desolate as Timber Falls, Montana sounded, Hadley promised us her log-style ranch home, which sat in a small field of wildflowers, was only a few blocks from the "hustle and bustle." I'm just wondering what her definition of hustle was.

I swore all signs of Westfield, Rhode Island cleared right out of her system with the first plaid shirt she purchased. I never would've imagined her happy in a place like this, with all its echoing silence and slow mornings. But, somehow, she was thriving.

I wondered if it had been hard at first. Maybe she missed some of my calls because she was adjusting to her own life changes. I should probably let go of some of that resentment. I obviously still loved her.

Maybe these next few weeks would help.

While we walked down a concrete sidewalk, which bordered an endless grassy pasture with cattle grazing lazily deeper in the field, I admired the rolling hills in the distance. It felt like we were walking through the cover of *Anne of Green Gables*. It wasn't the urban city life I preferred with Starbucks, large shopping malls, and maybe my favorite thing ever, a food truck park, but I guessed I could see why my aunt enjoyed this so much. It probably reminded her of the farm she spent time at when she was my age.

"I'm starving." I said, breaking the silence. Literally, beyond the echo of one rogue cow's mooing, we're surrounded by absolute silence. It is so eerie. Back home, silence included the noise of car engines idling in traffic with the occasional inpatient horn, dogs barking, and people talking on every corner. Not here. Here, silence was silence.

"I bet so. I went to wake y'all up but you looked so cute curled together on the bed. I figured I'd let you sleep."

"Did you just say y'all?" My head jutted forward in complete shock.

Hadley threw her head back and laughed so loud it practically echoed. "I guess I've been hanging around Marcus too much. He has a thick drawl and throws y'alls around like a football."

I smiled, seeing my aunt light up like that.

Despite the lingering resentment I hadn't fully figured out yet, there was something about her laugh that made my chest feel lighter. It was such a pure, unfiltered kind of joy – like she wasn't pretending or performing. Just happy. It was exactly what I wanted, too. Something real.

"I look forward to you meeting him at some point this summer. But no need to rush any of that." She looked like she wanted to say more but didn't.

After a minute she added, "Right around this bend is the start of downtown. First up, Pancake Patty's."

Timber Falls

An hour later, with full bellies, we were back on the main street ready to explore downtown. Pancake Patty's was exactly how I imagined it would be, with faded maroon pleather booths and tacky wall art. The waitress looked like she was not much older than Chloe and me; her hair divided into two French braids and her face painted with shiny lip gloss, dark eyeliner and slightly clumpy mascara. She couldn't care less about my aunt's introduction of us. In fact, every time she spoke, she sounded annoyed, like we were interrupting her or like it was our fault she had to take our food order.

So much for making friends in Montana. I'd been hoping she might randomly invite us to a bonfire or whatever they did around here, but I didn't even get a smile. First attempt: fail. But I wasn't about to give up yet.

Waitress drama aside, the breakfast was *delicious*. I had blueberry Belgian waffles with a side of thick cut maple bacon and Chloe had a farmer's breakfast bowl, which was a combination of crispy hashbrowns, eggs, and sausage, with peppers and onion held together by melted colby jack. My aunt kept it simple with a gooey cinnamon roll and a cup of hot tea. She must've eaten dinner without us based on how much less ravenously she ate.

We hadn't walked far when Hadley paused. I thought we were about to head into the Five & Dime store where we now stood, but instead she threw her hand up to wave at a family headed our way.

"What're the odds?" She mumbled with a big smile plastered to her face. "This is my second cousin... the one I just met a few weeks ago whose grandfather owned the horse ring my mom grew up around. I'm not sure who she's with but I imagine they're her kids."

As the family approached and I caught a better view, I slapped the back of my hand against Chloe's leg, trying to subtly get her attention. Who was *that*? Next to Hadley's second cousin were two teenagers. One a brunette girl with long legs and olive skin and the other an athletic, curly-haired broad-shouldered boy. His light brown eyes, which matched his sun-kissed skin, met mine as they approached and I couldn't help but smile.

"Hadley, what are the chances! It's so great to see ya." The woman looked like she was probably the same age as my mom. Her chestnut hair was cut in a simple bob, and she wore burgundy plastic sunglasses. Unsurprisingly, she was wearing a similar plaid long-sleeved shirt as my aunt. Someone ought to tell them it was 75 degrees out.

"These are my twins, Laurina and Lorenzo. They just finished their sophomore year at Timber Falls High."

"Renzo, ma. Everyone calls me Renzo." His raspy voice proved his disinterest in the conversation, though I swear his glance kept bouncing my way. He wore a dark green school t-shirt with a pair of black and white Nike basketball shorts with matching Nike slides.

"It's so nice to meet you two. We're distantly related... I think I'm your...second cousin, once removed? Which is a really weird way to explain family if you ask me."

Hadley must be nervous. She always rambled when she got nervous.

"Oh, I'm sorry, I should introduce these beautiful girls at my side."

Ohmigod, could this be any more embarrassing.

"So, this is Amelia," she grabbed my shoulders and shuffled me in front of her, putting me on display. "My best friend's daughter, though she's practically my niece since I've known her since she was four." Keeping me in front of her, she nodded toward Chloe. "And this is Chloe, her best friend. They live in Rhode Island where I'm from but will be spending the summer here with me."

Laurina nodded slowly, as if to decide if Rhode Island made us interesting enough to care about. What's with the girls in this town? She popped her hip to the side and shoved her hands in her Abercrombie mini shorts, which weighted them just enough to expose even more of the midriff that was already on display beneath her light pink cropped t-shirt. She looked like she woke up and did a hundred sit-ups and ran a 5K all before breakfast, which was probably a protein shake and definitely not Pancake Patty's. She had some fierce abs. I wasn't jealous or anything but, still, I hoped not all teenagers around here were built like that. Chloe would fit in, but my body was like my mom's, more curved than muscled.

"It's great to meet ya." Their mom extended her hand for us to shake. "I'm Teresa Romano but please call me Terri. I'm sure you'll be seein' me around town. I work at the Book Nook part-time and spend a lot of time volunteering for the high school between Laurina's cheerleading commitments and Renzo's soccer stuff. He made varsity this year." She bragged while elbowing him in the side.

He shrugged it off. "No biggie. They needed a strong leg and Coach said that I have a rocket for a kick. That and I have incredible stamina; I own that field."

Did he just wink? Did anyone see that? I looked at Chloe, but her eyes were fixed on his sister, who looked annoyed as heck.

"Real humble." Laurina said while she rolled her eyes at her brother.

"Facts." He smirked.

"Are you sure those weight plates aren't falling off the bar and onto your head? Who talks like that?"

"You're just jealous."

"Literally of what, though."

"Anyway." Their mom interrupted, stepping between them. "The twins are headed out tonight to the Summer Kickoff with some friends. I'm sure they'd love to have you girls join them."

"Mom." Laurina huffed.

"You can definitely hang out with us," Renzo offered at the same time. Laurina looked at her brother with disgust before she exhaled in defeat.

"Whatever, fine. We're meeting outside of Joe's at seven."

This could be our way in. Laurina was a cheerleader, and Renzo had already made varsity. There was no way they weren't part of the popular crowd. Which meant everyone they were meeting up with tonight probably was, too. If Chloe and I could blend in we'd all but guarantee ourselves a memorable summer.

"Thanks, that sounds fun. Hadley, do you mind?"

"Not at all. Let's continue with our tour of the magnificent downtown, though I may have oversold the hustle and bustle part." She said with a playful grimace. "But I still want to show you girls the creek and a few more stores. Then we can swing by Java Joe's for a drink, so you know where to meet up later. We'll make sure to head home with plenty of time for you to get ready. Sound good?" She was facing us now, which left the Romano family to stare and wait.

"Sounds good." I shifted to face Renzo and Laurina, though only Renzo was paying attention. "Thanks, again, for the offer. It was nice to meet you guys." I smiled my best smile, rolled my shoulders back a bit to put myself on display, even though I was mainly hidden inside a loose t-shirt, and tucked a stray curl behind my ear.

Once we said goodbye, we continued our walk. Hadley kept pointing and explaining different parts of town and its history as we walked but I was too distracted to hear her, busy trying to think of what I'd packed and what to wear tonight. As much as I wanted Laurina's attention, especially since she was a cheerleader and probably part of the popular crowd, I was more focused on impressing her brother.

Our Chance

"Are you sure this looks okay?"

I meant the question for Chloe, but directed it at my reflection.

I was wearing a pair of distressed cutoff white denim shorts and a light green halter top. I usually hated high necklines – too tight and suffocating – but this one had open sides that made my shoulders look great. The crocheted fabric also laid just right across my chest, which had fully developed by thirteen, way earlier than most girls in my grade. My mom had told me she was the same age when she hit puberty, that it ran in the family. She'd always tell me, *"All bodies are beautiful, especially yours."* I believed her, mostly. But it was hard not to feel weird when other girls, namely Jessica, whispered about me, like my body made me a walking scandal.

Besides Frank Plimpton, who was always a bit of a jerk to me, most of the boys weren't all that subtle about noticing me. They'd stare from across the lunch table, or try to sit close during assemblies. I never really knew what to do when I caught them looking. Smile? Say something flirty? I generally pretended I didn't notice. One time, my super short-term boyfriend, Bryce, brushed his hand across my chest when he hugged me goodbye. He played it off like it was an accident, and maybe it was, but I jolted like I'd been electrocuted. He looked offended, and I felt ridiculous for reacting like such a little kid. I'm pretty sure he told the wrestling team I was a prude after that. At least, that's what someone told Chloe.

And yet, standing here now, I wanted to be on display. Renzo was older. Hotter. He had that laid-back, effortless confidence the boys in my class only pretended to have. They were all scrawny arms and yo mama jokes. Renzo had broad shoulders, tan skin, and honey-brown eyes. Eyes I *definitely* wanted on me.

"You look hot, Meels!" Chloe tugged on the bottom of my shorts exposing a sliver of midriff and knocking me out of my daydream. "Even better," she giggled.

"Mm, I guess so." I chewed on my lip and looked over my shoulder to check out my back. My shorts were probably three sizes bigger than Laurina's but they still looked pretty good. I'm not used to feeling insecure and I'm not even sure that's what this feeling is, but a part of me was really nervous I'd show up to the party and everyone would look at me like I was Violet from Willy Wonka, after she chewed the gum and turned into a giant blueberry. I shook the thought off, remembering my mom's words. *All bodies are beautiful.*

Chloe stood next to me and brushed her hands down the front of her jean skirt before adjusting the thin straps of her cream and teal striped tank top. "Do you think anyone's going to care that we're not freshmen yet?"

"Who says they'll find out?" I smirked before grabbing my Covergirl mascara. Neither of our moms let us wear makeup beyond lip balm and mascara. It was totally unfair. But at least I had mascara to help draw attention to my bright green eyes, which already stood out thanks to my green shirt. I worked on applying the first coat to my lashes while giving

Chloe the side eye. "It's just a technicality, anyway. Eighth grade is over so the next time we're in school, it'll be high school. We just need to round up a bit."

"Are you sure that's going to work? I think it's pretty obvious that I'm not a sophomore. Lauren definitely looks older than me."

"Laurina." I corrected, for what reason, I don't know. "It doesn't matter, Chlo. Maybe you just have a baby face, they don't know. Nobody here knows us. This is our chance to be whatever and whoever we want. We can't have the best summer ever if we're kicked out of the first high school party we go to for being fourteen instead of sixteen."

"You're right, you're right." Chloe nodded while she continued to evaluate her appearance in the mirror. I don't know why she's so worried. Her thin legs and long torso would fit right in.

I added a bit more product to my hair, scrunching it with my hand, before I decided I had messed with it enough. I kept my hair down, hoping my red curls would help me stand out. Chloe, on the other hand, had her silky strands twisted behind her, held by a large claw clip. Her mascara emphasized the almond shape of her eyes, something she once admitted made her self-conscious, even though I thought it made her look effortlessly beautiful.

"Are you ready to go?" I grabbed her hand, eager to leave.

She nodded apprehensively as we slipped on our Chuck Taylors and headed toward the living room.

"Don't you girls look cute," Hadley gushed before her eyes softened and she shook her head. "Gosh, that is not what I looked like when I was fourteen. I wore old jeans that stopped at my ankle and boxy t-shirts most of the time. I was not this cute and put together." She laughed as she grabbed our hands and gave us both a spin.

"Thanks, Aunt Hadley. We weren't really sure what to wear tonight."

"Oh, it doesn't matter. Nobody's going to care what you're wearing. They'll just care that you're nice, polite girls."

"That's not how it works, Hadley. They will definitely care what we're wearing." I rolled my eyes.

"Well, they shouldn't," she dismissed with a wave of her hand. "Are you sure you girls don't want me to walk you there? I don't need you getting lost on day two. Your mom would kill me."

"How would we even get lost?" I bent down to give Little Foot a pet behind her ear. "It's like one path to town and the same path back. Which is, as far as I could tell, the only walkway in the town. I think we'll be good."

"Yeah, yeah. Small town in the middle of nowhere, I get it. Go have fun. Here, take this. If you need anything, find a pay phone or cellphone and call me."

I took the post it note from Hadley, folded it in half, and tucked it into my pocket as we made our way out the front door. If I had a cellphone her number would already be in my phone and I wouldn't need to rely on a number scribbled on a yellow scrap of paper. What if it got wet and became unreadable. I'd have to add that to my list of reasons to share, again, with my mom.

The moment we were out of sight, we paused so I could roll the hem of my shorts shorter and Chloe could tuck the bottom of her tank top under, making it a cropped top. My aunt was generally encouraging, but would've definitely stopped us if we looked "too grown for our own good" as she liked to say. We gave each other a quick once over before continuing the trek into town.

The air felt as warm as it had earlier in the day and even though we were only an hour from sunset, I had a feeling it wasn't going to get any cooler. Thank God, because neither of us even considered bringing a hoodie. As we rounded the end of the field, the main street came into view, with string lights bordering both sides of the road. It looked like half the stores had already turned their lights out for the night. This town was so sleepy.

"Look, there they are." Chloe pointed down the road at a group of teenagers standing outside of Java Joes, two girls and three guys. As we approached, it was easy to notice Laurina, who wore rolled down red Soffe shorts and an oversized t-shirt, of which, based on her exposed left collarbone and shoulder, she must've cut the neckline off. Next to her was an equally slender girl, with dirty blonde hair set in one long French braid, perfectly manicured makeup, and, you guessed it, rolled Soffe shorts. Her hip bones were as prominent as Laurina's collarbones. Great.

Renzo was one of the three guys standing there. He had on khaki cargo shorts and an American Eagle baby blue short sleeved shirt with a popped collar. The other two guys were dressed exactly the same, except one shirt was gray and the other a deep purple.

"Oh, you actually showed up." Laurina said with a surprised look.

"Of course they did." Renzo said as he draped a heavy arm around my shoulders. The weight caused me to dip slightly against him. "Ya'll want a sip?" He wiggled his water bottle in front of us with a goofy grin.

I glanced at Chloe, who shrugged back at me. "Uh, sure." When I brought the Poland Spring bottle toward my lips, I could smell the burn of alcohol. I looked at Chloe again, but Renzo's arm, still resting around my shoulders, had clouded any judgment left in me. I took a big sip and quickly brought the back of my hand to my mouth as my body released a quick shiver. Gross. I handed it to Chloe, who looked nervous, but took a sip anyway. She shuddered the same way I did which elicited an eye roll out of Laurina.

"I remember my first drink," she said, raising one perfectly arched brow and crossing her arms like she was too cool to be seen with us.

"We're used to mixed drinks back in Rhode Island," I lied, shrugging my shoulders hoping to come across nonchalant.

Laurina and her friend looked at each other and laughed.

"Anyway," Renzo said with a slow draw. "This is Matty and that's Carter. We're all on the soccer team. Next to Laur is Rylee. They're inseparable and annoying as all get out."

"As if, Ren." Rylee said as she swatted his arm and batted her eyes. "You love us."

"We sure do," Matty said before he grabbed her hips, pulled her into him, and kissed her as if there was a pot of gold lodged in the back of her throat that only he could dig up. I wondered what it was like to be kissed like that.

"They're dating." Laurina said with an eye roll. "Can we go now?" She looped her arm through Rylee, effectively dragging her away from her incredibly cute boyfriend. From what I could tell so far, all of the girls were definitely twigs and all of the guys were hunky and athletic. Chloe naturally fit in, though lacked the confidence to do so, and I had the confidence but was clearly more body than they were used to seeing.

"Shall we?" Renzo asked.

"Sounds good. We have no curfew, so we're game for anything."

Laurina rolled her eyes – again, but Renzo smirked before he stepped away and did some type of secret handshake move with Carter. They bounced chests at the end and broke into a fit of loose laughter.

"Think I can get a sip, sweetheart?"

Chloe, still holding the vodka filled water bottle, handed it off. "All yours." She seemed unimpressed by Carter's dark blue eyes and blonde boy-band faux hawk.

"Tough crowd," he laughed. "It's blueberry flavored, my favorite. If you girls are used to mixed drinks, you'll love the punch at Anders."

"Anders? Is that where the Summer Kickoff is?"

"Nah. The Kickoff is at Bennett's Orchard but Anders' family owns the farm behind it and the real party is going down in the barn that borders the properties."

"Yeah," Matty added. "It's not used as a barn anymore, so Anders' dad let us turn it into a hangout space. If he only knew what we actually got up to in that barn." He high fived Renzo with a big laugh before wiggling his brows and adding, "Right Ry?"

"Ohmigod, you're impossible." She giggled.

We started walking toward the party as the water bottle was passed around a second time. Renzo handed it to me and said to finish it since there was only a little left. I tipped it against my lips and emptied the end of the bottle into my mouth, this time keeping my reaction still.

"Atta girl." Renzo laughed. "Way to throw back."

I laughed cutely and grabbed Chloe's hand. I think we had successfully pulled off trying our first drink without drawing too much attention. I don't think Laurina believed us but she also seemed like a hater, so who even cared. Okay, maybe I cared. But she didn't need to know that.

It wasn't long before we were walking through the kickoff event on our way to the cool kids' party. I whispered "this is our chance" to Chloe, who smiled at me and squeezed my hand in agreement.

Summer Kickoff

"This setup is sweet," I said as we walked into the well maintained, but decommissioned, red wooden barn. I looked around and noticed the same type of string lights wrapped around the poles and rafters as we saw bordering town. There were several mismatched couches, two long coffee tables, a plywood board balanced on stands in the corner with Solo cups in triangles at either end, and a big bowl of punch on a table otherwise covered in bags of chips and popcorn. There were bales of hay stacked in the back corner but that was the only "farm" thing left in the place. It was way cooler than I could've imagined.

"Yo, Anders." Renzo hollered, waving over a short guy with a buzzcut and espresso skin. They did a choreographed handshake before Renzo introduced us. "This hourglass hottie is Amelia and that beauty is her friend Chloe. They're from Rhode Island but here for the summer." I blushed at the nickname and bounced my shoulder against his in playful acknowledgment. The random nickname was flattering, and even though it ran through me like a bolt of lightning, a small part of me wondered if it was meant as a cruel joke.

"Baller. Nice to meet y'all. Two minorities in one room? This almost makes Timber Falls count as diverse." He let out a deep laugh as he nodded to Chloe.

"What do you mean?" she asked as we followed Anders toward the punch bowl.

"Well, I'm black, that much is clear. And you're... Chinese?" He handed us each a cup and then began to ladle in the bright red concoction.

"Taiwanese. Is that like unheard of around here?"

"Well, sweetheart, look around and you tell me."

"Why is everyone calling me sweetheart?"

"She's just joking," I added with a fast laugh. I glanced at her and frowned at her tone. Why did she care if people were calling us sweethearts? Wasn't that a good thing? She shrugged slightly before she nodded an apology.

"Sorry, not tryna harass you or anything, just a polite term we tend to use as a blanket nickname around here. Heck, get Renzo drinkin' and he'll call *me* sweetheart." He laughed again.

I laughed too, but kept my eyes on Chloe who was smiling, but her eyes were roaming, likely noticing his point. Everyone at this party may have been built like her, with long torsos and long hair, but besides Anders, the next darkest skin belonged to the twins, who were sun kissed at best. I hoped that didn't bother her. We never really paid much attention to that back home, or at least I didn't. Honestly, the lack of diversity should've been expected since we're in the middle of the midwest in a random town named Timber Falls. It didn't even sound multicultural. If anything, it sounded like I-ride-my-cow-to-school culture. Anyway, I'd bring it up tomorrow to make sure Chloe felt okay, but for now, it was time to make some friends.

"Thanks for the drink." I smiled and took a big gulp. It was just as gross as the blueberry vodka but at least there was some type of Kool-Aid cutting the burn now.

"You got it." Anders fist bumped me then walked off toward a group of guys who seemed to be having a rowdy conversation full of obnoxious laughter and back slaps.

"Are you good, Chlo?" I whispered so Renzo, still next to me, wouldn't hear. She took a deep inhale before raising her plastic cup and tapping it against mine with a smile.

"That's the way to do it." Renzo lifted his own cup, tapping the air, before he took a big gulp. "Come on, I'll introduce you to more peeps. You two are both smokin' hot. It'll give me street cred to just roll up with you."

We both giggled.

"I doubt you need any street cred." I said, while his words – *smokin' hot* – bounced around in my chest like a pinball. It felt like I was starring in my own teen movie.

"Yeah. You right. You right." He smirked. "Come on, I bet there's a game of never have I ever starting soon."

"Fun!"

Chloe grabbed my hand and squeezed, no doubt because she was just as aware as I was that we would definitely lose that game. It was based on someone saying something outrageous they've never done and if you *have* done it, you put a finger down. It works best when you're with a group of friends because you can say things you know someone has done. When all ten fingers are down, you lose – but really you win. It's always better to be the fun one than the person at the end with all ten fingers up but zero experience.

After Renzo introduced us, we spotted an open blue corduroy loveseat and quickly sat. The space around the coffee table filled in with Renzo, Anders, Carter and a few other soccer guys. On the couch adjacent to ours was Laurina and two of her friends and next to them, in an oversized chair, sat Matty with Rylee curled in his lap.

"Now's your chance to back out, Cordelia. Hate for you to embarrass yourself." Was she talking to me? I looked around the room and realized she must've been.

"It's Amelia," I murmured.

"Isn't that what I said?"

"No." I straightened my shoulders before confidently continuing. "Anyway, thanks, but we're good to play." I gave Laurina my best smile, which she countered with an eye roll.

Forty-five minutes later we had lied our way through two rounds of 'never have I ever' and polished off two and a half solo cups each worth of mystery punch in the process. I liked how light and floaty everything felt, how I didn't overthink every judgmental look Laurina shot my way. But my head was both heavy and hollow, like a balloon filled with sand, and I wasn't sure if that meant I should stop or keep drinking.

Apparently instead of putting one of your fingers down when you've done whatever was stated, you just took a drink, which is how we ended up drinking as much as we already had. There wasn't an easy way to determine a winner. It seemed like everyone was using the game to air out dirty laundry and drink as much as possible. There were a few really specific ones, like *Never have I ever been late to science class because I was kissing in the east wing hallway* and *Never have I ever logged into someone else's AOL and changed their away message*. That second one made one of the girls next to Laurina storm off.

We obviously couldn't lie our way through the targeted ones, but the sentences that focused on sneaking out of the house, skipping class, and kissing in random places like behind the school, at the park, or in a movie theater were easy to pull off. By the end of the game my face and chest felt hot and I wasn't sure if it was from laughing at everything everyone was saying or from whatever this was I was drinking. Probably both.

To be honest, I've never had alcohol before so I wasn't sure if feeling hot was part of it. But, I mean, I was only fourteen so why would I know, right? No one in eighth grade really talked about drinking or partying, like that switch didn't flip until high school.

But older girls in my neighborhood, like Jessica, definitely bragged about sneaking out on weekends or staying out until eleven on a weeknight just to get late-night apps at Applebee's. They made it sound like some exclusive club, not a casual family chain that served mozzarella sticks and boneless wings.

Maybe this was my chance to finally catch up. I was only a few months away from being a freshman, and high school was a totally different ballgame.

Here, right now, in a room full of sixteen and seventeen year olds, *not* drinking would stand out. I mean, yeah, plenty of teenagers don't drink – obviously it's illegal, I'm not dumb, but we came to this party to make friends and have experiences.

So experience, here we came.

I took another sip, recognizing now that the more I drank the happier I became, and the louder my laugh. I was having so much fun and based on the red cheeks and the laughter-induced tears formed at the edges of Chloe's eyes, I knew she was experiencing the same uncontrollable joy.

With the game over and everyone dispersing to different corners of the barn, Renzo stood up and invited us to play pong, which was apparently the name of the game that was set up on the long piece of plywood. When I asked Chloe, she shook her head and squealed "Ohmigod, yes, we *have* to." I agreed but when I started to stand up I wobbled and fell back onto the seat. My cheeks flamed. I shot a quick glance around to see if anyone noticed, brushing it off with a laugh that came out way too loud.

Chloe cracked up, smacking her hand over her mouth to try to stop herself.

Renzo stepped forward with a chuckle and held his hand out for me. "Punch'll sneak up on ya." I nodded like an idiot and grabbed his hand, letting him help me up. This time I stood successfully, but kept hold of Renzo's hand. He didn't let go either, though. I leaned my body against his, not even on purpose, before I reached my free hand out to help Chloe up. The momentum of my pull caused her to fly right into me and Renzo. I wrapped her in a hug and we both started laughing.

"Alright ladies, you game for some pong? Amelia you can be on my team and Chloe you can pair up with whoever wins the current game. My money's on Carter. Anders talks a big game but he actually sucks." He laughed and guided us toward the game.

Every time one of them sank the ping pong ball into the solo cup across the plywood table, a small crowd erupted, everyone celebrating with a drink. I wasn't sure if more drinking was a good idea, based on how my vision seemed to be taking three seconds to catch up with my head whenever I moved it to the left or right. It was a really weird feeling.

But when Renzo handed me a new cup, full, and winked, I quickly brought it to my lips to hide the burning on my cheeks.

What Even Happened?

We played a round of pong and Renzo and I easily beat Chloe and Carter. I was reeling with energy, none of which helped me sink a single cup; Renzo definitely carried our team. Inevitably, though, we lost the next round. "I can only do so much," he had teased, which prompted more laughter to bubble out of me.

I looked around for Chloe but didn't see her anywhere. When had she stopped watching? I swore I heard her voice cheering me on. All the same, she was probably somewhere nearby, but if I was being honest, my vision was so hazy. Even though I was seeing everything blurry and doubled, when I squinted a bit I spotted Carter, who was arm wrestling one of his soccer teammates. When I asked if he knew where Chloe went, all he did was shrug. Ugh.

I finally spotted her on the other side of the barn alone on the couch, which was totally weird because she was high-fiving people left and right during the game not that long ago. I was pretty sure that was her but why would she be isolating herself? We were making so much progress – even if my head *was* starting to hurt. I tripped over my feet as I approached Chloe but righted myself before falling. Wait, was she sleeping? Ohmigod, so embarrassing. How was she even asleep right now with "Turn Down for What" literally blasting.

"Chloe? Wake up." I whispered and tapped on her shoulder. She was a light sleeper so it was weird she didn't wake up when I touched her.

I shoved her.

Nothing.

I grabbed both shoulders and shook.

Still nothing.

What's happening? Why wasn't she waking up? Panic flooded my system. Oh my god. "No, no, no, no, no... Chloe. Come on, wake up!" I shrieked, barely audible over the thumping bass of the music that filled the barn. I collapsed onto the worn-out couch next to her shaking her recklessly and calling her name, praying for any sign of life.

Renzo was now standing next to me. He must have heard me freaking out. "Renzo! Help me. What's happening?" My mind started to race as my words tumbled out.

"I told ya the punch'll sneak up on ya."

Why was he smiling? "That's not helping! What if she's seriously hurt? What if she doesn't wake up? Should we call 9-1-1? Does anyone have a phone?"

Overwhelmed, I struggled to think clearly. My vision blurred with the sting of tears, and I fought to keep myself together.

"Are you serious? If we call the cops we'll all get arrested."

"Renzo, she's not waking up. We have to." Desperation set in and the dam broke. Tears drenched the top of my shirt.

"You're right." He hesitated. "Here." He shoved his phone into my hand. Right as I was about to dial, Laurina rushed over with a bucket of water and dumped it on Chloe. I was about to freak out, because what the heck was that for, but Chloe gasped as the icy shock hit her. Then she leaned over and threw up.

Relief washed over me, mixed with a lingering fear. "Oh, thank god, Chloe!" I wrapped my arms around her, ignoring the vomit still clinging to the corners of her mouth.

She went to say something, but quickly pushed off me and bent forward to throw up in the bucket that had just held the water that woke her. She groaned and leaned back on the couch.

"Are you okay? What happened?"

Chloe groaned but said nothing. Anders leaned over the couch and handed her a Gatorade while Renzo returned with a paper towel so she could wipe her mouth. I jumped off the couch, and took a moment to steady myself, almost forgetting how much the room had been spinning a few minutes ago. Whoa.

I stepped toward Laurina and thanked her. "I didn't know what you were doing at first, but thank you. That was terrifying."

"Rookie mistake." She scoffed.

"What?" I shook my head confused how she could be making snide remarks.

"Never mind." She rolled her eyes but they landed in a sympathetic focus. "Listen, you need to drink water in between your alcohol or you're never going to survive this small town. Oh, and eat some bread, it helps absorb the alcohol. I think. Anyway, it's what we do." She shrugged and walked off, rejoining her friends.

Huh, she actually ate carbs. Good to know.

The bass music continued to thump, and the party continued as if nothing had happened. Was this a normal occurrence? Nobody seemed worried but me. I sat next to Chloe and made sure she was okay. She took another sip of the Gatorade and leaned against me.

"I'm going to sneak into the kitchen and grab some cookies. Are you sure you're okay?" I bit the cuticles around my thumb while I stared at her. Despite the shower she took as soon as we snuck in, grateful that Hadley had fallen asleep on the couch, the glaze coating Chloe's eyes remained.

"I'm okay," she shrugged. She was definitely *not* okay. Cookies would help. We always stayed up late eating junk food whenever her dad started a big fight with her mom or whenever I had bombed a test at school.

I pulled up the comforter so it rested against her waist and did my best to fluff the pillows behind her back. "Okay, I'll be right back. Promise." I ran on my tippy toes, feeling very sober after Chloe scared me half to death, down the hall and into the kitchen. Just as expected, Aunt Hadley had plenty of treats stocked in the pantry. I grabbed the package of Oreos and two bottles of water and rushed back to the bedroom.

"Okay, so what even happened?" I pulled back the foil lid and handed Chloe an Oreo before grabbing my own. We both took a minute to twist the cookie apart, she handed me the plain cookie and I handed her the side with frosting. It's the same thing we've done with Oreos ever since I told her I didn't love frosting in the third grade. I took a bite of my cookie from where I sat with my legs crisscrossed on the foot of the bed. She was still resting against the headboard, but we faced each other, the cookies between us.

"I don't know what happened. I was drinking just like everyone else, but I guess it just affected me more."

"Laurina told me we need to have carbs before drinking and to drink water between alcohol."

"So now you're taking advice from Laurina? I thought you hated her."

"I mean, she's not great, but the advice sounded smart."

"You're right. Sorry. My head just hurts and it's making me cranky."

"It's okay." I reached for another cookie, twisting it and handing the frosted half to Chloe. "We'll just make sure to have spaghetti or something before the next party."

"The *next* party?"

"Yeah, Renzo said they normally kick it weekly either at that barn or in this dude Ralph's basement whenever his mom is out of town for work."

"You can't possibly be serious! I could go my entire life without throwing up my guts like that again."

"Yeah, that's why we need to start with carbs. It's only the start of the summer, Chlo, how are we supposed to get ready for high school if we quit trying after the first party fail."

"Uh, were you the one who was passed out on a stranger's couch for God knows how long?"

"No." I soften my tone, despite her rising anger. "I'm sorry, we don't need to be talking about this right now. Finding you like that scared the bejesus out of me. We can figure out our plans tomorrow after we've had some sleep and hopefully some pancakes."

Chloe nodded but her lips kept in a straight, tight line.

"Let's change the topic." I took her second nod as permission to keep talking. "It looked like you and Carter were having fun during the game of pong." I wiggled my eyebrows which elicited a laugh.

"He was nice but totally self-involved. He cared more about making sure his muscles flexed every time he threw the ping pong ball than he did about landing the actual shot. It's why we lost." She shook her head but her smile was back.

"I only won because Renzo maintained perfect aim. I'm not sure how because I was seeing double the whole time."

"Yeah, same. I didn't like that feeling at all. It was dizzying."

"I agree. It should be easy enough to drink less next time. It's not like anyone was monitoring how often we refilled our cups." When Chloe's smile fell, I quickly added, "If we drink again, I mean. Big if..."

"Sure." She nodded. "Anyway, enough about Carter and his biceps. How about you and Renzo? You were practically glued to his side all night."

"Not in a pathetic new girl way though, right?"

"No," she laughed. "Plus, it takes two. It's not like he tried dodging his, what did he call you, hourglass hottie?"

I covered my face with a pillow, embarrassed and gleeful at the same time. "Ohmigod, who would've expected that. I spent the whole time getting ready for the party worried that my hips were too wide and my legs too short to garner any attention."

"Wait, really? Why didn't you tell me that?"

"And say what? Gosh, Chloe, your perfectly toned stomach and mile-long legs are going to fit in perfectly, while my curves and short frame are going to stand out like a sore thumb?"

"Yeah, if that's what you were feeling. I would've shoved you in front of the mirror and reminded you how beautiful you were."

"Okay, Mom."

"I'm serious, Meels. We don't need to be shaped the same. How boring would that be? Plus, I would kill for a chest like yours. I would need an entire box of tissues, maybe two, to fill a bra and look even remotely curved."

"You never know when you'll need a tissue. Allergy season and all." We both started laughing and the tension in the air felt lighter.

"Hey, can I ask you something?" I split another Oreo in half, focusing hard on the task, afraid to meet her eyes.

"Why do you look nervous? Did something happen while I was passed out?"

"No, nothing like that." I handed off her part of the cookie sandwich. "I was just thinking about what Anders had said earlier in the night."

"About what?"

"About the, uhm, lack of diversity. I never really paid attention to that sort of thing before but it looked like you were getting upset when you looked around the barn."

"Hm. That's hard." I nodded, leaving space for her to continue once ready. "I mean, I don't *always* think about it but it definitely makes me uncomfortable sometimes. You have these big round eyes, like most people, while mine are slivers. You can barely see my eyelashes, even with mascara."

"Oh. I love your eyes..."

"I know you do. I'm just saying. There's differences and sometimes I'm just... aware."

"I'm sorry. So it bothered you that you and Anders were the only ones who were—" I waved my hand in the space between us, not sure what I was even trying to say.

"Diverse?" She smiled and I said a silent thank you for the fact that she was forever patient with me. "It didn't bother me necessarily. Anders was really cool and super cute but the whole thing felt so basic. Like of course the one Asian girl is going to crush on the one black guy, keeping us as a diverse little duo instead of being mixed in with everyone else." She shook her head, shoving a whole Oreo in her mouth. "It's hard to explain what I mean."

"No, I get it. I guess it's not something I've ever had to think about."

"Yeah, my mom calls that privilege."

"You've talked to your mom about it?"

"I have before." She shrugged.

"Promise me next time you feel weird or whatever about anything, that you will come to me, too. I hate that you hid those feelings from me. I don't want you to think I can't help or listen, even if I can't relate."

"Deal. And next time you feel insecure about your body, you come to me."

"Deal." I smiled at her before I tilted my head in her direction, letting her know to move over so I could join her under the sheets. "Now that that's out of the way, let's back up to the part where you think Anders is cute."

"Oh okay, right after we talk about your growing obsession with Renzo."

I rolled my eyes while I tucked myself in next to her. We both shared a yawn, and after glancing at the electronic alarm clock that showed it was already 2:45 am, we decided we'd talk more in the morning. I rolled to my side as she rolled onto hers, our backs to each other, as we both quickly drifted to sleep. What I failed to see based on our positions was that Chloe lacked the smile that I couldn't wipe from my face.

About Last Night

I woke up to the smell of bacon and maple syrup. When I rolled over, I noticed that Chloe was already sitting up with a book in her lap.

"Morning," I groaned.

"Morning." She closed the book politely, but kept her right hand tucked as a bookmark. "I woke up an hour ago, which is wild because we only went to sleep like six hours ago. I didn't want to wake you, so I grabbed a book off your aunt's bookcase."

"Anything good?" I tried to see what it was, but the cover was face down.

"*The Cider House Rules*? It's kind of sad so far." She tilted her head slightly. "It's about an orphanage run by a doctor who helps kids and women in tough situations."

"Hm. Interesting." I nodded, relieved Chloe seemed okay after last night. "How's your head, because mine is pounding."

"Ugh, mine too. I think that's why I woke up so early."

"I'm hoping Laurina's theory on carbs works in reverse because I smell bacon and where there's bacon, there's pancakes." My eyes widen with hope.

"I guess we should get up and see." She pulled a spare hair tie off her wrist and slid it into the book, where her hand had been, before she closed it fully and set it on the nightstand. "I could dig into a large stack of pancakes right about now. I hope your aunt has peanut butter."

I stretched my arms out wide, leaning left and then right. "I always forget you like to put peanut butter on your pancakes instead of syrup."

"I am who I am." Chloe's laughter was music to my ears. "Is your aunt going to be angry that we got home after she was already asleep?"

"I don't think so." I shrugged, then slid off the bed, letting my feet feel the full weight of my body. "I don't think she believes in a reality where I would do anything wrong. If anything, I bet she apologizes to us for falling asleep."

"No way." She giggled.

"I'm telling you," I laughed. "Just wait."

We walked down the hall into the kitchen to see a giant stack of buttermilk pancakes and a platter of bacon. "Morning, Hadley! You cooked for an army." I set my hand on my stomach in response to its hungry rumble.

"I felt so bad that I fell asleep before you girls got home so I thought I'd make it up to you with a big breakfast."

I nudged Chloe and she smiled, slid onto the bench, and grabbed a forkful of pancakes. "Thanks for making all of this, it smells delicious."

"Anytime." Hadley smiled. "If I'm being honest, though, these are also guilt-cakes. I think I'm in the doghouse with your mom." Her smile turned to a grimace before she stacked a few onto her plate.

"Better you than me!" I smiled wide. "Why, though?"

"Well, you might be there with me. Apparently, I should've known a lot more information about what you girls were up to last night. She called to check in and say hi and when I mentioned you weren't home, we entered a fast game of twenty questions, where I knew none of the answers."

"Oof. Sorry, Hadley," I said, the words catching in my throat. "I didn't think – I mean, I had your number in my pocket and figured that was enough. I didn't mean for you to get in trouble with my mom."

"It's not your fault. I didn't know how involved I was supposed to be, until your mom made it very clear."

"You should've told her if she allowed me to get a cellphone then she could call me from anywhere and I'd be able to answer."

"Nice try. You know her stance on cell phones before you're sixteen."

I shrugged and mumbled, "just saying."

"So, tell me about last night. How was the summer kickoff? Were Laurina and Lorenzo welcoming? Did you meet more kids your age? What did you do?"

I looked at Chloe and we had a quick telepathic conversation on what we should share. I decided to take the lead, knowing she was more likely to overshare. "Yeah, the twins were both super nice. We met Laurina's cheerleader friends and Renzo's soccer friends. Everyone was... nice."

"Oh, that's great! Nobody gave you a hard time for being a year or two younger than them?"

I dipped my eyes, focused on cutting up my pancakes. "Well, uh, I mean we didn't exactly tell them our age, but they also didn't ask. Probably because they were immediately blown away by our killer personalities."

Hadley laughed and nodded. "Do anything fun? I felt extra dumb when I couldn't even say where you had gone after your meet up at the coffee shop. I knew the town had an event to kick off the summer, but I realized I hadn't even known where it was held." She rubbed the back of her neck and gave a small, sheepish shrug. "Your mom waited until all of 6:15 this morning to call me and make sure you girls were home safe and that neither were kidnapped or killed."

"Honestly, the fact that she waited that long is pretty hurtful. No midnight check-in for her precious baby girl?" I smirked, but my voice faltered just enough to give me away. Shouldn't she have called more to see if we had shown up?

"I'm glad you think you're funny," Hadley said dryly.

I let out a soft laugh, but it faded quickly as I glanced at Chloe. She was rolling the edges of her sleep shorts, keeping her eyes down.

"We met at the coffee shop and walked to the Summer Kickoff event, which was at Bennett's Orchard," I said, slower now. "We played some games, hung out, that sort of thing. Nothing crazy. Right, Chlo?"

"Yep." She smiled and shoved a forkful of pancake into her mouth, like it was the perfect excuse not to say anything more.

"Anyway," I jumped in. "Anything fun in the works for today, Aunt Hadley?"

"Well, I was thinking of introducing you to my, uh, boyfriend." She cringed at the title. "Man, that sounds weird."

"Fun!" My eyes lit up, Chloe's too. "What's his name again?" My lips twisted as I thought. "Mark?"

"Close. Marcus. He actually has a son around your age; you might've met him last night. Anders?"

"Oh, no way! We did meet him. *Super cool* guy, right Chlo?" I grinned mischievously.

"Yeah, he was really welcoming to us." She nodded, cheeks pinking just a little.

I smirked. "Welcoming, huh?" I bumped her shoulder and whispered. "You mean *cute*."

Chloe shot me a look but didn't deny it.

I was about to tease her more when something clicked.

Anders... Marcus's son... The farm.

My grin faded as the mental math caught up with me. *Oh no.*

"Um," I said, trying to keep my voice neutral, "Marcus wouldn't happen to, like, own that big red barn just past the orchard, would he?"

Hadley perked up. "Yeah, that's his place! How'd you know that?"

How did I know that? Chloe looked at me, alarmed by the hole I just dug. "We saw it in the background when we were at the party," I rambled, eager to recover. "Renzo mentioned it was Ander's family's land."

"Sure is. But Marcus is a widower. After his wife died two years ago – breast cancer, it became less of a functional farm and more of just a place to heal and exist. I don't think all of the barns and buildings are operational anymore."

I almost told her I knew it wasn't a functional barn, since we had just partied in it, but stopped myself. Chloe was still focused on her pancakes, not adding much to the conversation. I hated how deep we'd already gotten into lying, especially now that we had to worry about this new wrinkle – Anders' dad, AKA Hadley's boyfriend.

Wanting to get off the topic of the party barn, I switched gears. "So how did you meet him?"

Hadley set her fork down and smiled, as if a memory just played through her mind. "We met at the farmer's market, both reaching for peaches, and he asked me to the diner for breakfast. We ended up connecting, weirdly enough, over the conversation of cancer." She paused to sip her tea before continuing. "He told me about his lovely late wife, and I told him about how my mom died when I was thirteen from lung cancer, and how later on in my life, Dorothy, who meant the world to me, also passed away from cancer. It was a sad conversation but an easy one at the same time. We bonded and started meeting up for regular breakfast dates and eventually it progressed to more. He's a great guy, I'm excited for you to meet him."

"That's amazing, Aunt Hadley. I'm glad you found someone." I smiled and meant it. In the ten years I've known her, I don't think I'd ever seen her date anyone. She hung out with my Uncle Josh a lot, but they're just friends, so that didn't really count.

"Thanks, sweetheart. Why don't you girls finish breakfast and then you can spend time calling your parents. I'm sure they're antsy to hear from you. Proof of life and all." Hadley laughed before clearing her throat and continuing. "Then you can shower and get ready for the day. Marcus, and maybe Anders, not sure, will meet us at the diner for lunch. I figured it's an easy location and then if you want to walk around town after, we'll already be there."

"Sounds good. Thanks!"

Forty-five minutes later, we had both talked to our moms – mine was definitely way more dramatic than Chloe's. Mom was mad I hadn't told Hadley more about where we'd be and made me promise not to "try anything funny." No wool would be pulled over my aunt's eyes, apparently, especially since she was nice enough to host us. I tried bringing up the whole *maybe-if-I-had-a-cellphone-this-wouldn't-be-an-issue* thing, but that got shut down immediately. We ended the call with me promising to be thorough with my aunt. It made me cringe, knowing I was now lying to my mom, too.

Chloe's call was the opposite. Her mom hadn't noticed she never called yesterday. Chloe said she sounded distracted, like she was in the middle of something that totally took over her brain. It was weird. She didn't even ask if Chloe had started her summer math book yet, which was usually the first thing out of her mouth.

Chloe shrugged off her call, but I could tell it left her feeling a little off. I think part of her *wanted* her mom to be concerned, maybe even borderline mad, like mine had been.

After we finished dissecting our phone calls, we took quick showers, then stood in front of our still-half-unpacked suitcases, trying to figure out what to wear.

I held up a tank top, tilting my head. "Okay, so how excited are we that we'll see Anders today?" I wiggled my eyebrows.

"I'm actually freaking out a little." Chloe bit at the cuticle of her left thumb and sat on the edge of the bed.

"Like in a good way?" I sat next to her, positioning myself to face her.

"No, not in a good way." She wiped her hands down her face. "The last time I saw him I was barfing all over his couch!"

"I mean, you made it into the bucket, so you didn't actually get any on the couch."

"Amelia!"

"Sorry, I was trying to be helpful. There's no way you're the first person to have thrown up at that barn. Nobody even seemed phased, which honestly was kinda weird. I mean, I was phased—" I shook the memory from my mind. "Anyway, he lingered near you all night. From what I remember anyway. I'm sure he's going to be excited to see you."

"Maybe."

"My mom always tells me to focus on controlling the things you can control and let the rest go. She's usually referring to the way I should act and treat other people, but in this scenario, I say we focus first on the way we look. Let's get you looking peak cute."

"Peak cute?" Her nose wrinkled, unconvinced.

"Yes!" I wasted no time digging through her suitcase, tossing options over my shoulder until I found the perfect top. "Ooo, this one. This one fits you so well!" It held up a soft green peplum tube top with a faux corset detail and a faded orange and yellow flower border along the hem. I grabbed a pair of white jean shorts that I had thrown behind me a minute before and tossed them into Chloe's lap. "Put this on and then we can pull your hair into a high ponytail to better show off your perfect collarbones. Boys love collarbones!"

"They do?"

"I don't know – probably." I shrugged. I started rifling through my own set of clothing while Chloe stepped away to change. I settled on a fitted, charcoal Red Hot Chili Peppers t-shirt and a pair of cut off jean shorts in a medium wash. I cared less about my own outfit, wanting to make sure Chloe got the attention she deserved.

After our conversation last night, I noticed for the first time just how long Chloe spent trying to enhance her eyelashes with layers of mascara. "You look great, Chlo."

She nodded, taking the edge of her pointer finger and using it to help bend her eyelashes upward.

I focused on taming my curls with an anti-frizz cream before Chloe had a chance to notice me watching her. Eventually we were satisfied with our looks and headed toward the living room where Hadley was waiting.

"If Anders gives you the cold shoulder, which he most definitely will not, I promise to rescue you and fill in any awkward silence. Okay?"

"You're the best." She smiled at me before we turned the corner to the living room where Hadley, as expected, was sitting on the couch ready to go.

"You girls are always so cute! I'm going to need a makeover before the month's up."

"That would actually be so much fun, Hadley, but is there even like a mall in this town? Do your clothes come from, like... the farmer's market?"

"Geez! I know I wear a lot of plaid now, but we do have stores." Hadley stood up and grabbed her brown leather handbag and the keys from the hook by the front door.

I giggled. "Plaid looks good on you; I'm just being funny."

"Mhm. If I'm being honest, the better stores are at a small mall twenty minutes and a town away. Sounds like a fun girls' trip is in our future."

"Definitely!"

"We'll never say no to shopping." Chloe added.

"Awesome. For today, it'll be club sandwiches and awkward new boyfriend introductions with my niece and her best friend."

"Sounds just as fun." I smiled and looped my arm through Hadley's, resting my head momentarily on her shoulder. She threw her arm around me and pulled me into a full hug.

"Alright, girls, let's head out. I figured we'll drive because the heat today is gross, and you both look too cute to get all sweaty." We nodded and followed her out the front door and toward her lapis blue Dodge Neon.

Meeting Marcus

"Amelia, Chloe, this is Marcus and his son Anders. Anders, the girls mentioned they met you last night at the Summer Kickoff and commented on just how polite and nice you were."

I could feel Chloe's embarrassment as my own, maybe because it was. So much for playing it cool. When she didn't say anything, I quickly smiled and said hello.

"Of course, Miss Hadley. Amelia and Chloe were great company last night. They fit in with all the locals, whether that's a good thing is up for debate." He laughed a wholesome laugh and motioned toward the long booth we were standing in front of. Hadley slid in first on the left side followed by Marcus and Anders. Chloe and I split the right side. I made sure to slide in first so that Chloe would better line up with Anders.

"I mean, we didn't wake up spontaneously wearing flannel like my aunt seems to do, so we're still holding strong to our Rhode Island roots." I laughed and nudged Chloe to remind her to act normal.

"That's right," Marcus said while passing around the plastic menus that were stacked in the middle of the table. "Hadley has told me a lot about Rhode Island and where she lived before coming here. She mentioned she lived only a few minutes away from you, Amelia. How are you liking your first few days here in Montana?"

"It's a lot different than Rhode Island, but it's really pretty here."

"Yeah," said Chloe, "I'm excited to get to see a sunrise or sunset over the beautiful mountains and fields. I've seen some pretty ones in Providence, but the sun falls behind the city's skyline. I bet the sky gets beautiful here with the wide open land."

"Oh yeah, Chloe, it does." Anders nodded. "We actually hang out a lot on top of Copper Hill to toss the ball around and often we'll land ourselves in the middle of a sunset. You girls will have to join us sometime. Laurina and them love it."

"Sounds nice." Chloe nodded then raised her menu a bit, probably to hide the blush creeping across her cheeks.

A few minutes later, after Chloe and I ordered BLT sandwiches, Anders and Hadley ordered cheeseburgers, and Marcus ordered a French dip sandwich, the conversation returned to what the locals liked to do. "Oh, and on Thursday night there's a tractor race that should be fun," Marcus said.

"Wait," I glanced at Chloe, the two of us exchanging the same raised-eyebrow look. "Did you say a tractor race?" I turned to Marcus, but Anders beat him to the reply.

"Oh, it's amazing. There's a dirt track at the edge of town and a whole bunch of farmers and non-farmers get together with their tractors and race 'em. It draws a huge crowd. A few people paint themes on their tractors but the farmers are using their daily equipment so those are the standard green and yellow."

"Are you being serious?"

"Yeah." He laughed. "There's tractor pulls, too, not just the race. And vendors get together to sell popcorn and corn dogs. Java Joe even gets in on it and sells iced coffee and mini cupcakes. Anyway, it might sound stupid but I swear it's fun."

"I believe you." I shook my head, surprising myself with how much it *did* sound fun. "Super different from what we're used to."

"And what's that?" I was pretty sure he was asking me, since I was the one talking, but his eyes were on Chloe.

"A fun night out in Rhode Island? Um, walking around the mall and grabbing pizza, hanging at the community pool, or on special occasions, a bay cruise down the coast. Definitely no tractor races."

"Fair enough," Marcus interjected, with a smile. I took the break in our conversation to really look at him. He and Anders had the same caramel eyes and bright smile, though his skin was a shade or two darker. He was also a few inches taller than Anders, which made him at least half a foot taller than Hadley. He had broad shoulders and seemed fit for a grownup, and I imagined he was the type of dad who helped his son practice soccer in a hands-on way. He seemed really nice; I was happy for Hadley, of all the random wild west men she could've fallen for, she seemed to have found a really great match.

"You're welcome to join us Thursday if you wanna check it out. There's a group of us planning to meet for dinner at Carter's, his mom makes a mean spaghetti, before we head to the race."

I looked at Hadley who nodded in encouragement and then over at Chloe who was now smiling. "I mean, as long as Carter's mom doesn't mind two more mouths to feed."

"Yeah, we could always meet you after the dinner if it's too much." Chloe added.

"I'll ask if you want, but Ms. Conway loves to feed us, so I doubt she'll mind."

"Sounds good. Thanks for the invite. I think." I laughed, which made the rest of the table laugh, too. A minute later our lunches were on the table and we dug in. Halfway through my BLT, I realized I still didn't know all that much about Marcus. I wasn't sure what type of topics I was supposed to bring up with adults, but I figured it was safe to ask about his job, so that's what I did.

"For the past few years, I've been working as a bovine veterinarian but I started off as a traditional vet." He replied.

"Bovine?"

"Just a fancy word for cow. There's a lot of farms around here and in the neighboring counties so I travel during the day to do health checks, disease prevention, emergency care, that sort of thing. I am trained with other large animals, too, like horses as well as domestic pets."

"Oh, that's pretty cool. Hadley you've got it made if you ever need help with Little Foot!"

Hadley nodded and Marcus agreed. "Little Foot is a cutie. Hard to believe she's around thirteen years old. She jumps with the energy of a cat in her prime."

"Hey, wait, do you help the horses at that place my aunt rides at? The arena?"

He looked over at Hadley who clarified. "She means Steeplechase Stadium, Terri's place."

"Oh, right." Should he know where my aunt liked to hang out? "They have a resident veterinarian so I'm not there often, but I've filled in a handful of times."

"Gotcha. Hadley, can we go there one day to see the horses?"

"Oh, absolutely. I've been bonding with a horse named Gingerbread, a beautiful mahogany thoroughbred," Hadley said, pausing to swipe a fry through the blob of ketchup on her plate. "I teach a horse care and management program on Wednesday nights and volunteer my time over the weekend."

Her voice was a melody of memories as she continued to tell us all about the horses. As she spoke, she sat back against the booth, her fingers still loosely holding her burger. Her face lit up in that familiar way I'd seen so many times – like when I was little and begged her to tell me about Snow White, the horse she rode when she was my age, back after her mom had died.

"Wait, are you supposed to be at the horse place now, Hadley? It's Saturday." I asked, pushing a piece of bacon back into my sandwich.

She shook her head with a small smile. "No, I let them know a few weeks ago that you girls would be coming into town and that I'd need the week off to make sure you're settled in." She took a sip from her glass before adding, "I did the same with my job. I'll go back next week. As for the horses, I'll be back on Wednesday. And then maybe next weekend you can tag along and check out the stable."

"Thanks, Hadley. I'd love that," I said, brushing crumbs off my fingers and glancing next to me. "You, too, Chlo, right?"

Chloe looked up from where she was peeling the lettuce of her sandwich, her expression lighting with interest. "Definitely. I've never even seen a horse up close."

"Really?" Anders cocked his head.

"Yeah. Well, I guess once. When my parents took me to New York City to see the Rockettes for Christmas. Some of the cops in the park were on horses."

"What're the Rockettes?" Anders wiped his mouth with his cloth napkin before he dropped it on his empty plate and focused on Chloe.

"Oh, um, it's like a Christmas thing with really pretty dancers with impossibly long legs. They do dance routines in, like, perfect sync. They do these high kicks that I'm not even sure how it's physically possible, but they nail it."

"Oh, sounds cool."

"Yeah, it's magical." She nodded "I only saw them once, a few Christmases ago. I tried to convince my parents to take me again last year but, you know, life and all that. Maybe next year..."

I looked up from my sandwich when Chloe's voice trailed off. I knew by life she meant her dad and how he was gone most of December for work, or at least that's what he said, and when he didn't get home until late on Christmas Eve it started a big fight. I also knew how devastated she was when her mom dismissed her request to see the Rockettes again. Should I change the topic?

Before I had the chance, Anders spoke up, seemingly unaware of Chloe's shoulder tension. "We have a local Christmas pageant that the Church puts on, but that's about it. Unless you're into off-pitch singing and super basic dance moves, I wouldn't recommend it." His laughter made Chloe and I laugh.

"Yikes. Looks like we're not in Kansas anymore, Toto... or maybe we are!" I slapped my hand over my mouth as I let out a loud raspberry laugh.

"Yeah, yeah. Ask Renzo about it some time. Laurina and him were in the production up until they started high school. He loves talking about it," he smirked.

"That's hysterical."

Anders nodded my way in response and soon a mainly comfortable silence fell over the table as we finished the last of our fries.

"So girls, I was thinking this afternoon we could check out the Book Nook since I know you're both big readers, and if I'm being honest I need the next book in the Harry Potter series. The fourth one comes out in a few weeks and I haven't even started the third."

"Ohmigod, Aunt Hadley, are you a secret nerd?"

"Hey, there's nothing wrong with a little book escapism in the form of witchcraft and wizarding." Hadley waved off my wide-eyed slow nod. Of course she's a fantasy nerd. Honestly, I'm not even surprised. "Anyway, are you girls in or are you just going to keep making fun of me?"

"I started reading *The Cider House Rules* that I found on your bookshelf, but would love to look around."

"Great read," Marcus stated. "I wish Anders over here would read more, but unless it's a biography on David Beckham or Paul Scholes, there's no chance it's getting opened."

"Hey, I also like Ryan Giggs, or anyone in the Manchester United squad."

"I stand corrected." Marcus laughed with this easy, warm kind of charm that made him instantly likeable. There was something grounded about him. Something that seemed to balance out Hadley's sometimes-scatterbrained sparkle. Her smile proved it all.

When the waitress dropped off the check, he grabbed it without hesitation and handed it back with folded cash, telling her to keep the change. She gave him a grateful smile, and I watched as Hadley leaned against the back cushion, still grinning like her heart was suddenly lighter.

It was moments like that that made me jealous of what grown-ups got to feel.

"You girls in for the tractor race?" Anders interrupted my moment of envy.

I looked at Chloe and smiled, waiting for her to speak up.

"Sounds fun," she finally said.

"Sweet." He nodded, shoving his hands in his pockets. "See you Thursday. I'll make sure Hadley gets the address for the Conways. If you can meet us there, we can drop you off at the end of the night. If that's okay with you, Miss Hadley?"

"That sounds fine with me, as long as it's someone with a driver's license, common sense, and no funny business."

"Yes, ma'am."

"Anders, sweetheart, for the hundredth time, please just call me Hadley. Ma'am is my mama."

I cocked my head, not sure what that even meant. She rarely talked about her mom, who died when she was my age, so it seemed totally out of the blue. Whatever, she had a big smile on her face so I wasn't about to question it.

"Sorry, habit. Thanks for lunch, it was fun."

"Your dad paid for it." She laughed. "So thank him."

"Right." He shook his head. "Thanks, Dad. So, Chloe and Amelia, see you Thursday?"

We nodded in unison.

I loved this for Chloe almost as much as I loved this for me. Anders is definitely crushing on her and I already know she thought he was cute, too. Plus, no mention of the drunk event so clearly he was a gentleman. Although why would he bring that up in front of his dad and my aunt? All the same, he didn't seem to be acting weird and *he* invited *us* to the tractor race. How literally insane is it that I'm excited for a tractor race?

I just hope Anders and Chloe continue to gel so that I get more time with Renzo.

Honestly, I wouldn't mind cracking the code on Laurina, either. I saw moments of niceness from her so I know there has to be more to her mean girl facade. We'll see. For now, it's time to browse books. Maybe my aunt will treat us to a few. And maybe she won't know which ones my mom usually said no to. There was nothing more fun than browsing aisles of books and reading all the back covers until something stuck. The only difference was back home we'd grab Starbucks next door and then walk around Borders Bookstore with a Frappuccino in hand. Hmmm...

"Hey, Hadley?"

"Why does that sound like you want something?"

I smiled my best 'who me' smile. "I was just thinking about how whenever mom takes me & Chlo to Borders we'd grab Starbucks first. I know we just ate and that there's definitely no Starbucks here but there is a fancy schmancy Java Joe's we're about to walk past."

"And you'd like a drink?"

"I mean, if you're offering, sure! Thanks, Hadley!"

"Your mom warned me you're tricky now."

I giggled and grabbed Hadley for a side hug. She wrapped her arm around me and surprisingly, or maybe not, wrapped her other arm around Chloe. "You win. Let's grab some fun drinks and then we can head to the Book Nook. You can each pick out one book on me."

"Thanks, Hadley." Chloe said at the same time as I squealed out a "Yay, sounds good."

Dinner at Carter's

"How do we look, Hadley? Do we look like girls who go to tractor races?" I was wearing a jean skirt with a gray shirt featuring a Blink-182 band logo. I spent the morning cutting a new scooped neckline and making cuts into the sides so that I could tie cute little knots that worked as both a fashion statement and made the shirt more fitted. Gone was the oversized t-shirt my Uncle Josh gave me. I also threw on a stretchy black plastic choker and a bit of mascara, same as Chloe. That was the only part of our looks that matched, though, since she decided on a sky blue tank top stacked on top of a white tank top, a pair of low rise khaki cargo short-shorts, and her Adidas black and white slides. I was pretty sure she wore the sandals to impress soccer-loving Anders, because she usually opted for her basic Birkenstocks, but who was I to call her out.

"Did your shirt come like that?" Hadley grabbed my hand and twirled me.

"Not exactly. I was really getting into the *Confessions of a Shopaholic* book I picked out over the weekend and realized I probably shop too much, so why not practice a few fashion techniques and make old clothes new? Very economical, right?"

"Very economical indeed. And creative, Meels, I love it. Just be careful leaning forward, that scoop neck is a little, uh, scoopy."

"Hadley!" My eyes bulged as I yanked the neckline up with a nervous tug. I definitely wanted to show off a little, but not to *her*. The whole point was to look good enough for people who didn't know me yet to not see me as a little kid.

"I'm just saying. You're only fourteen and you're quite well developed – and don't get me wrong that's a whole blessing, but you have to pay attention to these things. Especially around a group where the guys are generally a few years older. That's all, sweetheart."

I crossed my arms tightly over my chest, heart thudding like I'd been caught doing something bad. Did I really cut the neckline too low? Was it obvious I was trying to look sixteen? I glanced down, the shirt now feeling way more revealing than it had in the mirror. Hadley wasn't trying to be mean, I knew that, but something about the way she said, "quite well developed" made me want to shrivel up and die.

"I didn't mean to embarrass you," she added quickly, her voice softer. "Honestly, I love it." She shifted her focus to Chloe. "You look great, too. If I had legs like that, I'd live in those shorts."

"You *do* have legs like her, Aunt Hadley." I muttered, rolling my eyes, though the words came out half-hearted. My heart still fluttered from utter mortification.

"Well, maybe when I was a teenager." She shook her head, almost like she was disagreeing with some conversation in her head. "I'll stick to my high waisted shorts." She laughed. "Anyway, you girls still have the Post-it note with my phone number, in case anything happens?"

"Yep." I patted my pocket for good measure.

"Perfect. Then let's head on out." She clapped her hands once, like she was sealing the plan. "I'll drop you at the Conways' house, then I'm going to swing by Steeplechase because I think I left my sunglasses there last night. After that, and maybe a quick swing by the China Palace for some takeout, I'll be in for the night. Easy to get a hold of, and will definitely be awake when you get home."

I laughed. "It's okay if you fall asleep. Anders told us when he called with the address that his neighbor would bring us home. He told me to promise you he was very safe and responsible."

"Thanks for letting me know. Make sure you're polite and thank him for driving you, okay?"

"I will be *howdy-dowdy* nice, promise." I held up three fingers in an exaggerated scout's honor pose.

Hadley laughed. "You're too much. I can't wait to hear how much fun you have."

We started walking toward her car, our sandals slapping softly against the driveway. As she unlocked the door, she added, "Oh, and don't forget to thank Mrs. Conway, too, for dinner. I can't imagine the patience it takes to host a bunch of teenagers."

"We will," I said, though my stomach flipped a little. It was one thing to hang out with Chloe, but tonight, we'd be showing up at someone's house. Someone we didn't really know. There'd be even more new people to impress. I wasn't sure if I was excited or about to throw up.

With stomachs full of delicious garlic and red pepper pasta with what had to be homemade meatballs, we migrated to Carter's basement to hang out for an hour before leaving for the event. I looked around at the wood-paneled walls, the dark green and beige berber carpet, and the plaid furniture, which was not unlike the set my mom had at home. There was a whole wall of floor to ceiling bookshelves, half full of board games and toys and the other half with books. There were photos in wood frames that speckled the back wall that were mainly of Carter and two blonde girls, elementary aged, who must be his younger sisters. There was a television that sat in one corner, muted but airing a soccer match.

One thing I was glad to not see when I looked around was Laurina and her posse. Renzo had mentioned at dinner that they were at some cheerleading volunteer event that I guess is meant to look good on college apps. They were already thinking about colleges...

Carter walked over to the boombox radio and turned it on, immediately filling the space with "Country Grammar" by Nelly. I quickly forgot about Laurina and started singing "I'm goin' down, down, baby, your street in a Range Rover" along with Chloe and half the room. We broke out into laughter at our spontaneous karaoke and settled into the seats, Chloe and I on a couch alongside a girl whose name, I think, was Amanda. Renzo was standing near the tv with two of his soccer teammates, Carter and Matty were still near the boombox but looked to be eyeing the couch across from us, and Anders plopped in the wingback chair kitty-cornered to Chloe's end of the couch.

"The rest of the girls should be here any minute," Matty announced and I rolled my eyes.

"Sweet." Carter nodded.

"So, Chloe," Anders leaned her way. "Tell me more about yourself. I didn't really have the opportunity to say much to you when we were out with Hadley and my dad."

"Oh." She blushed and glanced over to me. I couldn't tell if she was nervous because she liked him or because she was afraid of slipping up and mentioning we're not technically freshmen yet, let alone incoming sophomore. It was probably the first thing because nobody but me was thinking about what grades we were, or weren't, in.

I smiled encouragingly.

"There's not much to know," she finally said. "I've lived in Rhode Island my whole life, been friends with Amelia since we were five, um my favorite tv show is either *Friends* or *Will & Grace*, though I always watch *Who Wants to be a Millionaire* with my mom on Wednesdays, so I guess I like that, too. I don't play sports but do enjoy running. I know bits of Taiwanese but not enough to impress my grandmother. Oh, and I love peanut butter on my pancakes." She laughed, realizing how much she had disclosed.

"Awesome highlight reel. Ya'll have been friends about the same length as me and Renz. Laurina and I used to be tight, too, but she's a lot of... energy. She's nicer than she seems, though, just takes a bit of adjusting. Anyway, I guess I can highlight reel my—"

"Hey guys!" Laurina and her top-knot ponytail bounced down the stairs with Rylee and Morgan close behind.

"Speak of the devil," I mumbled. Anders raised his eyebrows and let out a light laugh.

"Oh, wow, Chloe, you actually showed face? Glad to see you're alive and well." She smiled in the most condescending way possible then turned to Morgan and laughed.

That snotty little bit—

"I remember when you threw up in the back of Dave's car like 2 months ago, Reen. Chill."

"Whatever, Lo-ren-zo." Laurina rolled her eyes at her brother and walked off with her blonde clones toward the bowl of trail mix. Although maybe they weren't clones because I noticed Rylee had mouthed *sorry* to Chloe. It didn't make much of a difference because Chloe had already sunk back into the couch, noticeably mortified.

I was about to ask her if she was okay when Renzo dropped into the recliner kitty-corner from the other side of the couch, where Amanda was, and winked at me. I smiled dumbly, not sure how to start a conversation. It sounded like Anders filled in the friendship gap I accidentally made by restarting his conversation.

"Ignore her. It's like she knew someone called her nice and she had to turn on her mean girl personality. I wish she didn't do that. Like, what's wrong with being nice."

When I looked over at them, Anders was shrugging and Chloe sat up a bit from where she had previously slouched. Feeling good about it, I turned my focus back to Renzo who was in a heated conversation with Carter about the match on tv. I had no idea how to participate, I definitely didn't watch soccer... or any sports, but I could sit here, smile, and nod.

Wow, soccer was boring.

It was apparently a re-airing of the Italy vs Netherlands game that aired earlier today as part of the UEFA Euro tournament, but that was about all I absorbed so far. All I could focus on was the sound of Renzo's laugh, which came out a few notes deeper than his speaking voice, and wrapped around me like a warm blanket. It was impossible not to laugh along with him. How could he be so warm and inviting when his genetic twin was an iceberg?

Although, wait. I'm pretty sure we learned in school that boy-girl twins don't share the same DNA, like same sex twins would. That explained it. He sucked up all the nice genes, leaving her dry and rude.

While I tried my best to care about the foul called against one of the Italian players, I found myself tuning into the conversation happening to my right.

"Have you thought at all about college yet? I know you've got time yet. I mean, I'm starting junior year and *should* have a decision made, but don't." He scratched the back of his neck. "Right now I'm thinking about sports management or kinesiology, but not sure what school I want to pursue. My dad and my school counselor keep reminding me the clock's ticking on application windows. Which, like, damn, I'm not even officially a junior yet. Can we just slow down a minute?"

He laughed, but the way his leg bounced gave away his anxiety.

"Sorry," he added, "you're making me nervous, and I keep rambling instead of letting you speak."

"You're nervous?" Chloe smiled.

"Yep... So, any thoughts on college or no college or whatever?"

"That depends on who you ask," Chloe said, leaning back against the couch like this conversation didn't make her want to throw up. "Both of my parents attended Columbia Law and got their JDs. My dad practices immigration law while my mom has an independent practice in intellectual property law – she mostly works from home. So yeah, they've had Columbia's pre-law program on my radar since I was in kindergarten."

I sat there pretending to smooth my hair then shifted my focus to the silent soccer match on tv, nodding absently like I cared who was winning. But really, I was tuned into every word Chloe was saying. I knew the story about Columbia, she complained about it all the time. Law was *not* her dream.

"Damn, you have some smart genes, huh?" Anders said.

"I guess." Her smile lifted, then dropped.

"Does Columbia actually interest you though?"

"No, not really. But try telling my parents..." she sighed. "Anyway. So, if you ask them, they'll saw Columbia. If you ask Meels," – my ears perked up – "she'd say Miami."

I blinked, turning slightly toward her, but not enough for her to notice how dialed in I was.

"We always talked about going there together. Getting degrees in sun tans and relaxation. Well, really, she's interested in communications, and me psychology, but people go to Miami for the sun."

My chest warmed. She remembered the major I decided on in fifth grade? We only talked about the sun tans and relaxation part a few times, generally late at night, in those half-silly, half-serious moods. I smiled at the TV.

"There's something so fun about a palm tree," Anders said.

"Yeah, for sure. It would be like a four-year vacation with my best friend! Plus all the education," she laughed.

"You said if you asked her, but what about if I asked *you*. Which I did, by the way." Anders smiled as he grabbed two Gatorades from the bag Matty passed around.

I stayed quiet, my hands suddenly fidgeting in my lap. She made it sound like Miami was *my* dream when I always thought it was *ours*. I wasn't sure what stung more, her doubt in our dream, or the fact that Anders was the one she was figuring it all out with.

Chloe twisted the lid open for a sip. "If you asked me, I would probably say GCU. Grand Canyon U. It's a small school in the center of Phoenix and so beautiful. I saw a brochure once. It would definitely be a quieter approach to college than Columbia or Miami."

"Quiet sounds nice." He smiled while my own smile distorted itself into what felt like a grimace. Quiet? Small school? *Arizona?* We always talked about Miami, and she seemed just as excited as me about going somewhere far away from home that was surrounded by palm trees and beaches. How did she so easily offer this info up to someone she just met and yet I never even knew. I thought we were best friends.

I should've bit my tongue and focused back on Renzo, but I couldn't stop myself. "Since when do you want to go to Arizona?" It came out harsher than I intended and a few previously distracted sets of eyes shifted our way.

"I mean, it's just an option." Chloe said, surprised by my abruptness. "Miami is definitely the front runner."

"I never even knew you were interested in GCU," I threw my hands up in defeat. "Why didn't you tell me?"

She shrugged.

I huffed and stared, not backing down.

After a minute, she finally conceded. "Because, Amelia, you never really gave me that chance." Her tone was the harshest I had ever heard. "Once you decided we should go to Miami, you created this whole plan for us. I didn't want to hurt your feelings by suggesting anything different. Plus, Miami *does* sound fun, I'm not saying I *don't* want to go there." She sighed. "We have plenty of time to figure it out, we haven't even started—"

"Stop." I yelled, knowing what she was about to say. It was bad enough she hadn't been honest with me, she'd ruin everything if she admitted we were younger than they all thought.

Chloe's eyes glistened with a combination of shock and sadness. Maybe even frustration.

"Sorry," I said, lowering my voice despite the edge of irritation. "I just meant, we'll talk about it later. No point in drawing a crowd over a stupid disagreement."

"Yeah, sure. No biggie." She said softly, slouching back into the couch the same way she had when Laurina showed up. Great, now I was the snotty jerk. Whatever, best friends should tell each other everything.

"Sorry, sweets, didn't mean to start a thing," Anders frowned. "I was just tryna get to know you."

Sweets? What, can't take the time to say sweetheart? Eye. Roll. Plus, she's always hated being called nicknames. Shouldn't he have remembered that from the barn party?

Wait a minute. Was she blushing? Unreal.

"It's okay," she practically gushed. "So, what exactly is kinesiology?"

Their conversation continued on as they learned a bunch of interesting facts about each other, and I was left there to stare at the back of Renzo's head since he and Carter had turned to watch the ending of the UEFA match.

The Tractor Race

After Italy defeated Netherlands, we all stood up to head out. It was only a few blocks from Carter's house to the tractor race so we decided to walk instead of figuring out a ride situation, especially since there were ten of us in total. Laurina, Morgan, Rylee and her boyfriend Matty took the lead, followed a few feet back by Carter, Renzo, Amanda, and me and behind us Anders and Chloe. I was about to strike up a conversation with Amanda when Renzo sidestepped and smoothly ended up next to me.

"What's the frown about, Hourglass?"

"Is that my nickname now?" I smiled despite myself, his perpetual good mood was infectious.

"When you wear shirts like that, yeah." His eyes dipped to my scooped neck. "You look amazing. I meant to tell you that when you first walked through the door but Mrs. Carter was standing there so that felt weird."

I laughed. "This old thing? Thanks." I pulled at the bottom hem of my shirt, making sure it was still sitting in place.

"So the frown?"

"Oh, nothing," I said, brushing a piece of hair behind my ear. "Chloe just caught me off guard earlier."

"Ah, yeah, I heard your little spat. Happens to the best of us. You okay?"

"I am now." I elbowed his side lightly, like it was no big deal.

It was easier to flirt than to admit I felt a little gutted. I could hear Chloe's laugh behind us, light and easy. I didn't want to dwell on it. I didn't want to wonder whether she still saw me as part of her future, or just as her until-we-graduate best friend.

So I shifted closer to Renzo. Not enough to be obvious, just enough to feel the space between us shrink. He wasn't where the ache came from, but he might be where I could forget it for a little while.

He smiled at me. "Carter and I added some booze to our Gatorades before we left. His cousin's in college and hooks him up whenever he's home. Want some?" He wiggled the bottle. I glanced behind me at Chloe and Anders, who were deep in conversation, probably about how amazing the Grand Canyon is, and looked back at Renzo with a nod. I unscrewed the cap and took a big gulp. It burned on the way down, but I steadied my reaction.

"Atta girl." He took the bottle back and took a swig. Knowing his lips were where mine were a second ago made my palms sweat.

"Can I get another sip?" I asked nervously. He handed me the bottle and I let the harsh bite calm me. Who cares where Chloe wants to go to college; the rest of the night I was going to focus on Renzo and the tractor race. "So people really get excited for tractor races around here?"

"There's not much else goin' on for us, so yeah."

"Cool..."

"I know it must sound stupid to you, but it really is fun. You'll get wrapped up in the environment before you know it. There's vendors that set up with cotton candy, popcorn, and corndogs, Java Joe's has a stand with coffee and desserts, and there's fresh squeezed lemonade that is hella bomb. Then there's a few games usually set up like a cornhole competition, balloon darts, and one of those Strongman games."

"Strongman game?"

"You know, like at carnivals." He mimed swinging a mallet down. "That game where you hit the base as hard as you can, hoping the weight would shoot up enough to ring the bell?"

"Oh, *that*. Can you make it ring?"

"I'm hurt." His right hand flew to his chest. "Of course I can."

I giggled. "You sure? Might have to prove it."

"Oh, game on, girl. I'm more than just charming good looks... I'm muscles, too." He curled his arm up to flex his bicep. Muscles, he was.

"And modest," I laughed. "Okay, so when do the actual tractors come into play?"

"So the game and stuff is all set up before the grandstand entrance. Like behind it. Anyway, you can sit wherever you want in the stands and there's a whole series of events from tractor tug-o-war to an obstacle course and even mud bogging."

"Do I even want to ask what the heck mud bogging is?"

His laugh enveloped me. "It's where the trucks plow through deep mud pits. I'm not all that sure how it's scored to be honest but it's really entertaining. Just don't sit in the first few rows because when they get into a big rut, the tires shoot mud all over the place."

"Good to know," I laughed lightly and accepted the spiked Gatorade he handed my way. When I glanced behind me, Chloe had furrowed eyebrows like she was wondering why I was drinking from Renzo's bottle. Guess we both had secrets.

After a few minutes, we approached the gates. My aunt had given Chloe and me some money for tickets, but surprisingly Laurina handed them out to all of us. "It's on my mom," she clarified. We all thanked her and headed through the entrance.

"We're going to grab cotton candy," Morgan called back at us. "We'll meet you guys at the stands in, like, twenty." They didn't wait on a response before they waltzed off, giggling between the three of them about who knows what.

Matty quickly walked off trying to catch up with the girls. Rylee immediately looped her arm through his and planted a kiss on his cheek. They were like magnets.

Carter, Renzo, Amanda, Chloe, Anders, and I were left standing in a circle figuring out our next move. Carter asked Amanda if she wanted popcorn and the moment she nodded, they walked off. I was trying to figure out who Amanda even was, because I hadn't recognized her from the party, but it was starting to seem like Carter invited her just so he'd have someone to flirt with. He came across as a bit of a playboy, I mean I saw him talking with three different girls at the barn party last week. Hopefully Amanda kept her guard up.

Chloe came up next to me and quietly commented, "Guess we're really about to see a tractor race."

I knew it was meant as an olive branch, and honestly, I couldn't help but laugh. It seemed the alcohol had stripped away my anger and left me with euphoria. I was happy to have my best friend at my side.

"Best summer ever," I laughed a bit louder than I intended and slapped my hand over my mouth.

Luckily she laughed, too, and repeated "best summer ever" while bumping her hip against mine. It caused me to crack up even harder.

"Okay, lightweight, let's get some corndogs," Renzo said with a wink.

"Lightweight?" Chloe's head tilted as she looked between us.

"Yeah, we split my Gatorade, which was spiked with Svedka." He wrapped his arm around my waist and I'm pretty sure I let out an audible sigh.

"Oh... is everyone... is everyone drinking?"

Things felt hazy but I could still register the worry on her face and in her voice.

"Nah, girl, no worries." Renzo shook his head. "It was just me and Matty being idiots and I offered some to Amelia. Just a bit of fun. But everyone else is straight."

"Oh, okay." She nodded but when she looked at me, her eyes were cloudy with concern.

"Best summer ever, right?" I giggled and leaned into Renzo. She nodded again, hesitantly.

"Anders, you good bro? I'm going to get us some food and then hit the Strongman game – I've got a point to prove. After that, we'll head to the seats."

"He *thinks* he's strong." I teased, squeezing Renzo's arm.

"You didn't even give me a chance to flex," he whined, tightening his muscles until my hand practically popped off. I laughed, but it wasn't just about the joke – it felt good to play along. To be wanted by him.

"I'm good, bro," Anders said, grinning. "I'm more than fine to hang with Chloe. We'll meet you guys at the stands."

I gave them a dramatic wave and flashed a wide smile as Renzo gently guided me toward the food vendors. A flicker of guilt tugged at my chest, I probably should've stayed with Chloe. This summer was supposed to be about the two of us, doing everything together. But when I glanced back, she looked happy, deep in conversation with Anders, her laugh unbothered. We'd meet up soon anyway so I'm sure it was no big deal.

Once Renzo and I had corndogs in hand, we got in line for the Strongman game. I scarfed mine down in probably the least cute way possible, barely breathing between bites. When Renzo offered me his second one, I didn't even pretend to hesitate; I gladly accepted. With each bite, I felt more like myself again. By the time we neared the front of the line, my vision felt clear, like the euphoric fog was lifted.

"Sorry I inhaled your corndog," I said, cheeks flushed.

"No worries, Hourglass," he grinned. "We all have our moments. Plus... it was kinda hot."

"It was *not*." I smacked his arm, but couldn't help but smile.

"Trust me, it was." He smirked, then added, "if you're worried about drinking, just double down on Mrs C.'s spaghetti next time."

Next time.

"That's funny. At the barn your sister made a similar comment about frontloading with carbs before drinking. I guess you guys are right. But to be fair, I wasn't planning on eating like a pig and had no idea we'd be drinking, so—"

"Fair, fair. For what it's worth, you'd make one gorgeous pig."

"Thanks?" I laughed. "I think."

We shuffled forward, reaching the front of the line.

"Oh, you're up, strong man! Let's see what you got." I stepped aside as Renzo handed a dollar to the attendant and gripped the mallet. He rested it on his shoulder, threw me a wink, then slammed it down like he'd be training for this moment his whole life.

The weight shot up and struck the bell with a loud, satisfying clang.

He made it look stupidly easy. *Okay, then.*

My palms were sweaty all over again, and I was *very* aware of how warm my face felt. "Nice" was all I managed as he walked back toward me, an extra swagger in his step.

"Told ya." He smirked, curling his arm up to flex. My eyes dropped to his arm, and stayed there a moment too long. "You like it," he teased. "Alright, girl, let's head to the stand before they wonder where we got off to." He tossed his arm back around my shoulders and guided us toward the stand.

"I can't believe I'm into tractor tug-o-war." Chloe marveled.

"I know, right?" Our eyes were locked on the two tractors that were currently hitched together back-to-back by a chain. The crowd was cheering them on as they attempted to pull one another across the center line. It was like the tug-o-war we played in elementary school but with huge tractors.

The once bright green tractor was edging away, dragging the yellow tractor toward the center. Chloe grabbed my hand and we both slid to the edge of our seats, mesmerized. Moments later the yellow tractor broke through the plastic center line and the crowd erupted. We jumped to our feet and cheered. When we looked at each other we started cracking up at the randomness of it all.

"You think that's entertaining," Anders leaned in. "Just wait. Up next is the mud bogging."

"Ohmigod, Renzo told me about this. Things are about to get dirty, Chlo." I laughed.

"Is that so?" Renzo said with a devilish grin.

"You wish." I swatted his chest.

"Sure do."

My eyes widened with my smile. I broke eye contact with him to hold a fast telepathic conversation with Chloe. I had no idea what to do next. Or even what to say. Based on Chloe's silent response to me, she was also at a loss. It was exactly what I wanted, a cute boy who was interested in me, but now that I got this far – and bonus, Chloe and Anders have equally hit it off – we had no idea what to do.

Before anyone realized how lame we were, an announcer boomed from the series of speakers that encircled the track to announce the first tractor to attempt to trudge through the mud. Anders leaned in again and explained that the winner would be whichever tractor traversed the mud the fastest and if nobody was successful, it would be whichever tractor made it the farthest.

We watched the first tractor dive right into the mud, leaving deep ruts behind every foot it traveled. *How Do You Like Me Now* by Toby Keith echoed from the speakers and mud flew in wide arcs behind the tractor's wheels, splattering the front two rows of people, who cheered and shouted with excitement.

I was glad to be ten rows up, this outfit was far too cute to get sprinkled with mud, but it didn't stop me from jumping up and cheering with the rest of the crowd. Even Laurina must've momentarily forgotten she hated me, because when the tractor made it through to the end, she turned around and gave me an enthusiastic high five.

Forty-five minutes later, the last tractor failed to finish, and the announcer crowned the second one as the fastest and the official winner. We let out a final round of cheering before filtering down the bleachers and toward the exit.

I nearly tripped when we stepped onto the grassy area and Renzo slid his hand into mine.

He didn't say anything, and neither did I. My heart definitely noticed, though. We walked that way, hand in hand, toward the popcorn stand, where Chloe, Anders, and I were supposed to meet Anders' neighbor for a ride home.

Renzo hung out with us, his fingers still laced with mine even while talking directly to Anders. The two of them launched into a full-on debrief about the match earlier, both shocked, apparently, at how Italy was able to win on penalties in an otherwise 0-0 score. They went back and forth predicting who would win the next round: Italy or France. Anders was all in on Italy, but Renzo wasn't sure.

"Oh, there's my neighbor now!" Anders pointed. "He had the blue and white painted tractor, one of the ones that made it through the bogging but nowhere near fast enough."

"I remember that tractor," I replied. "I thought the color combination was pretty. Especially since there were so many green and yellow ones. Those were super basic."

"That's 'cause those are John Deere and Caterpillars." Anders' neighbor, stated as he walked up. "The farmers don't paint their equipment because they'll bring them back to their property, power wash 'em, and then get back to work."

"Oh, I guess that makes sense." Chloe nodded.

"Yeah, guys like me are doin' this for fun with old equipment that we more-or-less enhanced for these types of events. I'm Phil, by the way." He extended his hand and we both offered weak handshakes.

"I'm Amelia, and this is my best friend, Chloe. Thanks for driving us."

"You got it. Anything for Mr. White."

"Your last name is White," Chloe asked Anders with raised eyebrows.

"Yeah, ironic, isn't it?" he laughed. "And for the last time, Phil, my dad wants you to call him Marcus."

"My mama would have my hind if I didn't call him Mr. White or sir, you know that."

"Fair enough. Well, thanks for driving the girls and me."

Anders turned and slapped Renzo on the shoulder. "I'll see you Saturday for a pickup soccer game, right?"

"Absolutely," Renzo said. He was standing close to me now... really close, his arm brushing mine. "You girls wanna come cheer us on?"

I swear his words somehow tickled my neck, like a breeze, creating goosebumps on my arms.

"I would love that," I pouted, "but we promised Hadley we'd join her at Steeplechase."

"Next time," he said, taking a half-step back. "Well, guess I'll let ya girls get goin'. We'll catch up at the next party?"

"Definitely." I smiled, dragging my bottom lip through my teeth as a surge of nerves bubbled up. Renzo let go of my hand, and my palm instantly felt too empty.

I glanced down at the space between us, my heart sinking just a little. But when I looked up, his eyes were already on mine.

And then he leaned in.

There was no hesitation in the way he closed the gap. His lips found mine like we'd done this a hundred times, and I instantly forgot how to breathe.

My lips moved in sync with his, following his lead without a thought. I was nervous at first, but then let the connection wash over me; my heart was beating so loud I was sure he could hear it. If he did, he didn't show it.

It ended almost as quickly as it began, but something in me had shifted. My skin buzzed. My lips still tingled. And my brain? Completely short-circuited.

Oh. My. God.

Anders cleared his throat behind us.

"Uh, okie dokie then," Renzo blurted, stepping back like he suddenly remembered we weren't alone. "See you girls soon."

He turned and walked quickly toward Carter and the others, while I just stood there, dumbfounded. I wasn't sure if I wanted to squeal, faint, or rewind time and make it last longer.

Chloe linked her arm through mine and gently tugged me forward, pulling me out of my daze.

This was a daydream, right? Because otherwise, it meant Lorenzo Romano just *kissed me*.

As we trailed behind Anders and Phil, Chloe leaned in and whisper-squealed into my ear, confirming this was definitely not a dream.

Family on the Line

"I still can't believe Renzo kissed you last night," Chloe pushed me backward from where I sat opposite her on the bed. We'd just finished our Pop-Tarts, mine frosted blueberry, hers brown sugar cinnamon, both eaten fresh out of the foil packet since we never wasted the time to toast them. This was our first chance to really talk because when we got home last night Hadley was in fact awake and had rented *She's All That* from Blockbuster for us.

Honestly, I half expected to see *Land Before Time*, my favorite movie when I was little and the reason her cat's name was Little Foot. My mom still tried to push it on me sometimes, probably hoping to keep me trapped in my childhood forever, but Hadley wasn't like that. She gave me room to feel older, even if she didn't fully realize what I was getting myself into. We'd never lied to each other before – me to her, her to me – so why would she suspect anything now? That was the part that made me feel a little sick inside. Lying to my mom was one thing. Lying to Hadley felt like breaking some unspoken rule.

Hadley somehow remembered *She's All That* was one of my current favorite movies, which made me smile, and even though I'd seen it a dozen times, I still leaned in, taking mental notes on what they wore and how they acted.

Anyway, now Hadley was at work and we had the house to ourselves until around 4:30. We could've stayed in the kitchen or moved to the living room to talk, since it was just us, but in true us fashion, we rushed back to the bedroom and jumped onto the bed.

"I completely froze. He probably thinks I'm a freak." I pulled the sleeves of my shirt over my hands nervously.

"I actually think he was just as nervous."

"How could you know that?"

"Well, he stared at you after in the same trance you were in until Anders cleared his throat and then he stumbled over his words and hightailed it outta there. He was definitely nervous."

"Ohmigod, maybe you're right."

"I'm always right," she laughed.

"You and Anders seemed to be getting close. How's that going?"

"Oh, I don't know. I mean we're only here for a month so what's the point in trying to get close to him? There's no easy way to date someone in Montana from all the way in Rhode Island. Plus, if he found out I'm fourteen and not sixteen, he'd probably drop me like a hot potato anyway."

"You don't need to date him to have a little fun. This summer's for fun and for experiences. You don't need to date him to get your first kiss or whatever. Let loose!"

Chloe pressed her lips together, like she was holding back something heavier, then flashed an exaggerated grin. "There's no part of me that knows how to let loose."

"Oh, please," I waved the air between us. "I saw you guys flirting. Plus you were comfortable enough to tell him all types of things in Carter's basement."

"Right," she said, sucking in her bottom lip. "Can we actually talk about that?"

"Yeah. Let me start though, okay?" I softened my gaze. "I'm sorry I freaked out. I think I was just shocked to hear you didn't actually want to go to Miami with me. I mean, we talk about it all the time."

"No, Meels, *you* talk about it all the time. I just agree with you because that's what I always do."

"What is that supposed to mean?" I huffed.

Her shoulders deflated and she blew out a sigh. "It means I don't always know how to use my voice. I'm shy and I'm quiet and you're not. You're bold and confident and it's easier for me to follow you than try to create my own path. I'm not trying to be mean, it's just, I don't know. It is what it is."

"I didn't know that," I mumbled.

"It's not a bad thing. If I didn't have you to force me out of my comfort zone, I'd probably be sitting in science camp right now, learning about DNA extraction or building a robot or something."

"Is that what you would've wanted to do? If I didn't convince you about this best summer ever idea?"

"Gosh, no. Science camp is lame, but you know my parents. Anything for the college apps."

"So wild. We're not even in high school and they're already trying to pad your future college apps."

"Yep." Chloe nodded dramatically.

"For Columbia..."

"If they had their way, yeah. I have no idea how to let them down and honestly maybe in the next three years I'll appreciate Columbia more and my mind may change. I could also end up wanting Miami U. with you!

I love the idea of being roommates in college together. I literally have no idea."

"I could look into Grand Canyon University. It doesn't always need to be my way."

"Thanks," she smiled. "But honestly, I cannot see you anywhere but Miami with the palm trees and wide open ocean. We've got time, we'll figure it out." I nodded, knowing she was right, I belonged with the seashells.

"Well, I'm sorry. I shouldn't have acted like that," I exhaled. "And then I started chugging Renzo's alcohol Gatorade mix just to spite you, because I was mad you were sharing things with Anders that you never shared with me. It felt like we weren't best friends. It's dumb, I know."

"It did catch me off guard when Renz said you guys were drinking. The last time they all saw me, except for Anders, I was passed out on the couch then threw up into a bucket. It was so embarrassing and really scary actually."

"I'm sure nobody even remembered that."

Amelia narrowed her eyes. "It was literally the first thing Laurina said when she walked in."

I cringed. "Yeah, well, she's a snobby monster. She doesn't count."

"All the same, it was embarrassing and scary. I don't know how I feel about drinking now because what if that happens again. So, seeing you drinking so casually with him, like you were happy and giggly..." She shrugged.

"Sorry if it freaked you out. I was controlled, though, I knew what I was drinking."

"How, though? It was random alcohol mixed into a bottle of Gatorade. You have no idea how much was in there or how strong it even was."

"Okay, Mom." I said sarcastically. She rolled her eyes. "I understand, Chlo. I get the point, but as soon as I had a corn dog, I felt like I came back down to earth, so it couldn't have been a lot."

She nodded but didn't say anything.

Okay then, time to change the topic. "So what do you want to do today? Hadley left a few movies out on the coffee table for us if we want to check them out. Or we could go for a walk?"

"I'm good with watching a movie for now, then we can stay in our pajamas." She smiled.

"Oh, love that idea!" I clapped my hands together. "Let's go see what she rented for us." I grabbed Chloe's hand and pulled her in for a hug, which luckily she returned.

Once we got to the living room and saw the short stack of movies, we quickly agreed on *The Wedding Singer*, since I knew Chloe loved it. Chloe loaded the VCR, because of course Hadley didn't have a DVD player, while I threw a bag of popcorn into the microwave. Two minutes later we had settled onto the couch and were swept away by the humor of Adam Sandler's character, Robbie Hart, dressed in eighties clothing singing wedding songs.

Twenty minutes later the phone rang. "I wonder if that's Hadley checking on us." I paused the movie, shrugged at Chloe, and then walked to the corded phone that hung in the kitchen. "Hello? Oh, hi Mrs. Zhang." I looked over at Chloe, who sat crisscrossed on the couch. I waved her over. "Sure, of course, one second."

"It's your mom," I whispered. She rolled her eyes but grabbed the phone from me. I walked back to the couch and flopped down, wanting to give her privacy despite us being only a few feet apart. I grabbed the bowl of popcorn and started tossing kernels in my mouth.

"Hey mom."

"Yeah, I've been working on my math workbook." We both rolled our eyes.

"Wait, what? What do you mean?"

Chloe was silent for what felt like an eternity. When I saw her eyes well with tears I jumped off the couch and rushed to her side. I mouthed "what's wrong" but she didn't respond.

"Mom, what's going on?" Chloe's voice wavered; I grabbed her hand. She shook her head confused.

"But it was a business trip—"

My heart started to race as I watched tears fall silently from Chloe's glassy, brown eyes. I swallowed hard, wishing I could hear what her mom was saying.

"I knew you guys were fighting, but doesn't that happen to everyone? How could you—" Her mom must've cut her off.

Her voice cracked. "But have you tried?"

Chloe glanced at me, her expression torn between shock and sadness. "Okay, but, why now? Did you guys purposely wait until I was as far away as possible so you could just call me on Miss Hadley's phone?" She sighed and her shoulders slumped.

"So, what does this mean? Where will he go?"

"Okay. I just, I don't get it, Mom."

Chloe sank to the floor, unable to stand any longer. "I can't believe this is happening."

"Yeah, okay. I'll try to enjoy the rest of the vacation."

"You too, Mom. See you in a few weeks, I guess." She hung up, and the rest of the tears she had been holding back spilled out in a gut wrenching sob. I dropped to the floor where she was and pulled her into me, wrapping my arms around her.

"What happened, Chlo, talk to me."

She gently pushed herself out of my embrace and wiped at her wet face with her sleeve covered hands. "My mom just told me that she and my dad are getting divorced."

"Oh, Chlo, I'm so sorry. I never would've made light of their fighting or encouraged you to give them space by coming here with me if I knew this was going to happen."

"Well, apparently my mom had divorce papers ready to go months ago and she was just waiting to pull the trigger. I guess it was easier to blow up my life when I'm halfway across the country."

"Wow. Is that why your dad didn't show up the day we left for here?"

"I thought it was because he was on a business trip but apparently he just didn't want to deal with any of it. Deal with me? I don't know. My mom said it wasn't my fault but I feel like it is."

"Why would it be your fault?"

She rested her head against the kitchen wall and kicked her legs out in front of her. I matched her pose and waited on her to continue, grabbing her hand again. "I don't know. I could've been better. Caused them less stress—"

"Chloe, stop." My stomach twisted just hearing her say that. "No offense, but that's insane. You're the best person I know and you never start trouble. You're like the ideal child. None of this is because of you."

"Thanks," she sniffled. "I always tried so hard to be perfect for them. Hoping it would make my dad go on less business trips or make them argue less when he was home, but it obviously didn't matter." She started crying again, but only for a minute.

Her heartbreak quickly turned to anger as she let out a loud, frustrated growl.

"I'm going to call my aunt. She'll know what to do."

"No, it's okay. She already took off work for us last week. I don't want her to get in trouble for leaving early."

"Okay. How about I call her and ask her to bring home pizza then." When Chloe nodded, I stood up from the floor and extended my hand to help her up. "I'll give her a quick call while you go grab the comforter off our bed. We can snuggle on the couch and finish the movie. Maybe it'll distract you for a bit until Hadley gets home later."

"That sounds nice. Thanks, Meels."

I responded with a small smile. I had no idea her parents had been fighting *that* badly. I thought it was run of the mill fighting. Definitely not divorce level fighting. And if her mom already had divorce papers ready, I guessed that meant it'd been pretty bad for a while.

I wondered if something specific had happened or if her mom was just fed up with all his business trips. He only started traveling like that a year ago. Before then, it was pretty rare. For all I knew, maybe he was traveling more on purpose, not wanting to be home. That would really suck. I hope it's not that.

I grabbed the phone and dialed Hadley's work number, which was taped to the side of the fridge. I quickly let her know what happened and promised her we were okay and not to come home early. She agreed to bringing home pizza and said she'd add on some brownies, too.

Satisfied, I set the phone back on the receiver and met Chloe on the couch. She was stuffing handfuls of popcorn into her mouth, I guessed trying to drown her sadness in the movie theater butter. I grabbed the corner of the comforter and slid underneath it, scooching over until our shoulders rested together. We laid our feet on the coffee table and turned the movie back on. We spent the next hour and sixteen minutes watching the movie in complete silence. Neither of us laughed or swooned where we normally would and we forewent our normal jokes about the crazy eighties clothing and hair.

When the credits started to roll, I paused the video and turned to Chloe, taking in her red rimmed eyes. "So, now what? Do you want to watch another movie? Talk? I think Hadley will be home in like an hour."

Chloe sat up and bit the side of her mouth as she weighed the options. "Let's call Anders."

"Wait, what?"

"I said, let's call Anders."

"No, I heard you. I meant why? Did you want to talk to him about the stuff with your parents? I swear you can talk to me but I won't be mad if you'd rather him..."

"Ohmigod, no, that's not what I meant. I want to do the opposite. I want to forget about what's going on back home. I don't even know what *home* means anymore. I want to call him and see if there's anything going on tonight. I want to go to a party."

"Are you sure? I know you're upset but—"

"I'm sure." She spoke with an edge. "I want to forget about all of this. At least for tonight."

"Okay, let's call Anders."

I'm Fine

Renzo waved us over as soon as we got to the barn and tossed his arm over my shoulder. "Two nights in a row, how'd I get so lucky?" I guess his assumed nerves from last night had settled.

"We needed a night out. But as far as my aunt knows, we're in the bedroom watching movies, digging into a pile of desserts, and having a super secret slumber party."

"Oh, how do I get invited to one of those?" He wiggled his eyebrows.

I shoved his chest and giggled out a "You wish." He nodded enthusiastically. "I'm just glad Anders was able to get his neighbor to pick us up without his dad finding out. If Anders' dad knew we were here then my aunt would definitely have found out in like point two seconds."

"How do you know your aunt won't come into the bedroom to check on you girls?"

"We left the television on for the noise. Plus Chloe's got some stuff going on so I trust Hadley to give us our space. We'll sneak back in later and she'll be none the wiser."

"Devil."

I smiled sweetly.

"Everything okay with Chloe? You said she had stuff going on?"

I looked around, realizing she had already walked off, and spotted her standing next to the punch bowl with her cup tipped against her lips. "She will be. In the meantime, she seems to have the right idea. I'm going to go grab a drink with her."

"Sweet, I'll come find you soon," he winked.

A while later, I was invested in a conversation with Amanda, who was telling me about how Carter admitted to flirting with not one but two of her friends, claiming he never wanted anything serious. Apparently he just wanted to hang out with her. I wasn't surprised, but I pretended to sympathize with her all the same. *Guys suck, amiright?*

I excused myself quickly when I noticed Chloe from across the crowded barn, her eyes looking a bit too glossy. The news about her parents' divorce had hit her hard, and I couldn't blame her for wanting to escape, but the way she was chugging that drink – I knew it was going to end badly.

"Chloe, slow down," I kept my voice low, but the music swallowed my words. I reached out to touch her arm, trying to catch her attention, but she yanked it away as if my touch burned.

I could have been cozied up next to Renzo, maybe even sitting on his lap like Rylee always did with Matty, but I wasn't. I'd gone out of my way to be here for her instead, to keep her from spiraling into some emotional self-destruction she'd regret later. So why was she being mean to me? Pushing me away? That's not how we ever handled things.

"I'm fine," Chloe snapped, her voice sharp but unconvincing. Before I could react, she stormed off, weaving her way through the crowd. My heart sank as I saw her make a beeline for Anders, practically throwing herself onto his lap, the fake cheerfulness plastered on her face not fooling me for a second.

This was supposed to be the summer of new experiences, the best summer ever. But watching Chloe spiral like this? This wasn't how I meant for things to go. I wanted her to have new experiences because she wanted to, or because I wanted her to, not because she was sad. I hesitated, my stomach twisting into knots, then forced myself to walk over.

"Chloe, you've had enough," I said softly, reaching for her drink. "Come on, let's take a break."

Chloe's eyes blazed with anger. "Back off, Amelia!" She yelled. "I'm fine!" She pushed my hand away with such force the drink almost splashed out.

Anders looked uncomfortable but steadied a gentle hand on Chloe's shoulder. "I'll keep an eye on her," he whispered to me, his eyes sincere.

I nodded, feeling a mix of relief and guilt. I couldn't drag her away; she'd just fight me. I needed to let go, at least for now. I turned and spotted Renzo across the room. Maybe a distraction was what I needed, too. I pivoted, ready to step away, but turned back, offering a sympathetic glance toward Chloe, silently praying she'd be okay.

"Best summer ever, right Meelia?" She smiled before tipping her cup back.

I smiled, my eyes shifting between her and Anders. He nodded and mouthed "It's okay" so I turned and walked over to Renzo, determined to salvage my mood. She could ruin her night, if she wanted, but no reason to ruin mine. I tried.

"Everything alright, Hourglass?" Renzo leant against one of the wooden pillars that supported the barn and took a slow sip from the red plastic cup in his hand.

"Yeah, I think so." I looked across the barn at Chloe, still on Anders' lap, laughing a little too loud. "I don't want to talk about it." I waved the whole thought off. "We came here to have fun, so let's focus on that."

"Okay, let's have some fun then." He smiled. "You wanna crank up the music and dance? Or... we could play truth or dare."

I narrowed my eyes nervously at the mischief in his. "Let's start with the dancing."

"You got it. Need a refill before we hit the floor?"

Looking around, I quickly nodded. "Uh, yeah, if I'm about to make a fool of myself, I definitely need another drink first."

He laughed and guided me toward the punch bowl. After a long gulp, I took a deep breath and set the cup down.

Renzo's energy was infectious. He flashed me that mischievous grin of his and said, "Come on." We found the old boombox in the corner, cranked it up, and before long, the barn was pulsing with the bass of DMX's "Party Up." Under the glow of the twinkling fairy lights, the dusty wood and hay-strewn corners faded away, replaced by the electric charge of a real club, just for us.

At first, my moves were small as I focused hard on not embarrassing myself, but Renzo quickly closed the space between us. His hand brushed my waist, lingering just long enough to make my skin tingle, and suddenly we were moving together, closer than I'd ever danced with a boy. I could smell the faint mix of his cologne and sweat and feel his breath on the side of my face. My heart thudded in my chest, louder than the bass, from how effortlessly he seemed to know how to guide me.

Hints of flirtation turned into a steady pull. His hands finding mine, then letting go only to graze my arm, his gaze locking on mine like he was daring me to keep up. Laughter bubbled out of me before I could stop it, mixing with the music until I wasn't sure if I was dizzy from dancing, drinking, or from him.

Before long, more people crowded the floor, a blur of moving bodies that made the air feel warmer. Out of the corner of my eye, I spotted Chloe still sitting with Anders, her expression unreadable. I waved both arms high, grinning and calling out, "Chloe, come join us!"

She hesitated for a moment, but then a small smile crept onto her face. She made her way over, and soon, we were all dancing together. Renzo's hands stayed on my hips, his body behind mine, but I kept my smile pointed at Chloe. It was just us now. I hoped she had forgotten about the divorce and everything else that weighed her down a few minutes ago. When she laughed, I breathed a sigh of relief, letting myself sink against Renzo while continuing to dance. Chloe and I laughed, twirled, and danced like no one was watching. Even though I was *very* aware that Renzo was watching each dip of my hip and tilt of my chest. It felt like everything was right in the world and we truly were on the way toward having the best summer ever.

"Hey girls," Anders stepped up, accepting Chloe's hand when she jutted it out in front of him. He gave her a spin, causing her to wobble slightly and land against him in a fit of laughter. He steadied her with his hand, before letting out a chuckle of his own. "Okay, giggles, I hate to ruin the fun but Phil just pulled up. He's gonna take you girls home before he heads out with some of his college buddies.

"Aw, already?"

"Unfortunately, yes, but I'm sure we'll be seeing each other soon."

"Promise?" Chloe whined.

"Of course. The Fourth of July is only four days away. I know my dad and Hadley want to go together to the town BBQ."

"You guys have a town BBQ?" I questioned.

"Yeah," he laughed. "Anyway, I'm sure we'll be able to break away to meet up with everyone. We usually head over to Copper Hill. There's a crazy view of the fireworks up there."

"Sounds fun," I said, though I twisted my neck so my response was directed at Renzo, who had his arms wrapped around my waist, my back tight against his chest.

"Oh it will be!" He murmured. "You girls gotta join."

"For sure," I smiled eagerly as I regrettably separated myself from Renzo's embrace to loop my arm through Chloe's. "See you then?"

He threw a surfer dude hand gesture my way, shaking it back and forth with a wink. Unsure how to even respond, I laughed then followed Anders toward the exit, dragging Chloe alongside me. We thanked him for arranging our ride, waving as we slid into the backseat of Phil's Honda Civic.

It didn't take long until Phil's car slowed. He dimmed his headlights and pulled over before reaching Hadley's driveway. I appreciated how quiet and careful he was being, despite how many times Chloe and I have broken out into a fit of laughter or begged him to turn the music up. He made sure to turn the music off, despite our protests, before he turned onto Hadley's street. "Okay, girls, we're here. Better get out before this car turns into a pumpkin."

"Wait, what?"

"Like in Cinderella?" He shrugged. "I have little nieces, sue me."

"Nice," I laughed. "Thanks again for driving us. I'm sure it's the last thing you wanted to be doing."

"No worries. I was on my way out anyway so this worked out. Plus Anders is a solid kid, I never mind doing him a favor."

I nodded and rambled off another thank you while I all but pushed Chloe out the car door. I stumbled out behind her, not realizing how buzzed I was, and tried not to laugh too loudly. The night had been a whirlwind, and we were both giddy, unable to control our laughter despite us both slapping our hands over our mouths. Hadley thought we were safely tucked away in my room, having a movie slumber party and I'd like to keep it that way.

"Shh, shh," I giggled, as Chloe tripped over her own feet, almost bringing us both down. The darkness made everything funnier. We finally reached the front door, and that's when I realized – the key! I fumbled in my pocket, feeling a surge of panic when it wasn't there.

"What's wrong?" Chloe whispered, her voice tinged with worry.

"I... I don't have the key," I admitted.

"You didn't bring the key, silly," she laughed. "You hid it in the bush, we just need to find it."

"Oh yeah!" My eyes lit up in relief. "I forgot." I crouched down to search and after the first few minutes, we both started frantically feeling around, our whispers more desperate. "Come on, key, come on," I muttered, hoping Hadley wouldn't wake up and catch us in the act.

Finally, my fingers brushed against cold metal. "Got it!" I whispered triumphantly, holding up the key. Chloe let out a relieved giggle. We crept inside, closing the door as quietly as we could. The house was dark and silent, the only sound was our suppressed laughter. We tiptoed down the hall, almost tripping a few more times. When we finally made it to my bedroom, we quickly turned off the TV and crawled into bed, still giggling.

I turned to Chloe, eager to talk about the party, but she was already asleep. That was fast. I sighed with a smile and pulled the comforter up to our shoulders, feeling a strange mix of relief and excitement. Despite our rocky start earlier, we had managed to have a bunch of fun and, bonus points, we made it back without getting caught.

With my eyes growing heavy, I whispered a half-hearted promise to myself. I wanted our month in Montana to be filled with parties, new experiences, and maybe a little more time with Renzo. But Chloe's well-being should come first, right?

I glanced over at her, sound asleep, her breathing steady. She looked so innocent, like she hadn't just found out her dad was moving out and her parents were getting divorced. I wondered if she'd wake up feeling as content as she seemed now. Maybe, just maybe, we could navigate the ups and downs together. But selfishly, I also wanted to keep having fun, to keep going to parties and living it up.

For now, it was enough to know we made it back without getting caught. The morning would bring its own challenges, but tonight, I allowed myself a mix of relief and excitement as I drifted off to sleep. Tomorrow, I'd figure out how to balance it all.

Steeplechase Stadium

I woke up feeling a bit groggy. Chloe was next to me, her eyes fluttering open as she stretched.

"Morning," I said softly, trying to gauge her mood. "How's your head? Mine feels like it's stuffed with cotton."

Chloe gave me a small smile. "A bit thumpy, but I'll survive."

I hesitated for a moment, then decided to dive in. "So, uh, how are you feeling with everything? You know, with your parents and all..."

Her smile faltered, and she looked away, focusing on the ceiling. "I'm excited for today. I've never been up close to horses before."

I sighed inwardly. "Yeah, it's going to be amazing."

Downstairs, Hadley was already bustling around, packing a soft sided cooler with sandwiches, individual bags of potato chips, and bottles of iced tea. She greeted us with a warm smile. "Good morning, girls! Ready to check out Steeplechase?"

We nodded eagerly, and soon we were on our way. The drive was filled with Hadley's stories about the arena, her favorite horse Gingerbread, and her mom's summers there. Chloe listened quietly, looking a combination of content and reserved, while I filled the pauses with enthusiastic responses and follow-up questions.

When we arrived, my jaw all but dropped. Steeplechase Stadium was massive, like something out of a movie. Renzo's family owned this?

There were rows of rustic stables, a big ring where horses could show off their skills, and a winding track that seemed to go on forever. The open fields stretched out under the blue sky, dotted with horses grazing. It had all the classic horse arena stuff that I was envisioning but seeing it in person made it feel like a whole new world. I couldn't wait to see everything up close.

Chloe's eyes widened in awe when she spotted the horses peacefully roaming the field. "They're so beautiful," she whispered.

Hadley led us to the stables, which smelled like hay and leather. The gentle sounds of the horses moving about were oddly comforting. As we approached the first horse, a gorgeous chestnut mare, Chloe and I both jumped back nervously when it snorted and shook its head. We looked at each other and burst into laughter, the tension between us breaking.

Hadley chuckled. "Don't worry, girls. Horses can sense your emotions. If you're nervous, they'll be nervous too. Just take a deep breath and leave all your worries behind." We nodded, trying to steady our breaths. Hadley demonstrated how to approach the horses, extending a hand slowly and letting the mare sniff it. "See? She's just curious. Now, gently stroke her neck."

Chloe hesitated but did as Hadley said. Her fingers hovered in the air for a beat, trembling slightly, before brushing against the mare's sleek neck. The horse's ears flicked, but she stayed calm, her dark eyes steady on Chloe.

"She's so soft," Chloe murmured, the tension in her shoulders easing as a small smile tugged at her lips.

Watching her, something in me tightened – part pride, part envy. Chloe was braver than she gave herself credit for. If she could do it, I wasn't going to hang back like some nervous little kid. I was just as grown, if not more, than Chloe.

I stepped forward, my pulse quickening, and held out my hand. "Can I?"

Hadley nodded, guiding my palm to the mare's warm coat. The texture was nothing like I expected – smooth over muscle, heat radiating beneath. My fingers moved tentatively at first, but when the mare dipped her head as if to invite more, I let myself linger, feeling the slow, steady rise and fall of her breath. A real, unguarded smile crept across my face before I could stop it. Okay, this was cool.

Hadley smiled at us. "Now, let's try mounting them, shall we? I'll be right here to help." She led us toward a few bales of hay, intended to be a step up for us. Hadley walked over a dusty gray horse for Chloe and pointed out the dark brown horse that I would mount next.

Chloe's face lit up as she prepared to mount the gray horse. Hadley showed her how to place her foot in the stirrup and swing her leg over. With a bit of a wobble, Chloe found herself sitting atop the mare, her eyes wide with amazement. I'd ridden horses a few times, so needed less help, though I also stumbled a bit when I tried to kick my leg over my horse.

"You're doing great, girls," Hadley said, holding the reins, one in each hand as she walked between us. "Just take it slow and enjoy the view." After a few minutes, she dropped the reins, giving us freedom to move at our own pace. I knew she'd be able to rescue us if either of us accidentally took off at a race speed. Hadley always made me feel safe.

Chloe's shoulders, which had been stiff all morning, finally loosened. She found the horse's rhythm, and the way her mouth curved into a small, genuine smile made it obvious she was actually enjoying herself. It was a total shift from the way she'd looked earlier – like the world was chewing her up.

I let my own horse keep an easy pace, more focused on watching Chloe than anything else. A weird calm settled over me. Today was... perfect. No boys, no drinking, no drama. Just me, my best friend, and Hadley.

And maybe that's why it hit me so hard. How rare this felt. How good it felt to have Hadley smiling like that, proud to be showing us this part of her life. It made me wonder if this was the kind of thing I'd remember years from now, when everything else about being fourteen had blurred together. Would I remember the details of the barn party? Or would it be moments like this that stuck.

Once we returned to the stables, groomed the horses, and secured them in their stalls, we moved toward the field, where a few horses were still grazing. We sat on the oversized blanket Hadley spread out, ready to enjoy the peanut butter and jelly sandwiches she had packed. The afternoon sun shone brightly overhead, casting a warm glow over the arena.

Chloe looked relaxed. Happy even. "Thank you, Hadley," she said softly. "This was exactly what I needed."

Hadley smiled and squeezed Chloe's hand. "Anytime, sweetheart. Remember, you're always welcome here." She reached out and plucked one of the many dandelions dotting the field. "Here," she said, handing it to Chloe. "Make a wish."

Chloe smiled, gently taking the flower so as to not disturb the poof of seeds on top. She closed her eyes and, after a moment, exhaled a breath that sent the seeds flying in a million directions, catching the wind. "I haven't done that in forever."

"Chloe and I used to pick dandelions in the backyard, making wild wishes for things like seeing a real unicorn, getting a pet teacup pig, and—" I tapped my chin, eyes narrowing as I searched the memory. "Oh, what was the one we always did?"

"I can't believe you forgot." Chloe laughed. "We wished that our parents would get a letter from the hospital proving you and I were actually blood related."

"Oh my god, that's right." I nearly fell to my side laughing.

Hadley chuckled. Once we regained composure, she added, "I remember seeing dandelions, and all types of flowers really, on Dorothy's farm, but I never knew to make a wish. I saved those for the stars."

"I think both ways work." I smiled.

We talked a bit more before we packed up and headed back to the car. I couldn't help but think about the fourth of July being around the corner. I was eager to party and spend some alone time with Renzo but today reminded me of the bigger picture. My goal this summer wasn't just making new memories and having new experiences, it was doing it all with Chloe. Today was definitely a new memory and a new experience. I loved seeing how uninhibited Chloe was, even if it was short lived. I knew I had to talk to her about her parents at some point, but maybe for now she just needed more of these types of moments.

"Oh man..." I said, my voice lined with a fake sadness, like I had just realized I forgot something important.

"What's wrong, Meels?" Hadley looked at me with real concern, while Chloe's brows furrowed with suspicion.

"It's just that we made a core memory today."

Hadley's concern turned into curiosity. "Oh, well that's a good thing, right?"

"Yeah, but it's missing something..."

Hadley's brows lifted, and she crossed her arms, patiently waiting. "Oh?"

"Ice cream!" I declared with a grin.

Hadley blew out a laugh, clearly relieved. "You're right. How could we forget the most important part?" Her eyes sparkled as she looked between me and Chloe. "Right, Chloe?"

Chloe's face lit up. "Yeah!"

Hadley nodded, her smile widening. "Well, that solves it. Let's go get some ice cream."

We piled into the car, laughing and chatting about our favorite flavors, and eventually about what a horse's favorite would be. Chloe guessed butter pecan, I said carrot cake, and Hadley confused us with her choice – peppermint. That was until she said horses loved peppermint candies, so naturally they'd love it in ice cream form, too. Who knew? The rest of the short drive to the ice cream shop was filled with silly banter and ridiculous questions. I bit the inside of my cheek, tempering my emotions, despite feeling a big rush of happiness.

4th of July BBQ

The morning light blasted through our window since we had forgotten to pull down the blinds before we crawled into bed last night. Normally I would whine about being woken up so abruptly, but today I woke up feeling the kind of excitement that rivaled Christmas morning. I buzzed with anticipation, mostly because today was a chance to hang out with Renzo again. Sure, I was happy to spend time with Aunt Hadley and all, but the thought of sneaking off with Renzo made my heart race. Did that make me a terrible person?

Chloe and I were getting ready in our room, our laughter mixing with the sounds of Hadley bustling around the kitchen. Chloe had been quieter since that phone call with her mom on Sunday. Her dad was moving out, and even though her mom promised things would get better, Chloe wasn't buying it. She told me about it but didn't want to talk too much because it made her upset. I didn't push.

To be honest, I wouldn't have known what to say anyway. My parents separated when I was too young to remember and all I've ever known was their incredible coparenting and overly friendly friendship. I don't know how to relate to the fact that Chloe's parents have been fighting constantly and often at her expense. I wanted to tell her how good it could be to have divorced parents but I knew better than to assume all divorces ended as happily as my parents'.

Anyway, it was great to hear Chloe laughing today as she weeded through our collective wardrobe trying to find the right outfit for the big town BBQ. What even is the dress code for a town BBQ? We were going with Hadley and Marcus, which undoubtedly meant Anders would be joining, too. I'm pretty sure that was the reason Chloe was tossing so many viable outfit options over her shoulder. She was definitely spiraling, knowing she'd see him again.

"Do you think Anders will notice me?" Chloe asked, holding a cream colored tube top against her skin and evaluating it in the mirror.

"Absolutely! You'd look awesome in that top, put it on," I assured her, trying to sound confident for both our sakes. "Besides, he's always finding reasons to be near you. There were like twenty of us at the barn last week and his eyes were only on you."

"I mean, I kinda planted myself on his lap so he didn't really have a choice—"

"And he wasn't complaining," I laughed.

We finished getting ready, and soon, we were in Hadley's car, a basket full of chocolate-lemon and pineapple-coconut muffins occupying the middle seat. Apparently, even though the local restaurants set up food stands with special deals, the main part of the BBQ came from the locals, sort of like a giant potluck. As we drove toward the center of town, I felt a mix of excitement and stress bubble inside me. I was pumped for today, but I also wanted to keep an eye on Chloe. She'd been through a lot, and I needed to be there for her. Her and Renzo. And Hadley. And getting to know Marcus. Figuring out how to split my time was really becoming difficult.

Hadley parked a block away on a road that was already almost fully lined with vehicles. I told her we'd be fine to walk from her house but she didn't want to risk having the heat of the sun melt her muffins, which was pretty funny considering they were about to be set outside on a table. I didn't dare point that out because she looked so proud carrying the basket toward the center of town.

We crossed a small patch of dandelion grass that separated us from the sidewalk that belonged to the main street – only street – in town. I'm not sure what I expected from a town BBQ, but what I saw as we rounded the corner made my jaw drop. There were tables up and down the street draped in brightly colored tablecloths, some under white pop up canopies, some with large yellow, tan, or blue umbrellas probably borrowed from backyard patios, and some left exposed to the high sun. The tables featured crock pots of pulled pork and chili, platters of cold deli pinwheels, aluminum foil trays of casseroles, potatoes, and the like kept warm on sterno stands, and elaborate displays of cookies, brownies, and cupcakes. I was suddenly starving.

"Oh, perfect, I see Marcus up ahead," Hadley pointed. "Looks like he's guarding table space for us." She giggled and led the way to a rectangle table with a turquoise plastic tablecloth. I loved seeing her smile.

"Hey Marcus." I smiled at him while Chloe stood at my side and waved.

"Hey girls, great to see you." He nodded at us then gave Hadley a wink before he wrapped her into the type of hug that you could melt into, which she did. At least temporarily. She quickly pushed herself free once she remembered that we were standing next to her. She gave his chest a playful slap before she smoothed her long blonde hair behind her ears.

"Okay, girls. Let's get these muffins set up and get down to business."

"What exactly is business, though?" My head titled, wondering what exactly was in store for us.

She laughed and tapped her finger against her lips pretending to be deep in thought. "Well, this is actually all donation based. The only things for purchase are from the different shops and restaurants." I nodded, waiting on her point. "So, I guess business number one is walking up and down the street to see what kind of treats you want to enjoy."

"Yum! I love that plan."

"Make sure you girls eat as you're walking. Most of the good stuff ends up gone in the first hour."

"Got it." I saluted. "Thanks, Marcus." I bounced on my heels for a moment. "So, uh, Hadley, should we all walk together or..." I looked left and right, bending at my waist dramatically to peer around Marcus, as if Anders was hiding behind him.

Chloe swatted at my arm. I shrugged. "Just saying, I wasn't sure of the full plan. Based on your I-haven't-seen-you-all-week embrace, I wasn't sure if you wanted us out of your hair."

"I never want you out of my hair." Hadley laughed.

"Oh, good. Then all together it is." I drew out the words and continued to look around.

"We must be totally embarrassing, huh?" Hadley asked a laughing Marcus.

"Seems like it." He shook his head with a grin. "Well good news, girls. Anders is only a few tables away helping Terri – I mean Mrs.

Romano, set up her table. She made homemade meatballs and brought Hawaiian rolls, shakers of parmesan cheese and crushed red pepper, and who knows what else."

My eyes lit up. Partly because homemade meatballs sounded amazing but also because that meant Renzo was there, too. "Yum." My eyes sparkled. "Well, I guess we should check it out. Right, Chlo?"

"Yep, I love meatball sandwiches." She nodded enthusiastically.

"Me, too! So you guys are okay by yourself?" I smiled sweetly, slowly stepping away before they had even responded.

"Very subtle, Meels," Hadley chuckled. "Yes, we're good. Just don't leave the block party and come find me in a bit so I know what you're up to."

"Sounds good!" I grabbed Chloe's hand and tugged her into motion. I looked back once to wave but Marcus and Hadley were already focused on making the perfect display of muffins, laughing at each other and clearly having fun. I couldn't wait to have that type of relationship.

"That must be them up ahead," I pointed. "I can see Mrs. Romano's poofy short hair from here."

"Yeah, she reminds me of Carmela Soprano with the way she styles it. Actually with the way she dresses and talks, too."

"When did you watch the Sopranos?"

"My dad likes it. Sometimes if it's late at night and I'm still awake, he'll let me lay on the couch with him," she said with a small smile. "I'm pretty sure he thinks I'm quick to fall asleep but I've seen a lot of it."

I nodded and smiled. "I've never seen the show but I've seen the commercials a few times and you're totally right. I guess when you name your kids Laurina and Lorenzo, you're pretty confident in your Italian roots."

"Yeah, for sure." We slowed down as we approached Mrs. Romano's table where sure enough Anders and Renzo were standing with two other guys from the soccer team. One looked to be Matty but I wasn't sure who the other guy was. "So what's our plan?" Chloe whispered.

"Uh, well we'll say hi and then see what happens from there."

"So, no plan then."

"Not everything needs to be planned, Chlo. Let's just go with the flow!" I smiled, my bright eyes meeting her hesitant ones. I was about to reassure her when we must've caught Mrs. Romano's attention because she started waving dramatically. "Go with the flow." I quickly whispered before plastering on a wide smile and waving back.

"Hey, Mrs. Romano. Your table looks great. Marcus told us you made meatballs. Is that what I'm smelling?" I inhaled theatrically, waving the scent toward my nose. "It smells amazing, right Chlo?"

"It really does. Meatball sandwiches are one of my favorites."

"Well now that's music to my ears," she announced. "Lorenzo, dear, make the girls sandwiches while the crockpot's full."

"Oh, you don't have to do that."

"Nonsense." She motioned for him to grab a plate for us. "Go on, Ren."

I smiled awkwardly at him, not sure how to act. I couldn't wait until this whole flirting thing started to feel natural.

"Make sure you get your aunt down here before it's too late," Mrs. Romano added. " I want her to try some since it's a secret family recipe. Though with her being family and everything, I suppose it's safe to share it with her."

"I keep forgetting Hadley's your aunt." Renzo said, handing me a small white paper plate with a single meatball sized sandwich. It looked delicious.

"Yeah, she's my mom's best friend so we're not related by blood or anything." I hoped Renzo didn't think I was his distant cousin, because ew.

"Right," he chuckled. "Well that's a relief." I laughed with him before taking a bite of the square sandwich in my hand.

"Oh man, Mrs. Romano, this is amazing." I spoke unabashedly through a full mouth. When I looked at Chloe to get her opinion I noticed she had already finished.

"Seems like you both liked it. So happy to see that."

Chloe's cheeks reddened. "Now I feel like a pig."

"Nonsense." Mrs. Romano wore a proud smile. It was as if she measured her worth based on how much we enjoyed her cooking. Which we clearly enjoyed so win-win.

"When I have meatballs at home they'd be frozen from the grocery store. I'm not sure I ever had them homemade. My mom's a great cook but she mainly makes things like dumplings, and beef noodle soup. I guess she makes gua bao a lot, which is like braised pork belly in a steamed bun... which is nothing like a meatball but that's probably the closest we're going to get. It's my dad who's the big Italian food fan and since he wasn't home, isn't, wasn't – uh, anyway, we didn't have it that often. So this is great, thank you."

Chloe blinked, almost startled at herself, like she'd just realized how far she'd wandered off-topic. Her mouth tugged into a sheepish half-smile, and I caught the faintest pink rising in her cheeks.

"Of course, sweetheart. I'll tell you what. I have an extra batch at home, I'll make sure to get them to Hadley so you can have more."

"Oh, you don't have to do that." Chloe fully blushed now. "But thank you."

"Nonsense." Mrs. Romano waved the air, dismissing Chloe's hesitation. "I wish my kids enjoyed my cooking the way you just did. Fooey for them, meatballs for you." That made us laugh.

"Ma, we're gonna go walk around now. You all good with the setup?"

"Yes, Dear. Thanks to you and your friends. Go on; have fun."

"Planned on it." He smirked.

"And keep an eye on these sweet girls. I'd hate to have to tell my cousin you went and got them lost, you hear?"

"Loud and clear. I'll be on them like glue."

Before I had even processed what he said, his hand was on my lower back, pushing me forward with a wink. I grabbed Chloe's hand, keeping her at my side. We quickly met up with Anders, Matty, and a few others.

"Without getting fresh." She hollered out after her son.

I'm pretty sure my eyes doubled in size. I bit the inside of my cheek, doing my best to look like I wasn't dying inside.

"No promises," he said under his breath, his hand still on my back. He seamlessly joined the conversation that Matty was leading.

"I promised Ry I'd meet up with her for the fireworks later," Matty stated. "We could all head to Copper Hill now if you wanted," he offered. "I know my parents and at least yours, Renz, are gonna be staying downtown to watch from there."

"Solid idea, man." Renzo nodded. "It's always a good time on the hill."

"If tradition proves anything," Anders added, "they're all gonna stay on main street and then end at Pepper's Pies."

"Even though they'll have eaten all day," Matty laughed.

"And they say teenagers are endless pits," Anders tacked on.

"I know, right." Renzo laughed. "Okay, solid plan." He turned toward me. "Girls, you in?"

I nodded eagerly. Chloe had yet to really say anything, but nodded.

"I just have to let Hadley know that we're going to hang out with you guys so she has a general idea." I hooked my thumb over my shoulder toward where we'd come from. "She won't care, though. To be honest, I think she's eager to watch the fireworks alone with your dad, Anders."

"Gross." He frowned. "But one hundred percent accurate. You girls wanna loop around together and we can let our parents know the plan and then meet back here with everyone in like an hour? That'll give us time to eat as we walk. I saw macaroni and cheese balls up ahead and I'm not about to miss out on that."

"I'll never say no to a macaroni and cheese ball," I laughed.

"Awesome," Renzo fist bumped Anders. "You do that and Matty and I will go meet up with Smith's older brother. He's getting us some more Smirnoff and the Bacardi Breezers we promised Rylee and Laurina we'd get." He winked and finished with, "Try not to miss me."

I smacked his shoulder with a playful eye roll. "I'll try my best."

"Okay, lovebirds, it's only an hour. Let's roll."

Blushing, I nodded, and Chloe laughed, looping her arm through mine. We started toward the next table, excited to see what else we could munch on. It sounded like there would be alcohol tonight for the fireworks, so we definitely needed to set a thick layer of carbs down first.

For a few steps, it was just us, moving in sync the way we always did. But my mind kept tripping over itself – half in the moment, half somewhere else. Was this supposed to be our day? A girls' thing? Or was it okay I kept nudging Chloe toward Anders so I could end up on Renzo's arm – maybe even kiss him again? And if that was okay, then why did jealousy flare every time I watched them together.

"Hey wait up!"

I must've said his name too many times in my head, like Beetlejuice, because here he came, jogging to Chloe's free side. "I was hoping to walk with you, Chloe."

It's fine. It was what I wanted.

"See?" I whispered. "I told you he wanted to be by your side," I winked a few times, laying it on extra dramatic. "Walk with him, I'll stick right behind you." I unlooped our arms, letting her shift toward Anders, knowing she'd get immediately lost in his honey-brown gaze.

"So, uh, how was your week, Chloe?"

Fireworks on Copper Hill

We walked up and down main street as a trio, though I did my best to stay a step behind. I also tried to not let the jealousy take over. She was my best friend after all, not his. I knew I was being totally unreasonable. I was the one who came up with this grand plan of having new experiences and was all but throwing Chloe in Anders direction, for the sake of me getting closer to Renzo, but now that they're seeming to bond so easily? It was a little annoying.

"Should we head up the hill?" *Where Renzo would be.*

Anders turned back to face me. "Solid idea," he nodded. "Everyone should be there by now."

I smiled and picked up my pace, stepping in front of Chloe and Anders, eager to no longer be the third wheel. The climb up Copper Hill was tougher than I thought but the burn in my legs only added to the rush in my chest. As we approached the top, I took in the colors that smeared across the sky as the sun slowly started to dip. The air felt breezy but for some reason my palms were still sweating.

I glanced back at Chloe, who wasn't saying much, but her cheeks were bright pink, and I caught her biting her lip like she didn't know what to do with herself. Anders must've made a joke then, because they both laughed. Chloe's was soft and didn't sound like her at all. She was trying hard to impress Anders even though he seemed totally smitten. It pulled at my nerves.

I saw the group before I heard them. Laurina was sprawled out on a blanket, two empty bottles of Bacardi Breezers by her side, laughing in that stupid, sharp way she had. I knew it was fake. Her friends were lounging beside her, acting like they owned the hilltop, their messy hair blew in the breeze and their cropped tops showed off toned midriffs in various sun kissed shades. Rylee was laying against Matty, who had his legs on either side of her. They looked like the coolest kids in school. Like they were a shoe in for prom king and queen. I wanted that.

Laurina caught sight of us and smirked, her gaze landing on Chloe first, then me. Noticing her judgement, I tugged at my shorts wanting to hide the curves that only felt out of place when I compared them to her model-like build. She brought out the worst in me – and my insecurities.

"Wow, look who *finally* made it," Laurina said, like we had kept her waiting.

"Chill out, Laur. This is the exact time we said we'd meet." Anders rolled his eyes before giving one of the guys a handshake that ended with a back slap.

I smiled at her, ignoring the way my stomach twisted, and tried not to let her bother me. Laurina rolled her eyes before returning her attention to whatever story Rylee was sharing. I looked toward the end of the pile of blankets and caught Renzo, who was leaning back on his elbows. He wasn't saying much but his eyes kept darting to me, and every time they did, I felt like I couldn't breathe.

Laurina's laugh grated against my ears, sharp and loud, breaking me from my trance. I pointed to the now third empty bottle at her side. "Save some for the rest of us?"

"I have a better idea," Renzo said suddenly, jumping up from his spot on the ground. I couldn't tell if his skin was flush from the last of the sun's rays or from the alcohol it seemed everyone had already dipped into.

All eyes turned toward him.

"Body shots." He said it like it was the best idea in the world. I almost swallowed my tongue. I didn't even know what that meant, but his grin was wide and easy, like he was suggesting we put sprinkles on our sundaes, and not whatever a body shot was.

Laurina let out an "ooo," standing up after grabbing the large plastic bottle of Smirnoff. She held it in the air like a prize. "Obviously, I'm in," she said, flipping her hair over her shoulder. She stumbled half a step backward before steadying, tossing a disgusted look at Renzo. "But, ew, not with you."

"Yeah, no kidding, Laur," he grimaced. "You weren't my target anyway." He laughed and let his eyes graze up my body, now completely on fire, from the inside out.

Laurina's eyes followed his stare and when they landed on me, she looked even more disgusted than a moment ago, her mouth twisted down. "I wouldn't, but whatever."

She turned to Rylee and they both giggled. Laurina got down onto the blanket, shooing Matty away so she could kneel next to Rylee. She looked around briefly, for what, I don't know.

"I got it, one sec." Matty popped up from the bottom of the blanket where he had sat and went over to a large canvas tote. He grabbed a shaker of salt and tossed it to Laurina. Her eyes wandered Rylee's body before zeroing in on her arm. She sprinkled salt below Rylee's elbow then filled a little plastic shot glass with alcohol, balancing it in Rylee's mouth. *What the heck.*

Laurina winked at the group of guys, all eyes locked in, before she licked Rylee's arm and captured the shot glass in her mouth, tossing it back without using her hands and without spilling a drop. The group cheered, and Laurina laughed, tossing her hair back like she was in a movie. I grabbed Chloe's hand, but my eyes stayed glued to the scene in front of me.

Rylee didn't miss a beat. She grabbed the bottle and turned toward her boyfriend, who was already grinning like he knew exactly what he was in for. She sprinkled the salt on his neck, quickly licking it up, but then Matty spit the shot glass from his mouth, letting the liquid drip down the side of his face so he could turn the moment into a gross makeout session.

The air felt heavier, harder to inhale. Renzo grabbed the bottle from next to the lovebirds, breaking their trance with a laugh. "My turn." His eyes flicked to me and my stomach flipped.

"Your turn," he said, softer this time as he stalked toward me, his gaze locked on mine.

I froze. My skin felt prickly, and I couldn't figure out why. The thought of Renzo leaning over me or kissing me while everyone watching – it wasn't thrilling like I thought it'd be. It was too much. Too personal. I suddenly felt very much like a fourteen year old and not like the rest of them.

"I–" the words stuck in my throat. Chloe's hand squeezed mine and I turned toward her. She didn't say anything at first, just looked at me with a quiet expression.

"You don't have to," she finally whispered. Her voice was soft but confident.

I turned back to face Renzo, who was now standing so close that I could feel his breath on me. Behind him, everyone stared, waiting. He lifted a confident brow in expectation but the tension in my chest snapped.

I stepped back abruptly, like I was crossing the street and just noticed a bus speeding my way.

"I'm good," I said, louder than I needed to, shaking my head.

Renzo's brows drew together, confused. I didn't wait for his response – I stepped back farther, turning away from the group, away from the spotlight I thought I wanted, and tried to breathe.

The first fireworks exploded in the sky seconds later, streaks of gold and blue cutting through the twilight. I nearly jumped out of my skin, my already fast heartbeat now in overdrive. Chloe followed me to the edge of the hill, Anders trailing behind like a puppy loyal to its favorite human. I dropped onto the grass, watching the fireworks crackle, my chest still tight. Chloe didn't say anything, but sat next to me. She slipped her arm around my shoulders but I shook it off, blowing out an "it's fine." She knew better, but didn't press.

The fireworks went off in bursts, splattering gold and red into the night sky, but the hilltop somehow felt quieter now. Chloe leaned against Anders, who sat next to her with his arm draped over her shoulder. They weren't talking, they didn't need to. She was smiling softly, her body relaxed despite the loud booms that vibrated the ground. She hadn't wanted to come here, hadn't wanted to drink or flirt, hadn't wanted any of this – and yet it was so easy for her. So natural. I was happy for her, but I hated it. Still, I didn't want her to feel the peer pressure or the heavy expectation that I suddenly felt. It all seemed unfair.

I heard Morgan giggle behind me, high-pitched and eager. "Renzo, I'll take her turn!" Her words looped together. I turned back just enough to see her pull at the hem of her crop top, flashing her stomach in a way that made the group laugh. Renzo looked up from his bottle, catching my gaze behind hers, and dismissed her with a "nah."

Morgan's giggle fizzled, but she shrugged it off, her attention quickly shifting to Carter. I let out a slow breath, trying to let the moment go. Renzo ignoring her was probably a good thing, I guessed. But the knot in my stomach didn't go away. I hadn't been brave tonight. I'd totally frozen when I should've been outgoing, when I should've shown I was one of them. I didn't even know why I was trying so hard.

Why was I so obsessed with growing up faster, like it would magically make my life better? My life wasn't even bad. It wasn't just Renzo and the dumb body shots; it was everything. The older kids with older mindsets, the drinking, the fake confidence – I suddenly doubted all of it. I just wanted my pajamas, Hadley's couch, and Little Foot curled up on my lap.

I glanced back at Chloe, still leaning against Anders like it was the easiest thing in the world. That pang of jealousy hit me again, sharp and unwanted. Maybe I do want that. Maybe this was worth it. I looked behind me, again, as if Renzo would be standing there waiting, but of course he wasn't. He was back with the group laughing and joking, passing the bottle around.

I looked ahead to the finale of fireworks before me and tried to decide what exactly it was that I wanted.

All the Attention

I startled awake, my heart pounding against my ribs like it was trying to escape. For a second, I didn't know where I was. My pulse raced as last night replayed in my mind like a CD skipping – Laurina's grating laugh, Renzo's suggestive grin, the sound of fireworks exploding. It was like my brain had mashed last night into a confusing blur.

I shook it all from my mind, the room coming into focus as my eyes adjusted to the slivers of sunlight illuminating the otherwise dark room. Chloe was spread out next to me on the bed, her hair perfect even in her sleep. Her face was soft and peaceful, like she hadn't been slapped by Laurina's judgy glares or overwhelmed by the body shots invitation. She hadn't, really, not the way I had. Chloe rarely let things get to her like that. Well, besides everything going on with her parents. Sometimes I think their constant pressure on her to get straight As in school left no room for other stressors to sneak in. I pulled my knees up to my chest, feeling a strange ache in my stomach I didn't know how to name. Chloe didn't drink last night, but not because she was being a wimp, she simply saw I was upset and stayed at my side letting me be the quiet one for once. We did everything together, even when it meant doing nothing. And yet, even though she wasn't plucky or boy-crazy like me, she still ended up in

Anders' patient, non-pressuring arms, while I felt isolated, like I didn't belong.

I let out a long breath, carefully untangling myself from the sheets so I wouldn't wake her. There wasn't much room in the bed, and as I stretched, I realized my legs were still sore from climbing Copper Hill. That part was real – the ache in my thighs, the gravel stuck in my shoes. But the rest – Renzo, Laurina, Morgan's giggle, the heavy feeling in my chest – it felt like it happened to someone else. No way that was me. I was supposed to be brave, outgoing, a curly-headed firecracker. Right?

Yeah, right.

The smell of pancakes drifted into the room and I could hear Hadley humming along to some old song on the radio. Her voice was light and carefree, like she had no idea the world cracked under me last night. But why would she? The rational part of my brain knew that I was making a bigger deal out of this than I needed to. The evening continued normally not even thirty seconds after I denied Renzo. But still, it felt big. It felt like ten steps back. They might not have given it a second thought, but I sure did, and still was. I grabbed Chloe's sweatshirt from the chair, shrugged it on, and padded out of the room, hoping breakfast would untangle the knots in my stomach.

I walked into the kitchen and watched Hadley at the stove, flipping pancakes in a floral apron. "Morning, sunshine," she said when she spotted me. Her smile was big and she sounded like she'd been waiting all morning for me to show up, even though I was only ever right down the hall. "I figured the smell of these would eventually get you up." She laughed.

I smiled and slid onto the bench, grabbing a handful of fresh sliced strawberries that sat in the center of the rustic table.

"You girls have been so good this summer," Hadley said, piling pancakes onto the plate and setting it in front of me. "It's so nice having you here. I don't know why your mom was so worried. You girls are about as innocent as it gets. I would keep you here forever if I could. Wouldn't that be fun?"

My fork froze halfway to my mouth. Great, now I felt even worse. Hadley thought we were innocent only because we had been lying to her about pretty much everything. Preventing me from an internal guilt spiral, Chloe shuffled into the kitchen, sleep still clouding her eyes. She wiped her eyes and yawned a "thank you" as Hadley handed her a plate. She sat next to me and poured syrup over her pancakes, looking content, completely unaffected by last night. Maybe I was being dramatic about the whole thing.

"Marcus and Anders might stop by later," Hadley announced. My stomach dropped and I forced my eyes not to roll. Chloe didn't say anything right away, but I saw the smile tug at her lips.

"Sure, sounds fun." I managed. Chloe tucked her hair behind her ear and nodded, like it wasn't the most thrilling news she'd heard all year. But I felt it. Her excitement. It's the exact way I wanted to feel about Renzo. Or anyone really. Except right now the feeling in my stomach was less butterfly and more sinking rock.

After breakfast, Chloe and I sat on the carpet in the living room, watching a rerun of *Beverly Hills 90210*. Chloe had already picked a bright pink nail polish, carefully brushing it onto her toes with the kind of precision only Chloe could manage. I wasn't as particular. I grabbed a shimmery gold shade and painted haphazard stripes across my nails. I was attempting a pattern, and failing, but instead of getting frustrated, a laugh bubbled out.

"Okay, that does not count as nail art," Chloe looked up at me, gesturing to my toes. "That's... interpretive, at best."

"It's abstract," I corrected her, holding my foot out like it was on display in a gallery. "You wouldn't get it, Chloe," I said, faking a snobby accent. It's *art*."

She rolled her eyes before we burst into laughter. I stuck my tongue out and leaned back against the couch, the sound of the TV mixing with Little Foot's quiet purring. It felt easy, normal, like it was just us here and nothing else mattered. No boys, no *new experiences*, just me and Chloe.

Knock, knock, knock.

There goes that. Chloe froze, her hand mid-swipe as the bright pink brush hovered over her toes. I looked at her, then toward the door. I pushed away the disappointment that clogged my throat. "Come in!" I called, trying to sound excited.

The door swung open, and Anders walked in followed by Marcus, who was holding a Home Depot brown paper bag. "We come bearing gifts," he said, lifting the bag like it was a prize.

"From Home Depot?" My head tilted.

"It's for me," Hadley said, entering the hallway. "My shower's been on the fritz so Marcus said he'd help."

"Oh." I blinked, feeling vaguely out of the loop, though why would I have needed to know her shower was having issues. I needed to get a grip and stop being so sensitive. Marcus reached into the bag and pulled out a red plastic pouch of cat treats. "For Little Foot," he said, tossing it to Anders, before heading toward the back of the house with Hadley.

Anders lingered in the doorway until his dad was out of sight, then walked into the room and dropped onto the couch, stretching out like he'd been here all day. "Don't let me stop you," he said, nodding toward the nail polish.

Chloe raised an eyebrow at him. "You want us to keep painting our nails while you just, like, sit there?" Her voice was laced with confusion. Honestly, I was wondering the same thing.

"Why not?"

We both shrugged at each other, not sure how to respond. Neither of us were used to having boys hang around, let alone one so laid back. Chloe reached for her color, ready to apply the second coat, while I grabbed the gold again. Anders flicked a laser pointer across the carpet, and Little Foot perked up instantly, chasing the red dot with fierce determination. Chloe laughed loud enough to make me grin as she watched the cat spin in crazy circles.

I let myself relax. There was no pressure in the room, no awkwardness. We were all laughing, watching the way Little Foot darted around. But then the little red light disappeared. Anders paused and turned his head toward me, clearing his throat. "By the way, Renz asked about you." He said it so casually. Was I supposed to be casual back? Asked about me how? Why?

Chloe glanced at me, her lips pulling into a frown.

"What do you mean?" I asked, feeling my stomach bubble.

"He thought maybe he'd messed up last night," Anders turned the laser pointer back on, a shared distraction. "He wanted to make sure you were okay. Said he was just having fun and didn't mean to pressure you."

I blinked at him, caught between relief and guilt. I tried to play off my panic last night but it must've seemed like I was turning Renzo down. I had probably embarrassed him. I was the stick in the mud. Was he asking about me because he cared or was he just saving face?

"Tell him I'm fine," I said quickly, my shoulders tensed. "He didn't do anything wrong."

"I'll let him know," Anders said, tossing Little Foot a treat. "Oh, and he mentioned that party next week. You girls going?"

I glanced toward the kitchen to make sure Marcus and Hadley weren't in ear shot. "Maybe," I said with a lowered voice. "Is he?"

"Renzo?" Anders laughed, "Yeah." He leaned back on the couch before adding, "I assume that's why he all but demanded I make sure you're still into him and that you'd go."

Chloe gave me an eager look, her eyes wide.

I rolled my skeptical eyes in response, but my cheeks felt warm. He's still into me. Little Foot meowed and pawed at the treat bag again, drawing Anders' attention back to her. This was good. *Really* good. Renzo was asking about me and wanted to see me again. Maybe it wasn't all that big of a deal that I walked off last night, and we could pick up where we left off before the fireworks. Before the body shots. If he was apologizing and checking on me then he must care. Right? Seeing the way Marcus doted on Hadley and the way Anders' watched Chloe, made me feel so left out. I wanted that type of attention. Not the loud, center of the room attention I thought I wanted. Laurina could keep that. I wanted the quiet, one-on-one, no expectation type of attention. The free flow of it all.

My mind drifted to my parents. They always seemed to get all the attention. The center of the room, all eyes on them type of attention, and the quiet inside jokes and private memories kind of attention. The actual prom king and queen of their high school – two years in a row.

They got divorced before I was old enough to remember them as a married couple, but they were still my best example of a happily ever after. They had so much respect for each other and showed each other, and me, a lot of love. There was absolutely nothing I could get away with because they were always a step ahead. Whenever I tried to trick my dad into believing I was allowed to go somewhere or do something, mom had already told him the truth. They had each other on speed dial.

I wanted someone on speed dial like that. Someone besides Chloe. My mom had my aunt Hadley and their friendship was really similar to mine and Chloe's. Totally inseparable. Well, I guess until Hadley moved here. Maybe that's what would happen when we left for college in a few years. We could be in separate states but stay just as close as we were now. I'm not sure why I was so worried about losing my best friend. We were only 14. Maybe it was why I was trying so hard with Renzo and everyone else lately. Making sure I mattered to more than just one person. Making sure I knew I'd be fine no matter who was surrounding me. I bet I could even get Laurina on my side if I plastered on a fake smile long enough.

"Amelia?"

Chloe and Anders were staring at me. I had no idea how long I had been talking to myself in my head. I looked at Chloe who giggled. "Where were you? Anders was asking if we wanted to walk to Java Joe's and you were just sitting there staring at Little Foot."

"Oh, oops… I guess I zoned out for a second. Probably a perfect reason to get an iced coffee." I laughed. "I'll go ask Hadley."

Chloe put her arm out to stop me before I had the chance to stand. "Are you sure you're okay," she whispered. "You've been looking at Anders like you hate him."

I have? "I don't hate him, that's just my face," I said flippantly. Last thing I needed to do was tell her I was annoyed Anders was here, ruining our girl time. "You can have the alone time with him that I know you've been dying for while I go talk to Hadley." I popped up from my seat.

"I don't need alone—"

"Be right back!" I waved into the air, cutting Chloe off. Of course she wanted the alone time. It was exactly what I would've wanted, too.

With a huff, I walked down the hallway toward Hadley's room. I could hear Marcus clanging on the pipes as I approached. Not sure what type of privacy I was supposed to give them, I decided to announce myself early and loudly. "Hadley?"

A moment later Hadley poked her head out of the bathroom, running her fingers through her hair. "Yes, Sweets?"

"Sorry for interrupting." I smirked.

"Nothing to interrupt." She assured, a bit too quickly.

"Sure, Hads. Anyway, would it be okay if we walked with Anders to Java Joe's for some drinks?"

"Yeah, no problem." she twisted behind her and called out, "Marcus, do you care?"

"Nope," he hollered back. "Let Anders know I'll pick him up in town in an hour or so. We're headed to my Aunt Symone's later."

"Can do. Do you want us to bring you back anything, Hadley?"

"How thoughtful, I'm good."

"You sure? Nothing cold... refreshing? You look flushed." I smiled, wiggling my eyebrows.

"Don't even." She shook her head, releasing a laugh. "We're fixing my shower so I can wash my hair without water shooting into my eyes at the same time."

"Okie dokie; if you say so."

"Go!" she teased and waved me off.

I laughed and walked back into the living room. Anders was standing about an inch from Chloe now, talking in a hushed tone by the front door. Nobody ever cared about love the way I had. Hadley always said she had all the love she needed in her friendships, in me. My mom said my dad was enough for her, even though they're "just friends." Chloe wanted to focus on school and her path toward a shiny college scholarship. I wanted the experience, the relationship, the inseparable bond of a couple. Why was I now being surrounded by puppy love, with none of my own.

I sighed and forced a smile for the sake of my best friend. I should've done the stupid body shot. "They said we're good," I gave them a thumbs up. "Your dad will meet you in town in an hour or two."

"Awesome. Ready if you are."

I nodded, looping my arm through Chloe's before she had the chance to loop hers through Anders'. She smiled at me, content to have me at her side, completely unaware of my insecurity and jealousy.

Not What I Thought

It had been one week since we went into town with Anders to hang out, and somehow those two hours clung to me like the sticky summer air. I couldn't shake it off – being the third wheel, sitting across from Chloe and Anders as they leaned subtly toward each other. Their conversation had no pauses, it was seamless. They talked about everything from soccer to college to what it was like in Rhode Island. I felt like I was blending into the Nora Jones background music. I stirred the straw of my Frappuccino and nodded when it was appropriate, and smiled whenever they laughed, but in my head I was *so* over it. Java Joe's was nowhere near as good as Starbucks anyway.

At least the weekend had been a break from all of that – no parties, no pretending to be sixteen, just me, Chloe, and Hadley. Even though my whole summer goal was about growing up, it had been nice to lean into the familiar. To watch *Seventh Heaven* reruns with Chinese delivery containers spread out on the coffee table for us to all split. To have an at-home spa day with fruit smoothies, face masks, and Hadley perfectly French braiding both Chloe's silken hair and my unruly curls. The best part was riding the horses again at the arena with Hadley. There was something so magical about a horse.

I had barely thought about Renzo – well, sort of. There was still the occasional curiosity bubble that popped into my mind of what would happen when we saw each other next. Whether he was mad at me about rejecting him on the Fourth of July or if he was cool with it, like Anders had mentioned. All the same, I hadn't brought him up much. I did my best to fully dive into girl time. Chloe, on the other hand, couldn't shut up. She found any excuse to say Anders' name. Even at Sunday night pizza, when Hadley invited Anders and Marcus over, she practically sparked to life. Quiet Chloe had become the center of the conversation, laughing, talking, effortlessly fitting into this world that I was still figuring out. I smiled through it, not wanting to be unfair to Chloe, but the comparison of her ease to my lingering uncertainty, felt unfair to me.

Now it was Wednesday, and tonight was the night. Hadley would be volunteering late at Steeplechase, and Chloe and I would be gone before she got back. We were going to leave her a note but not with the truth. What's one more lie? We planned to say Laurina invited us to a late night movie followed by apps at the diner. She'd be so happy to hear we're getting along with Laurina. Little did she know, we planned to avoid her at all costs. Tonight was my chance to get what Chloe had, but with Renzo. I would be bold. And if I felt hesitation, I would swallow it down with a drink.

Chloe tugged a sundress over her head, twisting in the mirror as she adjusted the straps. "What do you think?"

I sat cross-legged on the bed, sifting through my pile of clothes. She looked perfect. The soft blue made her skin glow, her legs looked impossibly long, and it all seemed effortless. She looked like a sixteen year old ready to party.

"Yeah." I said. "You look amazing."

She grinned, smoothing the fabric over her stomach. "You think Anders will notice?"

"When doesn't Anders notice? He was ogling you when you had on one of Hadley's oversized sweatshirts with pizza grease on your face," I teased, tossing a hanger aside.

"Oh my god. I had pizza grease on my face and you didn't tell me?"

"Chill out, I was just joking." I groaned, flopping onto my back. "I have *nothing* to wear."

Chloe rolled her eyes pointing to the massive pile of options I laid next to. "You're being dramatic."

I peeked at her, then at the heap of discarded outfits. "That's because I *feel* dramatic."

She shook her head, reaching for a black tube top from my pile. "Wear this with the skirt you like. It's simple and cute."

I sighed, taking it from her. It was fine, but I didn't want to be simple. Cute was for fourteen year olds. I wanted to look older. I wanted to feel older. I shrugged on Chloe's tube top, and realized this would work. I was a lot curvier than her and so what fit her normally ended up quite tight on me. Nice. This with that skirt Chloe just mentioned was a great idea. Now, where on earth had I tossed it?

Thirty minutes later, we were ready to go. Anders' neighbor was going to pick us up, which thank God, because it would've taken half the night to get to the barn by foot. I glanced at the note we left on the kitchen table, chewing the inside of my lip. I hated lying to Hadley. "Does this sound legit to you?"

Chloe leaned forward and read the note that we took over an hour to think up. "Yeah, it's totally believable." She smiled at me and grabbed my hand. "Are you excited to see Renzo?"

"Yeah, for sure. I just want to have fun tonight, no matter what. I don't want everyone to think I'm the lame drag from Rhode Island. I feel so stupid for not just doing a body shot last week."

"Don't do that. It made you uncomfortable and to be honest, it was kind of gross..."

"Yeah, I don't get the appeal. I guess maybe someday we will?" We shrugged at each other before a honk outside made her jump. I laughed. "That must be our ride."

The barn smelled like what I now knew to be spilled beer. There was a buzz of laughter and loud music, with even louder bass, making the whole place vibrate. It was crazy to think we were isolated enough that Marcus wouldn't be able to hear the music from his house. It was only a few acres away. I took a look around, seeing a lot of familiar faces, Laurina and her group, Carter, Matty, along with a few new ones. When I turned to the right, I noticed Renzo approaching with his signature smile.

"Wasn't sure you were coming," he said, brushing a cold plastic cup against my arm playfully before taking a sip.

I cocked my head, like confidence was muscle memory. "Of course we came." I said, casually scanning the room again to avoid looking too needy. "I'm always down for a party."

His eyes flickered over me, teasing. "Looking good, Hourglass."

My stomach twisted somewhere between excitement and nerves. Before I could respond, Chloe grabbed my wrist, pulling me toward where Anders had found them a spot near the old hay bales. It seemed the couches were already overtaken by Laurina.

Someone held up a pitcher, sloshing a mix of fruit punch and alcohol into red solo cups. Chloe waved it off, and while I hesitated, I eventually took one.

"You're being tame tonight," Renzo said, leaning in close.

"Pacing myself. We pregamed." I lied. Truthfully, I hadn't decided if I was going to drink. Not after last week. I mean I hadn't even drunk last week but everyone else was and the whole body shot thing is still making me feel really on edge. I ended up grabbing the solo cup concoction because I reminded myself of the goal – to fit in.

The night stretched on, laughter mixed with conversation. Laurina and Rylee were dancing on each other in the middle of the barn, drawing a small crowd, their drinks spilling with every hip bump. Chloe sat next to me but was angled toward Anders, completely absorbed in whatever deep dive they were in now.

"It wasn't even *that* impressive," Anders was saying, grinning as he rubbed a hand over the back of his neck. "I mean, it was a potato-powered clock. That's barely science.'

"Oh, stop," Chloe said, laughing lightly, nudging his arm. "You won, didn't you? You were only ten. A genius in the making!"

Anders chuckled, shaking his head. "A very humble genius."

A giggle tumbled from Chloe's wide smile. She was locked into the conversation like it was an extra credit project. I watched, annoyed. Since when did she care so much about making a boy laugh? Since when did she stop wanting to have all these fun conversations with me? I could build a stupid potato clock. The whole thing was weird. Shouldn't she want more than a conversation? This was like their eighth random topic and neither had moved in closer to the other. Shouldn't I want what she was having with Anders? What my parents had. An easy friendship without expectation. I couldn't help but chase something more. Something I didn't even want as much as I kept convincing myself I did.

Renzo threw his arm lazily over my shoulder, keeping me close. But still, I was watching Chloe. I had the hottest boy in his school hanging onto my side but I couldn't help but watch the way Anders' eyes brightened as he listened to Chloe's story about building a robot at camp. It was all so lame. And really sweet.

That was when the tension started, it itched at me like a mosquito. Maybe it was me, maybe it was the drink Renzo handed me after I apparently chugged the first one, maybe it was how easy Chloe made it look, enjoying the night without worrying about being anyone but herself. I shifted on my feet, leaning slightly into Renzo, but still keeping my eyes on Chloe.

"Come dance," I said, grabbing at her wrist.

She barely glanced at me before pulling away. "Hang on. Anders is explaining his fifth-grade science fair project. Apparently he won," she laughed.

I blinked. "Cool."

Chloe didn't notice my tone, or maybe she did but decided to ignore it. Her laugh bubbled out again, as she continued to focus on Anders as if his childhood victory was somehow equivalent to an Olympic gold medal.

I let go of her wrist. *Whatever.* I turned on my heel, already walking away before I realized Renzo was following me. I wasn't exactly sure where I was stomping off to, so I stopped and pivoted to face him.

"What's up with you?" His voice was playful but it felt laced with frustration. I wasn't acting like the flirt he was wanting out of whatever this was supposed to be.

"Nothing," I muttered. "Actually," I said, lifting my head with indignation, bringing my cup to my lips. Empty. I twisted my lips, then reached for his cup, finishing the rest without hesitation. It was warm from being held in his hands, syrupy from the juice, and burned just enough to make my throat feel raw.

Renzo raised an eyebrow. "Thirsty?"

Before I gave myself the chance to answer, I stepped in closer, threw my arms around his neck and brought my lips to his. It was meant to be flirty. Fun. Confident. Instead, it felt like a performance. Like something I did because I thought it was what I should be doing. Because Renzo had been flirting. Because I rejected him last week. Because I was supposed to be gaining experience.

His hands landed lightly on my waist, but something in his posture felt hesitant. Maybe this wasn't what he wanted after all. I pulled back, clearing my throat, embarrassment creeping in fast.

"Whoa," Renzo said, rubbing the back of his neck.

I forced a smile. "What? You didn't like it?"

He chuckled but didn't answer right away, his eyes scanning my face. Not in a wow she's beautiful type of way, in a trying to figure me out way.

"I mean," he said finally, smirking a little, "I wasn't expecting it."

I swallowed hard. "Oh."

"Amelia?"

I turned to find Chloe standing there, arms crossed, eyebrows pulled low. "Why are you acting weird?" She tilted her head in question.

"I'm not," I shot back quickly, and definitely too sharply.

She narrowed her eyes. "You just ditched me."

"You cannot be serious." I threw my hands up, just for them to fall back at my side. What does she want from me?

"I told you to wait a second, and you waltzed off without saying anything and now you're over here tongue deep in Renzo's mouth? In the middle of the room no less?"

"Whoa, hey now..." Renzo put his hands up in defense and took a few steps backward. Great.

"Leave him out of this, he has nothing to do with this."

"What *is* this?" Chloe questioned, standing straighter now.

I scoffed. "You tell me."

Chloe's arms tightened across her chest. "I don't know, Meels. But you're acting... off."

"I'm having fun," I snapped. "Isn't that the whole point of this summer? Best summer ever, remember?" I looked down at my still empty cup, wishing it had magically refilled. I needed all the liquid courage I could find. Even if it had just led me to embarrassment a moment ago.

"You didn't even let me finish my conversation before you stormed off. Best summer ever was meant to happen together."

"Oh my God, Chloe, since when do you care about some fifth-grade science project?"

Her lips parted slightly, like she wanted to shoot something back but didn't know what. She sighed. "It wasn't about the science fair," she finally managed. "It was just talking. Getting to know someone."

I exhaled sharply through my nose. "Right. You're just *so* good at that, aren't you?"

Her brows pulled together. "What's that supposed to mean?"

I could feel Renzo watching, standing at a safe distance now. I shook my head. "Forget it." I turned toward Renzo, lifting my cup his way in a silent plea. He went to grab it but Chloe wouldn't let this go.

"No," Chloe pressed, stepping back into my line of sight. "You've been weird all night. Ever since—"

She cut herself off but I knew what she was going to say. Since the Fourth of July. My skin felt on fire. "Maybe it's because you haven't shut up about Anders for the past week," I snapped before I could stop myself. The song on the boombox ended at the exact right moment, causing my words to reverberate against the walls. Laurina stopped dancing and was now watching our stupid fight unfold. Though the music quickly picked up with the next song, I heard none of it. I couldn't tell the difference between the bass thumping and my own heartbeat.

Chloe's mouth opened, then closed. Her eyes shot daggers. "You're unbelievable."

I shrugged like I didn't care, but the weight of her stare bore holes into me. I swallowed hard but held my head high.

"You know what, Amelia? Do whatever you want. Just don't drag me down with you." She turned, walking away before I had the chance to respond. Instead I stood stunned. She thinks *I'm* dragging *her* down? She's the one who would rather sit in the corner talking about molecules or whatever instead of kissing boys and having fun.

Kissing boys. Oh, God. Renzo.

I turned my head slowly, and yep – still standing there. This time with a full cup. He offered it to me, exchanging it for the empty one in my hand. I smiled at him, feeling one inch tall. I leaned against the rough wooden beam beside me, steadying myself. The barn now felt too loud, too packed, too everything.

Renzo leaned against the opposite side, arms crossed casually. "I didn't expect to see you two fight," he finally said, nodding toward where Chloe had disappeared. "You seem like extensions of each other."

I gave a half-hearted shrug. "We are," I sighed. "Usually."

He gave a slow nod, but didn't say anything.

I exhaled through my nose. "Sorry about the kiss."

"Oh, don't," he said quickly, shaking his head. "I was just caught off guard." A grin tugged at his lips as he leaned a little closer. "I wasn't sure if your head was in the right space, and didn't want to take advantage. Anyway, it seems like maybe I was right, based on, ya know..." He gestured vaguely in the air, where we stood a few minutes ago.

I groaned, dragging a hand down my face before taking another sip of my drink. "It was meant to be flirty, not—"

"Desperate?" He guessed, one brow raised.

If I could dig a hole and crawl into it, I would. "Yeah..."

He chuckled. "Relax, Hourglass. It wasn't bad."

I peeked up at him, catching the easy confidence that was Renzo.

"Redo?" I asked, tilting my head playfully.

His smile deepened, but I saw the flicker of hesitation, the moment he glanced toward the crowd where I was looking. Toward Chloe. She was laughing like we hadn't just fought. Our eyes connected for a split second; she was definitely keeping tabs on me too, even though she was pretending she wasn't.

When I looked back at Renzo, my eyes were full of the promise that I was fine. It was a lie, but he didn't need to know that.

"Come here," he said, leaning in, his hand warm on my chin.

I let it happen, tilting my chin up to meet him halfway. His lips were soft, faintly sticky from the drink. It was nice; easy. Exactly what I thought I wanted.

But the overwhelming rush I'd pictured – the effortless, all-consuming moment, like Jack and Rose in *Titanic* or Josie's first kiss in *Never Been Kissed* – never came. Instead, I was working at it. Trying to match his energy, to make it feel natural, to convince myself this was as exciting as I'd imagined.

I smiled anyway, leaning in a little closer, letting the warmth of it spread through me, even as a quiet part of me wondered why it wasn't coming as easily as I'd hoped.

Because you're not actually one of them.

I took a slow sip of my drink, exhaling a small breath of relief that, for now, the night had settled.

Chloe had the easy conversation and the natural connection. But I was the one gaining the experience. Exactly what I wanted. Right?

We're Just Tired

"Is everything okay?" Hadley leaned against the doorframe, eyes flicking between Chloe and me. Usually, by this time of night, she'd hear our whispers, giggles, dumb jokes. Tonight? Silence.

"Did something happen at the movies?" she asked, her forehead creasing.

Chloe's head snapped up, just for a second, before she quickly looked away, adjusting her pillow.

OH. *The movies.* The lie we wrote on the note. "No," I said quickly. "Just tired."

"Yeah," Chloe added, nodding a little too hard. "Really tired."

Hadley hesitated, fingers tapping lightly against the wood like she wasn't convinced. I didn't blame her, we weren't being very convincing.

"O-kay." Her gaze lingered a bit longer, like she was debating whether to push just a little harder. "Get some sleep. Big day tomorrow."

The door clicked shut behind her, like she was letting it go – for now. I knew better, though, Hadley was probably already in the living room, turning the problem over in her head, trying to make sense of something she wasn't even sure was something. That was just how Aunt Hadley was. Always stepping in, always problem-solving, always wanting me to be happy. That's why I told her everything. Until now.

I turned toward the bed to find Chloe already asleep. *Sigh.* I slipped into the bed and stared at the ceiling, listening to the steady rhythm of her breathing. It sounded peaceful. How was she able to fall asleep so easily when my brain was in overdrive? The fight played back in my head like some badly edited movie – cutting between Chloe laughing with Anders, me snapping at her, Renzo, the kiss. This was *not* how the night was supposed to go.

I turned on my side, away from Chloe, curling my fingers into the blanket, eyes locked on the closed door. Maybe I should talk to Hadley.

I usually told her everything. She always had an answer, always knew how to talk me down when I got too caught up in my own head. Would she even get this, though? I would have to admit we were at a party. Which meant telling her about the drinking, the boys... all of it would unravel. Plus calling out Chloe's crush on Anders would wreck the rest of her summer. And mine. What if Hadley avoided inviting him and Marcus over? It would cause a rift between Chloe and Anders *and* Hadley and Marcus.

I sighed, rolling onto my back again, debating. The house was silent but the occasional creak of the floorboards let me know Hadley was still awake, walking around. I could tell her a *version* of the truth, just leave out the partying, the bad stuff and focus on the fight, act like it happened at the movie theater. But what good would it do to lie even more to Hadley. At some point, she'd catch on.

I could fix this myself. I had to. I twisted my head, looking at Chloe, her back turned toward me and a blanket pulled up around her. Usually, things were easy between us. We rarely fought and if we did it was over trivial things and the whole thing would just resolve itself without much effort. So why did this feel different?

I let out a slow breath, pressing my face into my pillow. There was always tomorrow.

I woke up first. That wasn't unusual, Chloe was a deep sleeper and could sleep through basically anything. I wondered if it was a technique she had learned with how often her parents fought at night. Whatever it was, I never usually minded being awake first. I loved the way the sun softly lit my bedroom in the morning. But this wasn't my bedroom, not really, and nothing about the morning felt soft or peaceful.

I laid there, staring at the ceiling, listening to the soft clinks and murmurs of Hadley down the hall, probably making tea, humming along to the radio.

Chloe shifted beside me, rolling onto her stomach, mumbling something incoherent into her pillow before she settled again. She seemed so... *fine.* Like she hadn't given last night a second thought. I twisted the blanket between my fingers, debating. I could wake her up, say something now to end this fight. A joke, maybe.

Hey, were you fake sleeping just to mess with me? But what if it wasn't fake? Plus, it wasn't much of a joke. I couldn't think of a single funny thing to say.

I could go with something honest. *Are we okay?*

Or maybe something dumb, just to break the silence. *It should be illegal to fall asleep that fast.*

I opened my mouth, but nothing came out. I sighed and rolled onto my side, facing the door, letting the tension sit between us like some invisible barrier I didn't know how to cross.

Eventually, Chloe stirred, this time waking up. She stretched, exhaled, and sat up slowly. I could feel her looking at me, like she was sharing the same internal debate on what to say first. I didn't turn over, maybe she'd think I was still asleep. Now who was pretending?

"Morning," she said after a minute.

I hesitated just long enough for the pause to feel weird. "Morning."

Neither of us said anything else. I got up but she stayed in bed. I pulled my frizzy hair into a messy bun, ignoring the tension pricking my neck. Chloe got up next, following in my steps until we were both in a silent agreement to head to the kitchen.

"Morning, sleepyheads," Hadley greeted as we shuffled into the kitchen. Chloe grabbed an apple. She didn't look at me nor did she respond to Hadley.

I grabbed a bagel, slid onto the bench, and waited. Waited for Hadley to notice, for Chloe to say something, for anything really.

It didn't take long for Hadley to shoot me a look, like she was measuring the distance between me and Chloe, trying to pinpoint what was wrong. "You two are quieter than normal."

Chloe gave a halfhearted shrug, biting her apple.

"Tired," I muttered.

Hadley wasn't convinced. "Right," she said slowly, sipping her tea. "So, did the movie suck, or..."

There's that lie again. Chloe didn't react, she was clearly leaving this to be my problem to solve.

"No, it was fine." I took a big bite of my bagel, the cinnamon raisin flavor falling flat.

"Huh." Hadley blew on her tea, the smell of peppermint crossing the table. Her eyes narrowed on us. "I would've thought you'd be raving about it, based on how excited you seemed beforehand."

This time, Chloe did react – shifting slightly, like she could feel Hadley unraveling the lie. Before she had a chance to respond, Hadley continued. "Okay, what's up? This whole weird energy thing isn't exactly subtle."

I glanced at Chloe.

She glanced at me.

I could say something right now. Hadley could fix this. Chloe raised an eyebrow at me, like she knew I was on the verge of cracking. Then, to my surprise, she exhaled sharply, almost too dramatically, and leaned against the counter. "Ugh, honestly we're just exhausted. The movie was way longer than we expected, and then the diner service was slow and I think the pancakes we both ordered only made us feel more full, more exhausted. Like a food coma." She put her hand on her perfectly flat stomach. "That's why I'm only having an apple," she said suddenly. Like this part of her performance was a surprise, even to her. "Then we were up late talking about the movie. Amelia's opinions on the ending, by the way, are terrible."

Hadley's eyes volleyed between me and Chloe, like she wasn't sure whether to buy it. "Uh-huh," she said, sipping her tea.

I blinked, caught off guard by Chloe's production, but grateful. "Excuse me, my opinions were solid," I jumped in, pretending like this was normal, like we hadn't spent the night avoiding each other completely.

Chloe chuckled.

I smiled at her, it was small but real, like maybe, just maybe, this wasn't totally wrecked. One stupid fight, one night of tension, was not about to do us in.

"If you girls say so."

We nodded enthusiastically.

"After breakfast, why don't you get ready for the day ahead? I'm off work and we have big plans."

Chloe and I looked at each other, our heads cocked in tandem. "Wait, you said that last night, too. What exactly are these grand plans, Aunt Hadley? Like we said, we're kinda tired."

"Tired, schmired. We'll stop by Java Joes, if it helps. I'm taking you girls to Lake Palmer."

"Lake Palmer?"

"I don't need to explain a lake to you, Meels, do I? You have water in Rhode Island." Her eyes sparkled with humor.

I laughed. "No, I meant, I guess, I don't know what I meant. What are we doing there? Are, uh, Marcus and Anders coming?" I asked this second part while looking at my feet. Hadley's eyes flicked toward me, quick, almost unnoticeable. But yeah, she definitely caught that. She never missed anything. Except our lies this summer.

"Nope. This is a girl's trip! I figured it would be fun to go tubing down the river. It's really calm waters so it'll feel like a lazy river ride, like that one we went to in Virginia a few years ago for vacation. Anyway, it leads down to a public park with a big open picnic area. There's usually a food truck that makes the most amazing mini tacos."

"Wait, really?" My eyes lit up.

"Yes, really. Sound fun?"

"Yes!" I squealed. When I looked over at Chloe, her smile was just as wide.

"I've never been tubing before. That sounds so fun, Miss Hadley."

"You have got to stop calling me Miss Hadley. It's just Hadley, sweetheart. I've known you almost as long as I've known Amelia."

"Sorry," her cheeks reddened. "Habit."

Chloe slid onto the bench beside me, finishing her apple, leaving little room for the tension to sit between us. I moved my leg to press against hers, prompting her to look at me. We locked eyes, and for a second, we were back to normal, no words needed. We had always been good at that, like some kind of secret silent language only we understood. We nodded at each other and soon wide smiles broke across our faces. "Swimsuits," I declared. "We need to go pick out what swimsuits to wear!"

Hadley smiled, like she knew she just solved our drama, as always, and shooed us off to our room. This was going to be exactly what we needed.

Lake Palmer

Hadley rented us three massive black tubes, wide enough that I wondered if Chloe would fall right through. I wouldn't dare share that thought with Chloe, though, who by the looks of it, now regretted agreeing to join. We held our tubes at the edge of the water bank while Hadley explained how to fall backward onto them. Easy peasy. Except it felt exactly like those trust exercises we used to do in elementary school gym class.

And trust wasn't exactly Chloe's strong suit. I couldn't blame her, I mean her mom agreed to having Chloe come to Montana just to divorce her dad the moment she left.

"What if there's something gross in there?" Chloe asked, her eyes wide.

"Like what?" I eyed the water, it seemed clear enough, a little green but super calm.

"I don't know. Bugs? Fish? The Lochness monster?"

I rolled my eyes. It was a river, not the ocean and anyway I was pretty sure the Lochness monster wasn't real. Right? Without giving her time to overthink it, I dropped my tube into the water, bent my knees, and launched myself belly-first, like a frog. I hit the plastic with a dramatic splat and the momentum bounced me right-side up, legs kicked out, arms stretched wide.

"See? I'm alive!" I said, laughing so loud it echoed off the trees.

Chloe shrieked my name when I jumped but seemed amused.

Hadley chuckled and shook her head. "See? Totally fine. No river monsters."

"Promise nothing bad will happen?" Chloe asked, eyes bobbing between Hadley and the water.

"Promise," Hadley said, steady as the rock she was.

Chloe watched as Hadley took a few steps into the water, then held the tube in place for her. Chloe squeezed her eyes shut, turned around, and leaned backward. Her arms were stiff when she dropped onto the tube, but when she hit with a small bounce, she seemed to relax. I grinned.

Hadley slid onto hers next. Once we were all floating, our tubes tied together by a white rope, the river took over. This was not white-water rafting, an adventure my Uncle Josh loved. This was definitely a lazy river, and it pulled us slowly downstream.

The sun warmed my skin, sure to get burnt, the water rippled around us, keeping us cool, and for the first time in forever, I wasn't thinking about anything. I was fully focused on this moment.

Chloe grabbed the rope, pulling her tube closer to mine until we could grab hands. Even though our arms were stretched to their limits, I held on tight.

"Alright," I said, adjusting myself on the tube. "Let's get to the hot topics of the day."

"Oh, and what are those?" Hadley asked with a lazy tone. Her black oval sunglasses covered her eyes while she laid on her tube-like royalty.

"Glad you asked because you're up first," I smiled. "So, how serious are you and Marcus? And you can't lie!"

"Yeah, no lying," Chloe piled out.

Hadley laughed. "You really waited until we were tied together in the middle of the water to ask this?"

"No escapes," I laughed.

Hadley sighed theatrically. "Fine, fine. We're... seeing where it goes."

"What does that even mean?"

"Yeah, that's suspicious." Chloe added.

"Do you *want* it to be serious?"

"I'm not good at this whole dating thing, Meels. But yeah, I think so."

"Ooooo." Chloe and I both sang in unison.

"Enough of that." Hadley laughed.

"Okay, okay," I said, shifting gears. "You wanna know a couple who literally makes no sense?"

Hadley shifted her body toward mine, definitely taking the bait.

"Uncle Josh and Stephanie."

Hadley groaned. "Amelia, no gossiping."

"Oh, come on," I grinned. "I'm a teenager, Hadley, I see things."

"Oh, do you?"

"Yeah, and they're all wrong for each other."

Hadley sighed again, but I could see the intrigue in the way her brows lifted. "Okay, I'll bite. Why?"

"Stephanie is always adjusting things, making Uncle Josh change." I trailed my fingers through the water, watching the ripples chase after us. "And she never eats a full plate of anything; she eats like a bird. It's weird. I don't know." I tipped my head back, squinting up at the sun. "Plus, haven't they been dating for like ten years? Wouldn't they be married by now if they thought they were right for each other?"

Hadley hummed, like she wasn't sure if she agreed. Then she tilted her head at me, shoving her sunglasses to the top of her head. "You know, Josh is one of my best friends, right? I think I'd know if there was an issue."

I raised a brow. "Not if *you* were the issue."

Hadley shielded the sun with her hand and gave me a look. "Excuse me?"

I grinned again, knowing I had her now.

"He looks at you the way—" I paused for dramatic effect, looking to my left at Chloe, who was leaning in fully engaged. "Well, the way Marcus looks at you."

Hadley sat up way too fast, nearly knocking herself off her tube. "Amelia Marie!" She exclaimed. "Enough of that. We are just friends."

Chloe giggled.

"You girls are wild," Hadley scooped the water, splashing it my way. "New topic." Hadley huffed but relaxed back on the tube, sliding her sunglasses back over her eyes. "What about high school? Are you girls nervous to start ninth grade?"

We instantly exchanged a look, knowing the answer without saying it. That was the whole point of this summer — to feel grown up, to walk into high school like we belonged there, not like wide-eyed freshmen who'd get eaten alive by the Laurinas of our school. The Jessicas.

I smiled. "Not at all."

Hadley laughed. "Mhmm, sure."

Somewhere between thirty minutes and 2 hours later, we had reached the open picnic area. We dragged our tubes onto the ground and made our way up the incline and onto the grass.

"Should we have packed towels? How are we getting back to the car?" Chloe looked around. What about returning the tubes?"

Chloe was always good for a minor freakout.

Hadley lifted her brows, pausing to make sure nothing else was about to tumble from Chloe's mouth, before she responded. "This high fashion waterproof fanny pack has my car keys and some cash. And you wouldn't believe it but we're only like 100 feet away from where we parked. This whole thing is a giant loop."

"It is? It felt like we were going straight the whole time." I looked around but couldn't figure out whether this looked familiar or not.

"That's the magic of lazy river tubing," Hadley smiled. "There's a tube return stand right over there and they have a bin of towels we can borrow."

"Like *used* towels?" I crinkled my nose at her.

"Well, they're not hot off the Bed, Bath, and Beyond shelf, but they're washed, Meels."

"Right, duh." I let out a short laugh and shook my head, grinning at my own ridiculousness.

Thirty minutes later, we were bent over with laughter, the wooden picnic table littered with napkins and paper taco wrappers. "That was delicious, Hadley, thank you. This whole day was amazing."

Chloe smiled. "It really was. Exactly what we needed."

"You don't say." Hadley smirked, no doubt feeling proud of herself. "Why don't we head home and end the day strong with a pajama movie session and ice cream sundaes."

"YES!"

Retro Night

"I can't believe we only have two weeks left until we go home."

"Ugh, I know. I feel like we're really getting into the swing of things now. I wish we could stay until the end of summer instead of just this month." I had my hands full of Chloe's hair, carefully twisting it into a French braid.

"Yeah, anything sounds better than going back to my mom's house" Her shoulders slumped as she added, "I guess that's what I call it now."

My fingers paused, mid twist, but only for a moment. I quickly refocused and with a casual tone, pressed her. "How was it the last time you called home? What do you think it'll be like?"

She blew out a breath, shoulders dipping as I separated another section of her hair. "I don't know. She sounded happier." She gave a small shrug, and a few loose strands slipped between my fingers. I kept weaving them in, pretending to focus on the braid even though her voice had my full attention.

"I guess they worked out the hard parts. Dad's moving into some high-rise apartment in center city and I'm allowed to visit him whenever I want. I'm mad at him right now though, so I don't know what I'll do."

Her gaze dropped to her hands, fiddling with the hem of her shorts. I started on the next section, but my chest felt tight. I didn't know if she wanted me to answer or just listen.

"She told me it's up to me. It feels like it shouldn't be my choice whether I see my dad. Like... shouldn't it just be an obvious thing? A non-negotiable, as they'd say. Happy or mad, shouldn't they make me see him? Shouldn't he want me to visit? Shouldn't he be the one asking to see me?"

"That's heavy." I shrugged, not knowing how to help.

"Yeah, it is. But I just wanna ignore it for now and worry about it in two weeks."

I nodded, twisting an elastic at the bottom of the braid before starting on the left side.

"I do know one thing," Chloe smiled. "I'm excited for tonight. I've never been to a themed party before."

"We've never been to *any* parties before this summer, Chloe," I laughed. "Unless you count our roller skating birthday parties, but I'm pretty sure we shouldn't count those."

"Good point. I don't know if I have anything retro to wear, though." Chloe tapped her fingers against her knee, eyes squinting like she was picturing her closet. "Maybe a floral top and your orange skort for a seventies vibe?"

"I think my aunt has old dresses and stuff in her closet." I popped up from the bed. "Maybe we can find something! As long as we can sneak out and back without her seeing us in her clothes, we can just mix it in with our laundry, clean them, hang them back up, and she'll be none the wiser."

Chloe smirked, leaning back on her palms. "Always the schemer."

I grinned widely and wiggled my eyebrows. "Let me finish this second braid and then we can go look."

Hadley's closet smelled like her woodsy floral perfume and was filled with clothes that probably hadn't seen daylight since before I was born. I never knew her to be a hoarder, but it was literally jam packed in here.

"Oh this is perfect," I whispered, running my fingers over the fabric of a kelly green and teal patterned dress. It looked flowy and seemed close to my size, which meant my aunt was holding onto a dress that was definitely too big for her.

Chloe eyed it. "Are we sure she won't notice?"

"Not if we get them back in time," I said, already pulling it off the hanger. "Plus, these are way in the back of her closet. All her new flannel tops and plain colored tank tops are right here in the front. I doubt she even looks this far back."

Chloe nodded and placed her hand carefully on a strappy floral dress that was a smattering of reds and orange. "Okay, this is pretty cute," she admitted. "You know, for vintage."

We grabbed the dresses, ran back to our room, and changed, giggling like kids playing dress-up. Knowing my aunt was out for date night with Marcus, we were able to leave right out of the front door, hitching another ride with Phil. Anders was lucky to have such a neighborly neighbor, always willing to drive us around. At one point I thought it was kinda weird he was always hanging around with high schoolers, but hey, it helped us out.

I was also a little nervous about him spilling the beans to Marcus, but it hasn't happened yet, so fingers crossed.

We could hear the music thrumming through the old wooden walls of the barn before we even got out of the car. After a quick thank you, we waved Phil off and headed toward the entrance.

Thankfully everyone was dressed up to, mostly in seventies and eighties themed outfits. It even looked like a few girls were in flapper-style mini dresses, full of sequins and streamers. That was the twenties, I thought, so, *extra* retro.

Laurina approached and tilted her head, eyes scanning me like she was debating something. Her gaze didn't feel quite as judgmental or grating as usual.

"You know, it's kinda hilarious. Most people try way too hard to look retro, but you're actually pulling it off," she said.

Morgan snorted, flipping her hair over her shoulder. "Yeah, like straight out of an old teen movie."

"In a good way?" I asked, raising an eyebrow.

Morgan shrugged. "Sure."

Rylee giggled, leaning forward to touch the material pulled tight against my waist. "Okay, but real talk, where did you even find this?"

"My aunt's closet," I said.

Laurina's brows lifted. "Oh, like, actually vintage?"

I grinned. "Yep. Both of ours." I pointed at Chloe, standing quietly at my side.

Laurina nodded slowly, like she was almost impressed. "Anyway, drink up. It's time to have fun," she said, as someone appeared beside us, handing out cups filled with something bright red.

Chloe took hers hesitantly, fingers wrapping tightly around the plastic.

"Cheers," Morgan said, raising her drink with a loose smile.

"Wait! Hold up," Rylee interrupted, suddenly serious. "Not to be annoying, but like, just a tip – never take a drink from someone unless you saw them pour it. Could be anything."

Chloe froze, eyes darting down at the cup.

"Oh! Wait, no, sorry!" Morgan waved frantically. "This one's totally fine. That was from Matty. I meant, like, in general! Honestly not sure why I chose this moment to go all Party Safety 101 on you."

"Yeah, it's totally safe," Rylee assured, but Chloe had already spit the drink back into her cup.

Morgan wrinkled her nose. "Okay, ew, don't drink it now, though. Let me grab you a new one. Now I feel bad."

Chloe shot me a look – half embarrassed, half annoyed, but I nudged her side gently.

"Better safe than sorry," I murmured, desperate to keep this interaction going.

She sighed, begrudgingly letting Morgan replace her drink with a fresh one. Her eyes trailed her to the cooler and back like it was all a set up. "Thanks." Chloe politely smiled.

We had formed a circle, clinked our cups and laughed. I was definitely riding out a high from being on the inside. I took a long sip of my drink, cementing the feeling with the strong burn of 'jungle juice.'

Laurina leaned in slightly toward the center of the circle, still needing the attention to be hers. "So, anyway, have you seen the incoming freshmen?"

Morgan groaned. "Oh my god, YES! It's actually tragic."

"Yeah, pathetic, really." Rylee added, nodding dramatically, her drink never more than a few inches from her mouth.

"What did you mean?" I asked, leaning forward, eager to keep up.

Rylee rolled her eyes. "Just that they're all, like, babies. They're leaving middle school but might as well be fifth graders still. So embarrassing."

"High school's gonna chew them up and spit them out," Morgan added.

"Especially if I have anything to do with it," Laurina laughed, resting her perfectly manicured hand on my arm, like I was part of the joke. The part where I was definitely not about to be an incoming freshman at my own school.

I choked, mid-sip, coughing just once before catching myself. Across from me, Chloe's grip tightened slightly around her cup, eyes flicking to mine.

I swallowed, exhaling like nothing had happened. "Oh my god, so embarrassing," I said, laughing along, nodding too fast. "You should see the girls at our school. They look like they're twelve."

Laurina laughed, satisfied. "Tragic."

I widened my eyes at Chloe, tipping my cup in the air, a silent cheer for our successful lie.

As I gulped down the rest of my drink I felt Renzo's eyes again, slowly grazing from my Old Navy flip flops all the way up the form fitted dress. *Thank you, Hadley.* I wanted to turn, to head toward him, feeling his gravity, but I didn't. Not yet. Not when I finally felt like I was on top of the world. *This* world. The world where I was one of the popular girls, sharing gossip and laughing over rumors. They had luckily moved on from how they planned to haze the freshmen, to a rumor they heard about Amanda. The way they so easily shared gossip, laughing at Amanda's expense, I wondered how real their friendship actually was. Looking around, I didn't even see Amanda here. Interesting.

Her loss!

I nearly jumped when Renzo's hand grazed my lower back. When did he get here? His gravitational pull must not have been as strong as I first thought. "You scared me," I giggled.

"My bad, Hourglass. I saw your drink was empty so wanted to give you a fresh one." He nodded at the group of girls and after meeting Morgan's eyes he added, "And don't worry, I swear on my twin sister's life that I did not alter this drink in any form."

Morgan smiled. She must be known for giving safety speeches.

"Ha-ha. What are you doing here, Renz. Don't you have an arm wrestling contest to lose?"

"You mean win?" He bent his elbow and showed off his impressive biceps.

I quickly swallowed my flirty laugh with a drink once Laurina's eyes landed on me.

"Get lost, Renz. Or we'll start talking about our periods."

"Gross. Whatever." He turned his attention to me. "Just wanted to keep you hydrated," he smirked. "You good here or wanna go over to the haystacks and hang with me?" His eyes dropped to the neckline of my dress for a beat, before returning to mine. I was a moth to the flame of his smile, and yet I heard myself telling him I'd catch up with him later.

With a wink, he was off. I turned back to the circle and laughed at something Laurina said.

This was everything I ever wanted.

Chloe, though? She was hanging back, listening but not fully engaged, shifting her weight like she wasn't sure if she belonged here, maybe unsure she actually wanted to belong. Not me. I was so sure of this moment and was desperate to keep the momentum.

"I'm gonna go sit for a bit," Chloe said quietly. Laurina barely noticed, but I did. I watched as she made her way to the loveseat near the back of the barn, and, of course, where Anders happened to be sitting. I watched them settle into easy conversation, Chloe tucking her legs under her, Anders leaning in slightly, like they were locked in on whatever they were discussing. That's how it always seemed to be with them. So much talk, so much...conversation. So much – nothing else.

"Beach ball!" someone shouted, pulling my attention from my best friend. I snapped back to reality just in time to see a neon-colored ball flying through the air, bouncing between people, catching momentum.

"Coming your way, Amelia!" Morgan shouted, swatting the ball toward me.

I jumped for it, one hand reaching, but I was unexpectedly off-balance. My foot landed weird, my grip slipped, and before I could stop it, my drink sloshed forward, bright red splattering down my dress. Down Hadley's dress.

For half a second, my stomach dropped through the floor. I knew exactly what this meant – pending doom. If Hadley saw this, it would be game over. I suddenly wished I'd paid attention when my mom tried to teach me how to properly do laundry last year.

"Oh, crap," I gasped, blinking at the damage. It spread and soaked through quicker than I could process what was happening.

Laurina winced. "Oof. Well that's not coming out."

Morgan and Rylee laughed lightly, not to be mean, I don't think, but more out of surprise.

"Oh, well," I said, shoving down any panic, waving it off like it didn't matter. Like I was too cool to care. "Guess I'm really committing to the retro look – party stains and all."

Laurina laughed, throwing her arm around me. "You're too much. Let's grab a fresh cup. Unless you planned on sucking it out of your dress?"

"Your brother wishes." I laughed.

"Oh, gross, Amelia! But, you're not wrong. Based on his all but drooling face, it's clear he's a fan of the soaked dress look." She laughed, giving her brother the finger from across the room before she led the way, dragging me toward the punchbowl, its deep red liquid taunting me as she grabbed fresh cups.

"Refill time," she announced, pouring generously.

"Amelia's committed now," Morgan teased, nodding toward my ruined dress.

"Totally," I laughed.

The night carried on, conversations overlapping, with no beginnings or endings. I didn't know who or what they were talking about but I did my best to follow their cues, laughing or looking disgusted whenever they did. Renzo's eyes found mine every so often, and while I wanted to walk over to him, I wanted to stay more. I felt so wrapped up in the energy of being part of this group, hearing the inside jokes, absorbing their effortless confidence. They were everything I hoped to become once I started high school.

Before I knew it, another hour had passed and we were finally ready to leave, the night buzzing in my veins. It was Matty's cousin driving us this time, a guy whose name I barely caught – Scott, maybe? The girls swore he was trustworthy, so we went with it.

The ride was quiet, windows cracked, cool night air filtering in and out. Chloe leaned her head back, eyes half-closed, looking at her I realized just how tired I was, too.

She hadn't noticed my dress at first, didn't see the deep, unforgiving stain that spread across the entire front of my dress, but when she did, her panic was immediate.

"Amelia! No. No, no, no…"

Her voice was sharp, cutting through the sleepy silence as she snapped upright, eyes wider than I'd ever see them.

"Something wrong?" Matty's cousin looked at us through the rear view mirror, immediately turning down the radio.

"No, sorry, I didn't mean to yell like that." Chloe blushed. Turning toward me she gawked, "Your dress is – it's ruined. Oh my God, what did you do? What happened?"

I looked down. She was not wrong. It looked so much worse now, the red unmissable, like proof of every reckless choice I'd made.

I shrugged, waving her off like it didn't matter, mostly to prevent her brimming mental breakdown. If she freaked out, I would *really* freak out.

"Tomorrow's problem" I said, laughing, tossing the dress near my laundry basket the second we snuck successfully back into Hadley's house. "I'm exhausted, and a little drunk." I fell backward, in my underwear, onto our bed. "We'll soak it in a stain remover in the morning."

Chloe just kept staring, like she was committing this moment to memory. The moment everything went up in flames. "Shouldn't we soak it now?" She whisper shouted.

I shushed her, already feeling the haze of sleep weight my eyelids. "It's fine," I lied.

Chloe sighed, knowing she'd lose the battle, and tossed me a set of pink and purple swirly pajamas. She got changed, too, carefully folding her borrowed dress and placing it in the basket, ensuring it wasn't touching the stained dress, and climbed into bed next to me.

I was about to tell her just how much fun I had tonight and ask her what she and Anders were so wrapped up in talking about when I suddenly found myself in the middle of dream land, where my dress was perfect, my choices had no consequences, and nothing was about to fall apart.

The Red Stain

I woke up to a persistent backhand against my arm.

"Ow," I whined, blinking slowly, shifting under the sheets.

Another swat.

"Chloe, what —" I froze. She was way too close, our noses practically touching, eyes wide. I groaned, rubbing my face. "It's like six a.m."

"No, Amelia, it's 10:30," she whisper-shouted.

"Oh wow, I must've really been tired. What's going on? You're close enough for me to kiss you. I know this is a summer for experiences and all, but —"

"Amelia, this is serious. Look!" She thrusted her arm out dramatically, pointing toward the space near the door.

I squinted, confused.

Wait.

The laundry basket. Where was it?

Hadley must've come in earlier, saw we were asleep, and grabbed the basket, because it had been mostly full, and that's what she did, she always tried to make life easier. She certainly didn't know what was in that basket.

The dresses.

Her dresses.

Her *ruined* dress.

I bolted upright, the fog in my head gone in an instant. "Oh my God," I whispered.

Chloe was already pacing, chewing her lip raw. "She saw, she had to have seen," she yanked her hands through her hair, her voice pitching higher with every word. "What are we going to do? Why hasn't she come in here screaming at us yet?"

Good question. Terrifying question. Aunt Hadley rarely got mad, but when she did – watch out.

The room felt too small, like the walls were closing in on us. Every sound from the house made my stomach clench. We sat there, panicking in a silence that taunted us.

Finally, I shook my head, hands flying into the air. Enough was enough. We couldn't just sit here waiting for the explosion. We needed to pull ourselves together. Or at least pretend to be normal until the blast came.

We crept into the hallway, dying a little with every step toward the living room. When Hadley came into view, I stilled, throwing my arm out to stop Chloe.

I leaned around the edge of the hallway wall and saw Hadley sitting on the edge of the couch, the stained dress in hand, bent over like she was in mourning. But it was just a dress, wasn't it? Why did her eyes look red-rimmed, glassy, like she'd been crying, like maybe she still might be. I froze, gulping back my greatest fear. I hurt Hadley. But how? What have I done?

Unable to take the unknown anymore, I grabbed Chloe's sweaty hand, and stepped forward, entering the room. "Hadley?" It came out quiet, uncertain. She looked up at me, letting the dress drape over her lap. She didn't immediately respond. She just stared at me.

Here we go. I deserved whatever was about to happen.

"Oh, hi, sweetheart. I was just doing laundry for you girls and saw this," she looked down at the dress for a moment.

"Hadley, I can—"

"No big deal," she waved. "I'll go soak it." She stood up, frazzled, with a smile that didn't meet her eyes.

"Hadley, I can explain," I tried again, despite the thick layer of tension that clogged the air. "We," I looked at Chloe for a moment of strength, "were hanging out with Laurina and the girls and I accidentally spilled my Kool-Aid. It was a total accident. I was going to soak it myself this morning and get the stain out before you noticed."

She sighed, sinking onto the couch and motioning us over with two quick flicks of her fingers. Her eyes stayed on me, sharp but tired. "Why didn't you just tell me?" She shook her head slowly. "And why were you wearing my clothes in the first place?"

"It was a retro party... or I mean, well, Laurina had let us know to wear retro clothes for the girls' night." I twisted the hem of my sleeve between my fingers.

Her eyes narrowed, like she couldn't decide if what I said was believable. "And you don't own anything retro, obviously, but why didn't you ask me?"

"You had already left with Marcus for your date, and I didn't want to bother you." My voice was smaller than I meant it to be. "Honestly, I planned on washing them and hanging them back up before you noticed." My shoulders curled forward as I dipped my head, staring at the carpet like it might swallow me whole.

Hadley nodded slowly, fingers tracing the edge of the fabric, like she was deciding whether to speak or hold whatever this was in for herself. I looked at Chloe, her eyes growing wide with uncertainty. I let out a half shrug, also not sure what was happening.

Hadley ran her fingers over the fabric again, her hand almost hovering. "This dress," she murmured, "it was my mom's."

I inhaled sharply, the realization a sucker punch to the gut.

Chloe shifted beside me, suddenly still, waiting for Hadley to continue. She knew Hadley's mom had passed away from cancer, but not much else.

"She loved it," she finally continued. Her voice lingered between us, sounding removed, like she wasn't here with us but lost in a memory. "It fit her perfectly – flowy, breathtaking, one of those dresses people actually stopped her whenever she wore, just to share a compliment." She smiled faintly, her eyes still misty. "I thought my dad tossed it away after she died," she said with a hint of residual anger. "But then, on my first birthday without her, it was just... there," her head shook like she didn't believe the memory had happened. "Wrapped in a box waiting for me on the kitchen table." Her voice tightened but she continued. "I was so excited," she admitted. "Though, it never fit me quite right. She was curvy like you, Meels, definitely not the stick-and-bone body I ended up with."

I let out a small breath. That's why a dress that was clearly too big for her was still in her closet. She wasn't a hoarder, she was a girl who had lost her mom.

"I never could bear to get rid of it," Hadley continued. "Or the others I found later, when I packed up my dad's house. I don't wear them, but it's nice, it feels like tiny pieces of her, just hanging there in my closet."

I gulped back my guilt and watched as Hadley looked down at the dress again, running a thumb over the stain.

"This one was extra special to me, so seeing it like this just caught me off guard."

I leaned forward, voice small. "I'm so sorry, Hadley. I never should've taken it. If I'd known—"

Hadley's lip twitched into a small smirk as she interrupted my apology. "You know, my mom was the queen of girls' night."

I blinked. "What?"

"She had this amazing group of women, always dancing, gossiping. She never batted an eye when I spilled my milk martini."

Chloe's head cocked. "Milk martini?"

"Milk in a martini glass," Hadley clarified with a laugh. "I wanted to participate."

For the first time today, I smiled.

"She definitely wouldn't be mad to know you spilled your juice while hanging out with a great group of girls," Hadley said, her tone soft but her gaze steady on me.

The words should have let me off the hook, but they only made the knot in my stomach tighter. She thought she was reassuring me, and maybe she was, but she didn't know I'd only told her half the truth.

Hadley sighed, shaking her head like she was tossing away the memory. "It's okay. We'll throw some baking soda on it, let it soak with vinegar."

She stood, stretching her arms. "Breakfast?"

I didn't hesitate, I all but hurled myself into her open arms, hugging her tight, muttering another apology against her shoulder.

She squeezed back – warm, but not quite as tightly as usual. "It's okay, Meels. Accidents happen. Just next time, maybe ask before stealing from my closet, yeah?"

I laughed against her shoulder, but the sound felt brittle. "Yeah, definitely. Consider this a lesson learned."

When she pulled away, her smile was there, but so was something else – an edge that made my chest ache. It wasn't anger, exactly, but I knew she'd remember this. I'd chipped at the ceramics of our relationship again, adding one more hairline crack to the glaze.

Chloe cleared her throat, slicing through the silence. "For the record, it was all her idea."

A deep laugh rolled out of Hadley, pure enough to pull some air back into the room. "Now that I believe."

Chloe smiled, probably feeling the same shaky relief as me. "I wished my parents communicated like this. This was so... sane. Thank you for understanding and not murdering us. I'm really sorry for my part in it."

"Oh, sweetheart," her face softened as she shifted closer on the couch, tucking one leg beneath her. She reached out and rested a hand on Chloe's arm. "Fights are tricky. I'm sorry that you have witnessed so many." Her thumb brushed back and forth against the fabric of Chloe's sleeve, slow and steady. "My dad was no saint, he was actually quite mean, so I understand how you must feel."

She leaned back slightly, the corners of her mouth pulling into something between a smile and a sigh. "For what it counts, I forgive you both. Growing up is messy. You'll make more mistakes, but the best thing you can do is be honest about them." She gave Chloe's arm a small squeeze, her voice softening even further. "I'll always accept the truth, even when it's a red stain on my mom's dress."

We both nodded and followed her toward the kitchen, settling on the bench while she dusted baking soda on the dress before setting it aside and grabbing the carton of eggs.

Her words lingered, heavier than she probably meant them. She just wanted honesty. Simple, direct honesty. And yet, we hadn't even given her that much. Out of the corner of my eye, I saw Chloe glance down at her hands, and I knew she felt it too.

"Hey, Hadley?"

"Hmm?"

"Can you tell us more about her? Your mom, I mean."

Hadley paused, then smiled, the kind that was small but real. "Yeah, I'd love to."

And just like that, the morning shifted from guilt to nostalgia, from regret to connection. I let myself sink into it, the wonderfully detailed stories Hadley shared about her mom painting pictures I never wanted to leave. For a little while, I wasn't thinking about Laurina or Renzo, about the next part, or what came next. I was here. Fully here.

But even as I laughed along, the truth sat like a pebble in my sock – small, constant, impossible to ignore. No matter how sweet this moment was, the cracks I kept creating through my lies weren't going anywhere. Hadley was the role model I'd always looked up to, everything I wanted to be, and yet... I was failing her.

To love someone as wholly as Hadley loved her mom, that was the dream. I felt lucky to be able to have that with my own mom, and my dad. And Hadley, Uncle Josh, everyone. I curled my fingers around Chloe's hand, giving it a light squeeze as Hadley's stories washed over us. I knew she was thinking the opposite. While I was grateful, she was wishful. Wishing for the type of mom who never placed pressure on her to get straight As, to be obedient, to join the chess club and the debate club and somehow still volunteer at the dog shelter. Someone who just loved her as she was, letting her make all the right decisions along with the wrong ones. Ready to forgive, to guide, to love. Chloe wanted what I had. I suddenly felt so stupid for feeling jealous of her these past few weeks. Her connection to Anders was intellectual at best. My connections back home, they were deep rivers of love all interconnected and permanent.

I smiled, letting my head fall against Chloe, grounding her in my world. She was one of my rivers; always would be.

Bear Creek Trail

Hadley was making pancakes again and honestly? That was enough to convince me today was going to be a good day. From the outside looking in, everything was back to normal. Laughter in the kitchen, the warm smell of batter on the griddle. But underneath, I could still feel it. The thing she hadn't said. The tiny pause before she smiled, the way her sentences sometimes landed just a little too neatly. It wasn't enough to ruin the morning, but it was enough to remind me the stain on her dress wasn't the only thing that hadn't fully come out.

She hummed softly as she poured the next batch onto the griddle, the tune catching for just for a second before she picked it up again. I told myself I was imagining it.

I was also certain I'd be in pancake withdrawal once we headed back to Rhode Island at the end of next week. "I'll go check on Chloe." I smiled, shuffling down the hall while Hadley flipped her latest masterpieces.

I laughed when I walked into the bedroom and saw Chloe still dead asleep, tangled in the blankets like she was trying to become the bed. "You're gonna miss pancakes," I warned, nudging her lightly.

She groaned, flipping from her back to her stomach, burying her head in the pillow. Classic Chloe. I shook my head, chuckling quietly, and turned to leave. "There's strawberries and whipped cream, too.

If I don't get to it all first!" I giggled and left, hearing her mumble a response. That oughta get her out of bed.

Yep, she was only a few steps behind me, rubbing her eyes, not bothering to change out of her plaid pajamas.

"Are you girls ready for a hike?" Hadley asked, flipping another golden pancake onto the plate like suggesting extreme physical activity at nine a.m. on a Tuesday was totally normal.

I paused mid-bite, chewing slowly, processing what she had just said. "Like, actual hiking? Outside? In nature?"

"That's usually how hiking works, Meels," Hadley said, grinning.

Chloe, on the other hand, looked absolutely thrilled, like Hadley had just offered us a free vacation to the Bahamas instead of an uphill battle with dirt and sweat. "Oh my God, yes!" She gasped, actually clapping.

I shot her a look. "You're... excited?"

"Uh, yeah? Look at this place," she pointed toward the kitchen window. "We're only in Montana another week, we should take full advantage."

"Or we could not climb things and just appreciate the view from literally anywhere else. My legs were sore for like two days after we walked up Copper Hill. *Hill* Chloe, not mountain."

Hadley laughed, shaking her head as she dropped on the bench across from us with her own plate of pancakes. "Marcus showed me this particular trail. It's got killer views, but it's not too hard... promise. Plus, if you survive, I'll buy you double bacon cheeseburgers after." She wiggled her eyebrows. "Deal?"

Chloe gasped, again. "Okay, well now we have to go," she said, digging into her pancakes like she hadn't eaten in days.

I sighed, accepting my fate. I never would've expected Chloe to get so excited over a hike, though I guessed her long legs were made for it. I sprayed another swirl of whipped cream onto my stack, accepting this as my final meal. I was definitely not surviving a full-fledged hike.

A warm breeze whipped through the car, tangling strands of my curly red hair as we sped down the winding road toward the mountains. The windows were rolled all the way down, the scent of pine flooded my senses.

The radio played *Oops... I Did It Again* and we quickly begged Hadley to crank it up so we could do bad car karaoke, competing for who could match Britney's energy the worst, hand movements and all.

"Okay, okay, you girls are killing me," Hadley laughed, turning the volume down.

Chloe smirked, adjusting her thin-strapped tank top. "You're just jealous of our natural talent."

"Exactly, Hadley," I nodded. You're jelly times ten."

Hadley rolled her eyes but smiled, shifting gears as the road narrowed. The closer we got, the more I could see the peaks in the distance, rising up huge and untouchable. It was hard to believe they were real.

All of my hesitation flew right out the window, replaced with excitement. The air felt lighter and despite everything I'd complained about earlier, this was about to make for an epic story to tell everyone at the lunch table next year.

Hadley pulled past a wooden *Bear Creek Trail* sign and into the gravel parking lot, the tires crunching beneath us. The sign listed the elevation, distance, and difficulty level of the trail but we drove past before I could process any of it. For the last twenty minutes, this had been fun – windows down, music blasting, Chloe hyped beyond belief, which made me hyped beyond belief. But now?

Now I was standing at the bottom of the trail, staring up at what looked less like the simple hike Hadley promised and more like some twisted Olympics qualifying endurance test. "Oh," I said, dumbly, looking up.

"It's going to be fine," Hadley grinned, grabbing her water bottle.

"Fine?" I repeated. "This hardly looks fine. This is—" I gestured wildly at the incline ahead of us. "—basically the stairway to heaven, minus the Heaven part."

Chloe laughed, adjusting her high ponytail, absolutely unbothered. "You're being dramatic."

Hadley just smirked. Smirked! "Marcus brought me here for the first time this past Fall. Trust me, once you get started, you'll see it's easier than it looks."

I did not believe that, but also, I didn't have a choice, so here went nothing.

Hadley clapped her hands together like the world's most annoying camp counselor. "Alright, troops. Ready?"

Chloe cheered.

I groaned.

At first, I walked like someone trying to delay an inevitable death – slow, dragging my feet a little, still highly suspicious about this whole situation. But after a few minutes, something shifted.

The dirt path stretched ahead in bends, lined by towering pine and fir trees, their trunks thick and rough, making a solid wall of nature. Wildflowers popped up along the edges – bursts of purples and yellows, swaying slightly in the breeze.

It smelled fresh, too, like the trees had their own kind of air, cleaner than anything back home. Almost like one hundred of those little tree shaped air fresheners hung around us, except so much better.

Without realizing it, I started walking faster, not running, but I was actually hiking now, not just dragging myself forward. I grinned, stepping over a tree root, setting the pace for the three of us. "Okay, I kind of love this," I admitted, surprising even myself.

Hadley shot me a knowing look. "Yep, told you."

Chloe laughed, barely winded. "You're welcome for forcing you into greatness."

I rolled my eyes, definitely winded. "I said I was having fun, not that I was about to take up professional hiking."

They both laughed. "Baby steps," Hadley said.

The sound of her laugh was a breath of fresh air. Or maybe it was the actual fresh air – the wide-open sky stretched above us. It was almost enough to make me forget the splinters I caused in our relationship. *Almost.*

More than anything, I wanted things to feel totally, completely normal. And I knew exactly how to get there. We'd always bonded best over my ridiculous stories and gossip, the kind that left her laughing so hard she'd wipe at her eyes. I just needed the right one.

Got it.

"Did I ever tell you about the time Uncle Josh and Stephanie tried to take me on a hike in Vermont?" I asked, grinning, already knowing this would be comedy gold.

Hadley raised an eyebrow.

Chloe laughed. "This oughta be good."

"Oh, it was basically a scene right out of *Parent Trap*, except I didn't actually do anything awful." I threw my hand over my heart before adding, "I solemnly swear that Mother Nature acted all on her own."

Chloe snorted.

"First, Stephanie's hiking boots? Brand new, like right out of the box. She was so proud of them and kept saying 'aren't these cute?'"

Hadley groaned. "Rookie mistake."

"Yep. She had blisters in under ten minutes," I confirmed, shaking my head. "Then," I held up my hand. "I accidentally knocked the snack bag into the creek with the way I was pumping my arms. Believe it or not, guys, I'm no athlete."

Chloe giggled, "Nobody thought you were."

"Rude," I laughed. "*Anyway*. So then Uncle Josh started chasing the granola bars downstream, like we'd never see food again if he didn't catch the Ziplock baggie."

Hadley covered her mouth, laughing.

"And then!" Their reactions egged me on. "Stephanie, already half-starving, because she never eats enough, decided to sit down and rest her blistered feet."

"No," Chloe gasped, already sensing disaster. Maybe picturing that scene from *Parent Trap* when Meredith had a newt placed on her.

"Rock – covered in ants." My voice and hand gestures were theatrical, like I was starring in a one-woman production.

Hadley lost it. "Oh my God."

"I swear, it was like the universe was personally trying to ruin her day."

The laughter rolled through us, bouncing between the trees. "Needless to say, the hike ended shortly thereafter and she never asked to go on so much as a neighborhood walk for the whole rest of the year."

"Okay, *that's* hysterical." Hadley wiped tears from her eyes as we restarted our climb, having paused during my reenactment. It felt so great to be in this moment, future shin splints aside, not having to pretend like I was anything other than a dramatic fourteen year old kid.

"Look!" Hadley pointed in front of us. "We're just about at the top. I can't wait for you girls to see this view. It's going to be breathtaking, you just wait."

I laughed. "My breath was taken like half a mile ago. Why am I alone on this struggle bus?"

"Long legs," Chloe deadpanned, making me roll my eyes.

But then I saw it.

The moment we stepped past the last stretch of trail, the world opened up, like I had just stepped into a secret level of Super Mario 64, minus the floating blocks.

I stopped short, my brain short-circuiting a little, forgetting how to make words or even sounds, as I took in the view. Holy cannoli. This was ridiculous. Everything stretched so far and wide, it was endless – like something out of one of those nature calendars my grandma always hung, the views that felt too perfect to actually exist.

Rolling green hills spilled into deep valleys, thick pine forests spread out like someone had dumped an entire bottle of green paint across the landscape with rivers that cut through it all like wavy strands of silver.

And the sky? Absurdly blue, streaked with just enough white to make it obnoxiously postcard-worthy, the sun sitting high with pride.

"Whoa," Chloe whispered, dropping her hands to her hips, bending backward a bit, letting the breeze hit her face like she was Pocahontas.

Hadley smiled, arms crossed, taking it in. "Worth it?"

"I mean, yeah," I admitted, eyes still scanning the distance. "I think I get why people willingly climb things now," I murmured. "Though, honestly? Someone should invent an outdoor escalator for moments like this."

Chloe laughed. "It was *not* that bad."

I shoved her lightly, but laughed with her.

Hadley pulled out her disposable Kodak camera, aiming it toward the horizon. "Memories," she said simply.

I nodded, pausing to stamp the view into my brain, already knowing I'd never forget this.

"Get together, girls," she motioned at us.

We happily obliged, using up the rest of her film with our ridiculous poses. I couldn't wait to hang one in my locker.

"Alright ladies, picture time is over," Hadley announced, tucking the camera back in her bag. "Time to head back down," She pointed down the trail. "We can swing by the pharmacy, drop off the camera to get developed and then grab dinner as promised."

"Or hear me out," I said, wagging my finger in the air like I was about to announce the next greatest invention, "we just tuck and roll all the way down. Faster, easier, and highly entertaining."

Chloe burst into laughter, shaking her head. "Of course that would be your suggestion."

Hadley laughed. "It's always easier walking down than up, Meels. Gravity is your friend."

"Yeah, well, gravity better deliver me straight to a double bacon cheeseburger, or I want a refund."

"Noted," Hadley said.

We laughed, the mountain already turning into a memory, the cheeseburgers now the next great adventure.

The Girl's Mine

It was finally here. Our last Friday before heading back to Rhode Island. Sure, we had all next week to hang out, but as for parties, tonight would be the last big one for Chloe and me.

"Can I borrow this?" I held Chloe's broccoli-colored tank top, running the fabric between my fingers. Her clothes fit me like a second skin, exactly what I wanted. Plus, not only does green look really good against my pale freckled skin and red hair, but the color had a mirror effect on my eyes, making them extra emerald.

"Yeah, of course." Chloe barely looked up, still tunnel-visioned on finding her own clothing combination. We were both on a mission: one last impression before heading home, back to party-free Rhode Island.

She yanked a black halter top off its hanger, holding it against her body, twisting side to side. "Thoughts?"

"You'll look like an Abercrombie model," I said, loosening the thin straps of the green tank top slightly, to better accommodate my body. "You always look great in black because of your hair. It's a moment."

"Exactly the goal." Chloe grinned and slipped into a denim skirt.

We spritzed Cucumber Melon spray on each other, focused carefully on applying mascara and lip balm, and last minute swapped necklaces, ensuring we both looked perfect.

"Okay, final check," Chloe said, stepping next to me in front of the mirror.

"Are we, or are we not, about to make history?" I smirked. "I mean, look at us." I ran my hands down the sides of my torso.

"Killer." Chloe grinned.

With that, we ran out the door toward Phil's car, ready for one last legendary night.

Twenty minutes later, we were bouncing down Marcus's dirt road, windows down, Destiny's Child blasting from the radio. Phil's car smelled like Dr Pepper and whatever body spray he had bathed in that day. The barn came into view just as the sun started dipping behind the mountains, streaking the sky with orange and lavender.

This was the last one. The last barn party before we went back to the reality of homework, curfews, and parents who chaperoned our every move. Rhode Island would feel like a cage after this.

"Do you think Anders is already here?"

"I mean it's *his* barn," I said, adjusting the green tank top. "Plus, I doubt he'd miss a chance to talk about the Mars landings and robotic whatevers with his favorite debate partner?"

She gave me a look. "You make it sound like we're dating or something. He doesn't like me like that."

"He definitely does."

She didn't argue, which basically meant I was right.

Inside, the barn smelled like the citronella candles someone had lit near the corners. The boombox blasted a Blink-182 remix that made the floorboards vibrate. The whole place had a golden haze from the twinkle lights, which I felt certain made my skin glow in the best way possible.

Renzo was leaning near the hay bales, laughing with some of his teammates. His T-shirt clung to him in the best kind of way. He looked up, catching my eye and held it just long enough to turn my insides into soda fizz.

"Amelia!" Laurina called from across the barn. She was sitting with her friends, who had taken over the couch and love seats. Her legs were crossed, the platform sandal on her top leg swinging as she sipped from a red plastic cup, her smile mischievous. "Come on, we're starting something."

I wondered what that meant. Eager to find out, I shooed Chloe toward Anders, who hovered near the loft ladder with a sketchbook tucked under his arm. They always talked like no one else existed, so I'm sure Chloe was more than excited to see whatever was inside his spiral notebook. I wouldn't be surprised if she already knew what it was.

I settled into the circle with Laurina, channeling the bold version of myself that I wished was permanent. Others started to gather, sitting on the floor or the arms of the furniture.

"Ever play suck and blow?" Laurina held up a slightly bent playing card. "It's a classic around here."

"And it's not the kind Rylee likes to play," Matty joked.

"Ew, Matty, could you not?" Laurina stuck her finger in her mouth, mimicking a gag.

I raised an eyebrow. "A card game?"

"Not exactly," Morgan laughed.

We made a loose circle, now all on the barn floor. Someone killed the music for dramatic effect. I heard Chloe's voice behind me, followed by footsteps as she soon sat next to me, Anders on her other side.

"The game is simple," Laurina smirked. "Hold the card to your lips with your inhale, pass it to the next person. No hands. You blow it to the next person, who sucks it in to hold it. If it falls, your faces collide."

I nodded, eyes wide. *Okie dokie then.*

Matty was on my left, but before I had a chance to even speak up, Renzo and he had swapped spots. Laurina kicked off the game without another word, passing the card with ease. The second girl fumbled, but made it to the guy next to her, who passed it off to Rylee, then Rylee to Renzo. His eyes flicked to mine, and he leaned in. The card hit my lips and I successfully sucked in, heart hammering.

Chloe was next. I moved toward her, careful. She leaned forward at the same time, and despite our best effort, the card dropped.

The circle erupted in a combination of gasps and laughter. Carter let out a wolf-whistle.

Chloe's face was strawberry Jell-O. "That was a physics fail," she muttered.

"I knew you guys were close, coming here as besties and all, but maybe we read the room all wrong." Matty had tears in his eyes, laughing through his comment.

I was fully aware that Chloe was prepared to crawl in a hole and die so I quickly let out a super casual laugh, waving my hand in the air. "Oh come on, like you haven't seen two girls kiss before? I thought Montana was cool."

"Damn, hourglass," Renzo said, nodding his head with approval.

"Okay, okay," Laurina jumped in, not wanting too much of the attention to fall off her. "Back to the game. Chloe, it's still you."

Chloe nodded, cheeks flamed, as she positioned the card back over her mouth and slowly leaned toward Anders. I half wondered if he'd rip the card down just to finally kiss her, but he didn't. Of course he didn't. Instead they transferred it successfully and it was already on its way back around the circle. When the card reached Laurina, the whole group shuffled spots for round two – everyone except Renzo. He just slid from my left to my right, close enough for his knee to brush mine.

Soon enough, Amanda blew the card to my lips. I sucked it, it held, and someone booed, wanting me to kiss another girl. I laughed, the card slipping to my lap but I caught it and turned toward Renzo.

I leaned in, sucking the card until I was close enough to blow it toward him, but before I could, he had flicked it to the floor and closed the space between us in one move. His mouth was on mine, firm and certain. We kissed longer than a few seconds – long enough for the chatter around us to dip – my breath gone, my heart off to the races. When we separated, my lips stayed parted, frozen, while he smirked and announced to everyone, "Just clearing that up. The girl's mine."

I'm the girl? The girl that's his? Oh. My. God.

Out of the corner of my eye, Laurina's expression tightened, sharp enough to make me wonder.

I floated on clouds for the end of the game and all the way to the spiked punch bowl, where Renzo refilled my drink without asking. With the game over, a few new couples were off in corners making out, Chloe and Anders – now with drinks – slid right back into whatever conversation they'd been lost in, and Laurina and her friends were dancing dramatically to the music that Carter turned back on.

Renzo's arm stayed locked around my waist, anchoring me to his side. I half listened to him and Matty talk about his cousin's busted four-wheeler and how they'd taken it over the frozen pond last winter "just to see if it'd crack the ice." Matty snorted so hard punch shot into his nose, sending him into a fit of coughs and laughter.

I watched, sipping my drink. The first one, paired with Renzo's very public kiss, left me light and floaty. This one settled heavier, weighing down my legs, making my head spin just a little more.

Across the barn, Chloe and Anders were deep in conversation, gestures flying between them as Chloe used both hands to explain something. I caught her laughing, her head tipped back, and it hit me how different she looked compared to a few months ago. She was happier, despite the mess with her parents. Braver, even if she didn't know it. More... herself.

I turned back to Renzo and let myself lean against him, knowing he could support my weight.

"Hey," he said low in my ear. "You good?"

"More than good."

His lips brushed against my skin as he asked if I wanted to dance. I nodded like an idiot, feeling my pulse in my throat. He topped off our drinks without asking, his hand warm but firm at the small of my back as he steered me toward the makeshift dance floor.

Laurina, Morgan, and Rylee were already in the middle of a choreographed routine to "No Scrubs," their laughter ringing over the music. I caught Laurina's eyes flick toward us, pointed enough to sting. Then she flipped her hair and spun back into step, like she hadn't just made it crystal clear she wasn't okay with me choosing her brother over her.

I tried to shake it off. Renzo's arm was tight around my waist, holding me close like he wanted everyone to know I was his. I liked it, more than I was ready to admit, but the burn of Laurina's look lingered.

We swayed back and forth, caught in our little bubble, while the girls switched tracks to P!nk's "There You Go," yelling the lyrics like they were mad at every boy in the barn. It made me laugh, even as a flicker of unease crept in under the warmth.

Someone found sparklers, or maybe brought them, and started lighting them right outside the barn doors. A bunch of us ran out, laughing and ducking through smoke, waving tiny fireworks in sloppy circles. A boy named Drew took a picture of us with his disposable camera, and I was already mentally planning on how I could get my hands on a print. I wanted to remember this moment, and even more so, wanted to make sure everyone back home saw just how cute the boy with his arm draped around me was.

A moment later we heard a crash inside. We walked in to see someone had knocked over the punch bowl. The room was loud with laughter and bass and nobody seemed all that phased by the mess. "Time for beer," someone announced. Where the beer would come from, I had no idea.

Renzo kissed my cheek and said, "Be right back, Hourglass," before jogging over to where some kid from the soccer team stood by the boombox. I spotted Chloe by the corner table, holding a cup and talking to Laurina, which was weird because those two had barely spoken all summer. They were smiling so I guessed it was going okay. I stood back, spinning the empty cup in my hands, trying to lock it all into memory. The lights, the voices, the dusty floor, the smoky air. Renzo's kiss. Chloe's smile. Laurina not being mean anymore. Everything felt so right.

And then, the barn door slammed open.

I Trusted You

Hadley stood there, winded like she'd run the whole dirty road, her eyes blown wide, like she couldn't register what she was seeing.

Marcus, right behind her, jaw clenched, took in the crowd, the drinks, the music, the… everything.

No one spoke.

No one breathed.

"ARE YOU KIDDING ME?" Hadley shouted, her voice slicing through the barn like nails on a chalkboard.

Marcus didn't yell. He didn't have to. He walked straight over and yanked the stereo cord from the wall.

Silence.

For a second, the barn was completely still. Then it was chaos.

Some kids bolted, climbing out the barn windows, while others grabbed their bags and made a bee line for the entrance. Some tripped over bales of hay and the ones too drunk to process what was happening just stood there.

I didn't move.

Neither did Chloe.

Neither did Anders.

Marcus's eyes locked on his son. "What the hell is going on?" he asked, voice low but sharp. "Is that *alcohol?*"

Anders opened his mouth, closed it again. Swallowed hard. "Dad—"

"It's bad enough you're throwing parties at *sixteen*. But these girls?" Marcus pointed toward us, his voice rising. "They're *fourteen*, Anders. *Fourteen*. You knew that?"

Anders looked like someone had punched the air out of him. "They said... I mean, I thought—"

"You *thought?*" Marcus snapped. "You thought wrong."

Behind us, I heard Renzo mutter something before he took two big steps back like he'd burst into flame if he stayed too close. I trained my eyes on the floor, refusing to look at him. At anyone.

Then Hadley's voice, quieter now, in the worst way possible. "Oh my god." Her eyes found mine when I slowly looked up. She didn't even look angry, just wrecked. "I trusted you, Amelia."

Everything inside me sank. I couldn't breathe. My arms felt numb. I could hear Chloe sniffling next to me, trying to keep it together.

Marcus turned back to the crowd. "Party's over. Anyone I know, I'm calling your parents. Everyone else? Out. Now."

The barn exploded into another wave of motion. A few kids tried to say something, explain or joke to lighten the moment, but Marcus cut them off. "I SAID NOW."

Hadley grabbed our arms, not rough, but not gentle either, and steered us toward her car. Her lips were pressed so tight they were turning white. She didn't speak. She didn't even *look* at me. I quickly realized that her silence hurt more than if she had yelled.

The ride back was silent. The kind of silence that makes your ears ring. I stared out the window, but everything looked like static. I half expected the sky to open into a wild thunderstorm, matching the way my gut swirled, but it didn't. I was stuck thinking about the first party, the one where Chloe passed out on the couch after one drink too many. That could've gone so wrong. What if she had hit her head? What if nobody had noticed? What if tonight someone else had passed out or gotten hurt?

Hadley pulled into her driveway too fast, slamming the gear shift into park. She still didn't speak.

We climbed out, heads down. My knees were jelly, my throat constricted like that time I tried kiwi and realized I was allergic. She unlocked the front door, stepped inside, then finally turned to us. "Bed. Now. We'll talk tomorrow." Her voice didn't shake, but it didn't need to. The look in her eyes, which were rimmed in tears, will haunt me for the rest of my life.

I'd broken something so much bigger than a rule or curfew. I had broken her trust. And I wasn't sure I'd be able to fix it.

We kept our heads down as we walked down the hall to our room. I wanted to grab Chloe's hand, comfort her, myself, but my arms wouldn't move.

We didn't brush our teeth. We didn't change into pajamas. We just climbed into bed and while I stared at the ceiling, Chloe was curled up on her side, pulled so tight into herself she looked like she might shatter. I continued staring straight up, my heart thudding too fast, my mouth dry like I'd swallowed cotton balls. My body felt shaky, hot and cold at the same time, and it had nothing to do with the alcohol in my system.

"I'm so sorry," I whispered, my voice cracking around the edges.

She didn't answer. Not right away. Her shoulders did this small, hiccuppy twitch, and I realized she was crying. It was the quiet, no-sound kind of crying. The kind that makes your throat hurt just from watching.

"She trusted me," I said. "Hadley. She trusted me and I completely blew it."

Chloe wiped at her face, still turned toward the wall. "You didn't completely blow it." She paused. "Just, like, *mostly* blew it."

It was a joke, and though she didn't laugh she did turn her head toward me and offer a small smile.

I let out a half-laugh, even though my stomach felt like a lead balloon, and grabbed her hand. "I thought we could pull it off," I admitted. "This summer, this whole pretending-to-be-a-highschooler thing. I thought we had it in the bag." What Hadley didn't know couldn't hurt her, was what I thought. Until now. Now I realized just how immature I really was for the whole thing.

"Yeah," she mumbled.

We fell into silence again for a few minutes, hands held tight. I could feel the guilt crawling across my skin, knowing this was my big plan and I brought Chloe down with me. She probably would've been better off back home at her science camp, out of trouble, safely adding extracurriculars to her future college resume.

"I just wanted to feel grown up," I said. "You know? Like I'd, we'd, had an experience. Something we could bring to freshman year and be bold and brave about. Be the girls everyone else wished they could be. Sounds kinda stupid, now."

Chloe turned her head, finally meeting my eyes in the dark. Hers were puffy and red, and I probably looked the same.

"It's not stupid. But, you know what I think was the best part of our *best summer ever?*"

I shook my head.

"Tubing with Hadley and riding the horses at her arena. Or, going on the trail hike that you swore would kill you. Even making ridiculous wishes on the dandelions like we did when we were seven, laughing until we couldn't breathe."

I swallowed hard. "Did I mess up our summer?"

"You didn't mess it all up," she sighed. "We went into this together and I'd be lying if I said I didn't enjoy the sneaking around parts, too." She sighed. "We definitely grew up this summer."

"Yeah." I swallowed hard then added, "I'm sorry about that first party, by the way."

"How would you have known? Neither of us ever drank before. We should be glad it wasn't worse."

"Yeah. I also feel bad about trying so hard to be friends with Laurina. I don't even know why I cared. I guess she was just popular in the way I thought I wanted to be. I mean, she's nice now, but she was so rude to us in the beginning. I never should've pushed you aside to get her attention."

"You didn't. Once I worked up the nerve to talk to Anders, I'm pretty sure I was the one pushing you aside. I've never talked to someone so easily."

"Hey..."

"You know what I mean. He's a *boy*."

"That he is," I laughed. "Though I think I ruined that for you. Based on the way he and Renzo looked at us after Marcus announced our ages."

We didn't say anything after that. Just laid there. Eventually, I fell asleep with my heart still pounding, wishing I could hit rewind on the night – but knowing full well I couldn't. I assume Chloe eventually fell asleep, too. We'd have to face this head on in the morning.

Definitely Grounded

I woke up with the same pit-in-my-stomach feeling that I had when I lied to my mom in sixth grade, when I told her I studied for a test when I hadn't, and ended up royally failing. It made my body feel like it was made of wet sand.

The room was stuffy, and my head was pounding from an emotional hangover. And maybe a real one, too. Chloe was still curled in a ball, like an alleycat protecting herself from a harsh winter night. Her eyes were shut peacefully but her blotchy face told the real story. I didn't want to wake her, knowing what was coming our way, so decided to let her sleep it out a little longer.

I walked to the edge of the bedroom and gingerly opened our door, careful to not let it creak. I crept into the hallway like I was on some stealth mission, my bare feet silent on the floorboards, desperate to catch a glimpse of Hadley, delusionally hoping she was somehow in a better mood. A forgiving mood.

And that's when I heard her. She was pacing the kitchen on the phone. Definitely *not* in a better mood.

"I just needed time to think, Marcus." Dramatic pause for I guess whatever Marcus had to say. Then with a sharp tone, I heard: *"No, I haven't punished them yet. They're still asleep."*

My heart lodged somewhere between my throat and my ribs. I tried to swallow it down, but it wouldn't budge.

"I know. I do. I'm not excusing anything but yelling the second they got in wouldn't have made a difference. I wanted to talk to them when they, and I, could actually think straight."

There was a long silence. Too long.

"I called Josh last night," Hadley said softer, defeated.

Oh no. I sucked in a breath and took a step back. Her voice dropped even more, sounding completely wrung out. *"Because I needed someone who knows her. Knows how she thinks. I didn't call to flirt, Marcus. I called for help."*

Something inside me twisted. She wasn't being dramatic nor yelling. This was worse. Her voice was bruised, like one of those bananas that turns soft and spotty when nobody's looking. Too far gone to save. I hoped she didn't actually feel that way. Not when I was the one who felt completely rotten.

"I can't talk about this if you're going to make it about that."

I definitely ruined whatever good thing they had going. Great job, Amelia. I didn't want to hear the rest. Couldn't hear the rest.

I turned around and slipped back toward the bedroom, my breath trapped somewhere outside of my lungs. I needed my best friend. To heck with letting her sleep. I had already ruined her summer, might as well ruin her morning, too.

When I opened the bedroom door I saw Chloe awake, sitting in bed, with her back against the headboard. She looked at me, eyes squinting; I lifted and dropped my shoulders, unsure what to even say. I plopped on the bed next to her and after a minute of blowing out a slow breath, trying not to cry, I managed an update. "She was on the phone," I said quietly. "With Marcus."

That was all it took. Chloe's face crumpled a little. She pulled her knees up and wrapped her arms around them. Neither of us spoke.

"That's not even the worst part. They were obviously talking about last night but then I think they started arguing about Uncle Josh."

"Your uncle?"

Before I had the chance to explain we heard a knock at the door. We stared at each other, eyes wide in panic.

"Girls? Can you come out to the kitchen?"

Her voice sounded calm. *Too* calm. Chloe and I exchanged a silent stare, the kind that said *this is going to be bad*. After a minute, we pulled ourselves off the bed like we were about to walk the plank.

Hadley was already waiting by the table. No tea, no phone, no distractions. She just sat there, spine straight, hair in a too-perfect ponytail, face unreadable.

We shuffled in. I sat first, Chloe tight against my side like we were trying to become a single unit and maybe escape this together. Hadley looked straight across the table at us and I wanted to hold her gaze, knowing I needed to be accountable, but I couldn't help but stare down at the table. This felt horrible and we hadn't even begun.

"You both know you messed up," she said, no drama, no raised voice, just facts. "But that's not what scares me most."

I felt Chloe shift beside me. My throat felt constricted, my heart going a million miles an hour.

"What scares me," she continued, "is that I don't think you understand how dangerous that was. Or how fast that could've gone bad."

Immediately, I thought of Chloe after that first party – how pale she looked, how violently she threw up after she blacked out. How I tried to play it off afterward. But instead of admitting that, I heard myself say, "Okay, but nothing *did* happen. Everyone was *fine*."

Hadley's expression didn't budge. She let out a slow breath. "When I was your age, or maybe a little older, my dad started drinking heavily. The kind of drinker that made people, *me*, walk on eggshells. I remember being afraid to breathe too loud. I used to sit on the stairs and pray he'd pass out before dinner just so I could eat in peace."

Chloe opened her mouth, then shut it again. Like she wanted to say something but didn't know what. I stayed silent, too, my stomach twisted.

"As you know, my mom died when I was your age." She didn't look at us when she said it. "So it was just me and him. And the alcohol. And I hated it. Hated him for letting it swallow him whole."

That... wasn't the story, or the lecture, I thought we were getting.

"I used to love watching my mom and her friends, I called them the Pink Ladies, like in the movie Grease." A smile crossed her lips for half a second. "They'd dance around the living room with beautiful, flowy dresses, with martinis and bad music and laugh until they cried. For a while, I thought *that's* what drinking was. I couldn't wait to grow up and have friends like my mom had. But after she died? Everything flipped. Alcohol turned into something else entirely. It caused so much fear, so much anxiety."

My brain didn't know what to do with any of that, so naturally, my mouth went rogue. "You've never even been drunk," I blurted. "You don't actually *know* what it's like. You don't go to parties, and never even dated anyone... not until Marcus. You barely even try to have fun. Like, ever."

Chloe jerked slightly beside me, like she'd gotten whiplash just listening.

Hadley looked at me, but she didn't seem mad. "You think that was a choice?" I opened my mouth, but she kept talking. "I avoided parties, heck, I wasn't even invited to parties. I was too busy surviving. I was afraid of becoming my dad, so even as a young adult, I steered clear of anything that felt like him. But you know what I missed most? Being a kid. Growing up slowly. Enjoying the little, silly things."

I suddenly felt very, very small.

"I'm not telling you this for sympathy," she said, voice softer now. "I'm telling you because I want you to *know*. I want you to understand what you're reaching for when you party or sneak around or drink just to feel older."

There was a long pause. I finally looked up but it was Chloe who broke the silence. "We didn't mean to mess up this badly." Her voice cracked. "We thought we were in control. But we weren't."

Hadley nodded slowly. "That's the whole point. Slow down." She chewed the side of her mouth while she considered her next words. "I guess what I'm trying to say is drinking can be part of a happy life. A happy *grown-up* life. But only when you're ready. When you're old enough to know who you are without it. And you girls are fourteen. You're way too young to even be testing the waters."

I swallowed around the lump in my throat. "We're grounded, huh."

"Oh, you're *definitely* grounded," Hadley said, letting the corner of her mouth twitch. "For the rest of the time you're here, at least."

I hesitated, then asked: "Does that mean... well, I guess... if we asked nicely, could we maybe still have pizza tonight?"

Chloe looked at me like I had lost my mind.

Hadley raised an eyebrow, then tilted her head. "You know, I used to be terrified to ask my dad for pizza, even on my birthday."

I waited, not sure where this was going. Was I being presumptuous assuming she'd let us still have pizza like we talked about the other day? Grounded probably meant no pizza. Cereal for every meal.

"I love that you even *feel* safe enough to ask me," she said. "So yeah. We'll order pizza. And we'll make it a girls' day. Because grounded or not, this conversation isn't over. I have a *lot* of questions and you girls better get ready to dive into all the messy details of this summer. I have a feeling I overlooked a lot."

Oh.

Chloe let out a shaky little laugh.

I couldn't quite bring myself to smile yet. But my shoulders dropped just a little and I nodded, admitting the obvious. She definitely over-looked a lot but it was only because we lied to her and spent this summer sneaking around her back.

"Why don't you both go take showers, wash last night off of you. Then put on sweats and we'll load up a movie to decompress. After, we'll sit on the couch with some snacks, and get to talking. I want you to trust me and continue to feel safe with me so we can make the living room a judgement free zone. No consequences—" she held up her pointer finger, "no *new* consequences I should say, as long as you are honest. Deal?"

We both nodded, though I definitely didn't feel confident in this judgement free zone plan. If we really told Hadley all the details of this summer, we'd probably be on the next plane out of here. No way she'll forgive us, me especially. I guess we'd find out.

Safe Space

10 Things I Hate About You ended with the type of predictability that I craved: Kat got the guy, the band played on the roof, and for about five seconds during the credits, everything felt light. We laughed, we choked back tears, we sang along to Heath Ledger's bleacher scene. But as the screen dimmed, so did our smiles.

With the movie over, the room became far too quiet. I shifted uncomfortably; my stomach felt acidic. Like all of the sour powder from my Sour Patch Kids had just hit bottom, or more likely, it was from the looming lecture we were about to get. I hated disappointing Hadley, and I knew if we told her what we had been doing, she'd be crushed.

Hadley stood up, stretched, and turned off the TV. "Okay," she said, brushing invisible lint off her shirt. "That was a great movie. Awesome choice, Meels. So, it's safe to say that now we're all happy and cool, right?"

Well, we *were*. "I guess."

"I'm refreshing our iced teas." She grabbed our glasses and started toward the kitchen, glancing back at us with the kind of look that hovered between *I love you* and *this is just the beginning*. "And then," she added, "let's get to business. I want to know exactly what's been going on under my nose."

I barely had time to blink before my stomach bottomed out completely. There was no way she'd honor this whole "the living room is a safe space" concept. This would get messy so fast.

I looked over at Chloe, who was already staring my way. I bit my inner lip but said nothing. She scooched closer to me, leaving the right third of the couch open. I was relieved for her move because maybe Hadley would sit over there and I wouldn't have to make any direct eye contact.

Nope.

She set our iced teas down like we were about to enjoy a nice, casual chat, then grabbed the wingback chair, dragged it into position, and sat across from us. It suddenly felt like she was the therapist and we were the court-mandated patients, in therapy to avoid jail.

She sat there like she had all the time in the world. She took a long sip of her iced tea, set it down on a coaster, and crossed her legs casually like she was about to kick off this month's book club with her besties. "Okay," she said, voice gentle. "Let's start at the beginning."

Chloe looked at me like maybe I had a plan.

I very much did not.

Hadley cocked an eyebrow. "When did this whole partying thing start? Was yesterday the first of it?"

I gulped but didn't respond.

"Because from where I'm sitting, it looked like you girls had been having an innocent little summer. Going to the movies, baking cookies, having slumber parties, coffee at Joe's, breakfast at Pancake Patty's. And now I'm thinking I've been completely delusional."

Chloe sat up a little straighter and when I didn't immediately respond, she did. "You weren't delusional." Her voice was quiet. "We were just lying to you. That's on us."

I nodded slowly. "Yeah. We made it seem innocent on purpose."

Hadley fiddled with her ponytail, probably giving herself time to stay calm. "Okay. So the beginning of this lie was?" She looked between us. "Day one?"

Silence.

"Okay so how about the tractor race the other week. Did you really go or was that a cover?"

"We really went." I'm not sure why I didn't expand, probably because I had no idea what was happening here or how much to say.

"And the Fourth of July, when you girls walked off with Anders? What really happened there? Did you go up the hill to watch the fireworks?"

I shifted on the couch. Of all the moments for her to hone in on, that wasn't the one I wanted to talk about. "We really did go to the fireworks. But we left out a few details."

Hadley raised an eyebrow and waited for me to continue, but when I froze up, she let out a sigh, dropping her shoulders. "Listen, girls, I meant what I said. This is a safe space. You are already grounded, you won't get double grounded for being honest with me now. I want you to trust me. I want to hear the good, the bad, the ugly. Whatever the truth is." She shifted her gaze directly to me before she added: "That is the only step you can take that will head toward earning back my trust."

I looked down at my hands, picking at a hangnail like it might help me time travel. I wanted to go back to day one and do this all over. Skip all the parts that are now about to get me in trouble. Chloe was completely still beside me like she might've frozen for real.

Hadley leaned forward just slightly. "Okay. So. Start once you're ready and I won't interrupt."

I nodded, and then, because I wasn't ready to talk about the Fourth of July, I decided to jump off the cliff and go all the way back in time. "It actually started before the Fourth of July and before the Tractor Race."

Chloe's head turned toward me, surprised, but she didn't stop me.

"It was kinda right from the very start. Or, maybe even before the start? Like back in Rhode Island." I gulped.

"What do you mean?" Hadley asked.

"Our goal for coming here, besides of course spending time with you, was to get some experience. Find a party, meet a boy, prepare ourselves for high school."

"Ah, I see. Experience." I could tell she was trying hard not to panic. "And what kind of... experience... did you—"

"Not *that* kind of experience." My eyes bulged, realizing what she must've been thinking.

"Okay." She exhaled. "Okay, so you had a grand plan for the summer, and your parents and I fell right into the trap."

I nodded, feeling absolutely awful hearing it said out loud.

"Then what?"

"When you were walking us around downtown for the first time, we ran into Mrs. Romano, and she introduced us to her twins?" I started, my voice sounding too bright in my own ears. "They invited us to the Summer Kickoff."

"I do remember. But that's a big community event, how could you have gotten in trouble at Bennett's Orchard with the entire town there?"

I hesitated, the details tumbling over each other in my head. This wasn't about the orchard. It was about the way I'd felt that night. like I belonged, like I was older, like I could keep up with anyone in that barn. "We met Laurina and Renzo like we'd planned. You knew about that part. But instead of staying at the orchard, we... drifted. Through the woods. Over to the barn."

"And I, unfortunately, know which barn you mean considering I just dragged you out of it last night."

I smiled weakly. "Right. And we didn't plan for it to be... what it was. But when nobody asked how old we were, we didn't correct them. We let them think we were freshmen heading into sophomore year. It worked, too. At least until Marcus opened his mouth."

And that was the part that hit me hardest, saying it out loud – how dumb it was to want to be seen as older. Like someone she could trust to make my own choices. Clearly, I wasn't. I hadn't fooled anyone, least of all her. And now, sitting across from Hadley, I felt younger than I actually was.

"You understand why he did that, right?" Hadley questioned, her arms crossed.

"Yeah, of course," I nodded. "I didn't mean it like that."

"So, at the barn you were drinking?"

"Yeah." I looked at Chloe, unsure how much she wanted me to admit about that first party.

"Our first ever drink," Chloe added.

"I thought a few drinks would be totally fine," I cringed. "It wasn't."

Chloe's voice cracked. "I thought I could handle it. I couldn't." She looked at me like a deer in headlights.

I shrugged.

We both looked at Hadley, who looked back at us with blessed patience.

Chloe blew out a breath and grabbed my hand. "I, uh, I sorta blacked out."

Hadley's breath caught, like an elephant fell from the sky and landed directly on her lungs. "You what?" She asked, her voice tight and sharp around the edges, even though she was clearly trying to stay calm. "Chloe, you blacked out? Like, passed out completely?"

Chloe gave a tiny nod. Her face flushed a deep red as she tucked her free hand inside the cuff of her sweatshirt sleeve.

Hadley leaned forward, eyes suddenly glossy. "What happened? Were you okay? Where were you? Did anyone touch you?"

"No," Chloe said, her voice trembling. She rubbed the edge of the couch cushion between her fingers; eyes fixed on the fabric. "Nothing bad happened, nothing like that. Amelia saw me as soon as it had happened, I mean, I think. I just drank too much too fast. I had no idea what was a safe amount and it was making me feel a confidence I've never had before. It felt freeing to not be in my head like I usually am."

Hadley nodded.

"I found her on the couch and at first thought she was asleep. I shook her and was instantly terrified. I wanted to call the ambulance but apparently that would've made me a 'buzzkill'. I was about to demand it, when Laurina dumped a bucket of water on Chloe, which woke her up."

Chloe cringed. "I think I threw up everywhere, but then I was fine."

"You should've told me." Hadley's voice cracked. "Both of you. You should've told me the moment it happened. That could've ended so much worse. Do you understand how lucky you were? That no one took advantage? That you didn't hit your head or choke or—"

"I know," I said. "I know how lucky we were that it didn't end worse. I was too afraid to tell you, but Chloe wanted to. Our summer had just begun and I was selfishly wanting to keep going. I wanted to go back and party more even after that happened. I wanted to become one of the popular girls, even if just for the summer."

"Yeah, and Renzo gave her a lot of attention. I think that played into it, too."

"Thanks for that, Chloe." I blushed, horrified.

To my surprise, Hadley let out a soft laugh. "There's always a boy. So you and Renzo?"

"Yeah, I guess. We've flirted and stuff, nothing crazy. I've never gotten that type of attention before. I had a boyfriend for a quick second last year, but it was more like a boy who just sometimes held my hand in the hallways. I don't think either of us knew how to date or what it even meant to date."

"It takes a while to figure out the whole dating thing. You might not have thought I ever dated but I have. There were boyfriends before Marcus, it just took a long time to trust someone plus I needed to spend a lot of time working on myself."

"Yeah. I really liked Renzo, but I'm pretty sure that's not going any-where now."

Hadley swirled the last few ice cubes at the bottom of her tea glass, the clinking the only noise between us. She wiped at the sweat running down the side before setting it back on the table.

"Well, to be fair, Meels," she finally said. "You lied to him. It's one thing to be a bit younger, but you'll never know now if that would've been okay with him. Whether it's a friendship, relationship, whatever, you still started it off with a lie. It's hard to trust someone after that."

"I know," my voice dropped along with my head. "I definitely learned that lesson. Renzo backed away from me last night like I was a nuclear bomb."

Hadley nodded sympathetically. "So, we can definitely come back to this whole boy thing, because I have a feeling there's more there, but I want to get back to the drinking and partying." She waited for us to offer up a new story, but we stayed silent. I picked up my tea glass to buy time, and Chloe followed suit.

"You talked about your first party, you referenced some other stuff. What else happened?"

I glanced at Chloe and did half a shoulder shrug. Neither of us knew what exactly to share. It was my grand plan that blew up, and it was my aunt now staring at us, so I knew I had to take the lead.

"Well, to be honest, the other times we drank, it went pretty well. Laurina told us to eat more carbs ahead of time and to have water before each new drink. That seemed to help."

"Those are definitely good tips, but still not a safe idea until you're twenty-one. There's a reason they made it a law." She crossed her legs and looked between us. "So things went well? No other scary moments or getting sick?"

Silence.

"There was the whole Fourth of July thing," Chloe blurted.

"Chloe!" I shot daggers.

"What? She said it's a safe space." Chloe rambled. "Right, Hadley?"

"Yes, of course. This is a completely safe space."

I sighed, twisting the ends of my hair. "Okay, well, do you think this could be a safe space with pepperoni pizza? The Fourth of July was a little rattling but nothing bad happened, I swear. I promise I'll tell you. I think I just need some greasy motivation first."

Hadley smiled, patient as ever. This was the Hadley I grew up with and loved. She let me say whatever I wanted and always made me feel validated and normal. I remembered telling her about my third-grade crushes and my plan to go to a Backstreet Boys concert and get Nick Carter to fall in love and marry me. She didn't make me feel silly. It's why I always went to her, instead of my mom, when I needed help.

But now, the words in my throat felt heavier. I didn't want to ruin this by telling her everything. I didn't want her to look at me differently. As much as I kept saying I wanted to be grown up, I suddenly wanted to slow down and be the little girl laying on my aunt's lap watching *The Land Before Time.*

Safe. Happy. Innocent.

All things I wasn't sure I could get back, even if I wanted to.

Pizza Confessionals

Thirty minutes later we were digging into the extra-large pepperoni pizza and container of buttery garlic breadsticks, our birch beer bottles clinking every few minutes as we reached for another greasy slice like we hadn't just shared the worst parts, which were also some of the best parts, of our summer to Hadley. I honestly felt too weird to ask for birch beer because there was beer in the title, even though it was just soda, but luckily Hadley knew it was my favorite and offered it. She sipped her cream soda laughing through a story about something that had happened to her at work last week.

Chloe was in a better mood now, too, pausing her laughter to wipe marinara from her lip. I was working on my third slice, letting the cheese burn the roof of my mouth because I was not quite patient enough to wait for it to cool down. We hadn't mentioned the words *Fourth of July* since Chloe blurted it out earlier. Not since I made it very clear I was going to need carbs before talking about *that* night. The conversation was focused mainly on us asking about the horses at Steeplechase and hearing funny stories about her work. I had safely avoided all things related to this summer. I knew it wouldn't last but naively hoped it would.

Sure enough, a moment later, Hadley cleared her plate and announced she was going to put some break-and-bake cookies into the oven, stating "I figure if we're going to do the next round of conversation, we need dessert support."

The next round. Great.

I exchanged a glance with Chloe. She mouthed, *Are you going to tell her?* and I shrugged.

It was either that or lie more, and honestly, I was getting tired of pretending to be someone I wasn't. And even more tired of lying to my aunt. She had always been so inherently trusting of me, and I wanted that back. If telling her the whole truth would set me in the right direction, then here went nothing. Or everything.

Chloe and I moved back to the couch, her on the left side and me in the middle, while Hadley started baking the cookie dough. I heard the oven door open and shut, followed by the clicking from her setting her old-fashioned white timer. Timer in hand, Hadley joined us in the living room, but instead of returning to her wingback chair, she joined us on the couch. Nice and close. No escape in sight.

"All right," she said gently. "Fourth of July."

I stared at the timer, now sitting on the coffee table faintly humming, wishing it to go off, despite the fact the arrow pointed at the seven-minute mark.

"We left the barbecue to go to the hill for the fireworks, like we told you and Marcus, that was all true." She nodded. I looked at Chloe, then back to Hadley. "By the time we got there, everyone had already started drinking. Like, really drinking. They were loud, laughing, seemingly having the times of their lives. I wanted to feel that."

"Feel what?" She pried gently.

"I don't know. Like I was having the time of my life. Like I was one of them."

"Okay. That's a fair feeling to have. So, what happened next?"

I looked at Chloe, who slow-blinked her agreement for me to continue. "So, Renzo, uh, said he wanted to do body shots and everyone pretty much erupted with excitement like it was the best idea ever." I rubbed my thumb along the edge of the couch. "I didn't know what that even meant but I smiled and acted like I was excited, because *they* were excited."

"Neither of us knew what it meant," Chloe added. "Until Laurina went first."

I swallowed hard. "Right. Laurina volunteered and suddenly she was licking Rylee's shoulder and taking the shot right out of Rylee's mouth. Then it got... intense."

"Yeah. Rylee and her boyfriend went next," Chloe said, quietly. "It turned into a whole thing. Like a full-on make out sesh. Everyone was watching like it was a performance."

I felt my ears burning. "Yeah, and I mean honestly, they always make out so that wasn't all that bizarre but it also made it really clear what a body shot was meant to be. Two people, one shot of alcohol, and a random body part."

Hadley nodded, but didn't interrupt.

I exhaled dramatically. "So after that whole spectacle, Renzo called my name. He was like, 'Amelia, you're up.' Like I was next in line at the deli counter or something. He said my name like an obligation." My voice broke a little. "Honestly, it was everything I wanted. Or, I guess, everything I thought I wanted. You know, this super cute boy who's older than me, paying me all this attention, calling me cute nicknames, picking me out of everyone for the game.”

“Of course he’d pick you, you’re a beautiful, kind, young lady.”

I know she was trying to help, but it definitely wasn’t helping.

“Yeah. Well, I might’ve thought I wanted *that* attention, but it felt too... adulty? I don’t know; it was just too much.”

Hadley was silent, but not in a scary way. She wasn’t judging me, she was just waiting for me to continue.

“I panicked. Like, full-on flight mode. I all but shouted no and bolted. Pretty much ran into the darkness like I was in a horror movie and Freddie Kreuger was behind me.”

“She wasn’t alone, though. Anders and I followed her,” Chloe quickly added. “We sat with her on the rock and watched the fireworks in silence.”

I nodded. “I felt stupid. And embarrassed. And really, really young. Like I was the only one up there who still owned a stuffed animal and didn’t know how to flirt or be chill.”

I looked at Hadley, forcing myself to meet her eyes. “I know I made a mistake by lying about my age and lying to you about what we were up to. Drinking. Being a flirt. All that. But that night? In that moment, I felt like the only kid at an adults-only party. And no one even noticed when I left.”

I left out the part where that feeling faded fast, replaced by the same pull to keep up and dive into the next party.

The timer rang, shattering the heaviness in the room. I guess the cookies were ready. I wasn’t sure if that was perfect timing or awful.

Hadley glanced at the timer, then nodded slowly. “Thank you for telling me.”

I unraveled like a balloon losing air, relieved to have gotten that off my chest.

"You did the right thing," she continued. "Walking away was brave. I know it didn't feel like it at the time, and may still not have felt like the 'thing to do,' but I promise you that was the right move. That's what knowing your limits looks like. I'm proud of you for that."

With that, Hadley stood to get the cookies.

I expected to drown in humiliation and guilt, but all I felt was relief. It was a reminder that my relationship with Hadley wasn't ruined. I wasn't ruined. I was learning and growing. Maybe this is what it felt like to be older. How, as it turned out, it was perfectly fine, and normal, to slow down and just enjoy where I was in life. Maybe fourteen wasn't the death sentence I thought it was.

Hadley returned with a plate of cookies and a stack of napkins, looking like the mom from *The Brady Brunch*, except with beautiful long blonde hair and a smile that I'll forever envy. I immediately smelled the still warm chocolate chips, confident the center would be slightly gooey, exactly how I loved them.

I had just confessed to being a liar, a faker, and to almost doing a body shot with a boy and yet Hadley set the platter down with a smile so pure you'd think I had just told her about my playdate with Barney the dinosaur.

She sat back down, this time in the wingback chair, and tucked her legs underneath her. She balanced a napkin with a cookie on her thigh. "Is there anything else you want to talk about?" She asked. "That night, or anything else? Do you want to talk through the Renzo stuff?"

I picked up a cookie and stared at it, just in case it was about to sprout lips and answer for me. It didn't. "Maybe," I said, then shook my head. "I don't know. Not right now. I think it's ruined anyway, honestly. Once Marcus said our ages out loud, I'm pretty sure Renzo lost all interest."

Hadley smiled sadly. "Maybe it's ruined. Maybe not. But you're learning. That's part of all this. You make mistakes, you survive the fallout, you figure out how to handle it better next time."

Next time. I nodded, chewing slowly. "Does that mean we're not grounded? Since we're learning and growing?"

Hadley laughed, quickly covering her mouth with her hand when a few crumbs flew rogue. "Nice try, Meels. Part of your specific fallout is most definitely being grounded."

I shrugged with a smile. "It was worth a try."

Hadley shook her head, laughing again. Then Hadley looked at Chloe with a playfully raised brow. "So... what's going on in your world, Miss Chloe?"

"What do you mean?"

"Aside from all the bad choices you've girls collectively made." Hadley waved her hands through the air like an umpire declaring the player safe. "I noticed Anders name came up a lot. And I mean, he is a great kid, *and* I'm technically dating his dad, so, what's going on there?"

Chloe's face flushed faster than I thought human skin could manage. "Oh my God," she whispered, pressing both hands to her cheeks. "Don't make me do this."

Hadley grinned. "Too late."

"Yeah, Chlo, you're up." I goaded.

Chloe squirmed on the couch but eventually exhaled through a smile. "I like talking to him. He's smart. Like, actually smart. And he listens really well. We've just clicked. It's not like anything happened, I just, I like him."

"It's definitely mutual," I said, mouth full of cookie. "You should've seen the way he looked at you when you were quoting *Dead Poets Society*. Like he was ready to write you a sonnet of your own. Or when you were explaining whatever that science experiment was that you did last year. Pretty sure he was prepared to build you your own robot if it would've made you happy."

Chloe groaned. "Please stop talking forever."

"Amelia not talking?" Hadley teased.

"Stranger things have happened," I shrugged.

"Have they, though?"

"Yeah, you're probably right. There's no chance of me becoming a professional mime." I started moving my hands theatrically, as if I were suddenly stuck in a box.

This made us all laugh. Without saying anything else, or forcing the conversation to go deeper, Hadley passed the cookie plate around again and let the moment settle around us.

Friendship Bracelets

The next morning, we were crosslegged on the living room floor surrounded by paper bowls filled with tangled colored string and mismatched beads that probably hadn't seen daylight since 1995. Hadley had pulled out an old friendship bracelet kit from her closet and held it up to us like she was displaying Simba to the wild.

There was something healing about looping the string around my fingers, knotting it tight and watching my arrow-like pattern come together. I used to love making bracelets with Hadley when I was little and she would babysit.

Chloe sat next to me, hyperfocused, already halfway through her second bracelet with surgeon-like precision, while I was still deciding if I wanted to add a turquoise bead or a seafoam one. Hadley sat nearby on a pillow, sorting through tiny silver charms shaped like stars and hearts and a weird alien head. We didn't ask.

I waited until Hadley selected a crescent moon and resumed braiding her pink, purple, and beige strings.

"So..." I started, casually. Probably too casually. "I kind of overheard you yesterday morning on the phone."

Hadley looked up, still holding a strand of thread. "With Marcus?"

I nodded.

She didn't seem mad, just looked like she was buying herself time. "What did you hear?"

"I'm not entirely sure, but it felt tense. Like you guys were fighting? Like it was probably my fault."

"Definitely not your fault." She set her bracelet down and her mouth pulled into a soft line. "We're okay. Things were tense, you're not wrong, but that's part of dating someone who sees the world differently. It's okay to disagree. I'm trying to aunt the only way I know how. I lost my mom before any of the messy teenage years and my dad was a lost cause, preventing me from even having the experiences, good and bad, that you're now getting mixed up with."

I sat quietly, not sure what to say.

"I'm doing my best, without much experience, but in Marcus' opinion, based on *his* own experiences, I was being far too gentle by letting you girls sleep in and not forcing a conversation and punishment immediately."

I nodded.

"For what it's worth," Chloe started. "I have loved being here and having you take care of us. Even when we got in trouble with staining your dress and again with the partying stuff... I didn't feel horribly terrified like I would've with my mom or dad. I could never talk to my parents the way you've let us talk to you. You make us feel heard and seen and safe. That's a win."

"A total win," I added.

"Thanks, girls," she smiled.

"It does, though. Sound like my fault, I mean. He wouldn't have any reason to judge the way you parented us if we weren't off getting drunk in his barn."

"Fair. But, it was more because I called Josh for advice instead of him. He wasn't so thrilled with that."

"Why?" I asked. "If he's my uncle and you're just friends..."

Hadley smiled. "Want to know a secret?"

My eyes bulged, Chloe's too. We set our bracelets down and leaned forward. It was never the adults sharing secrets, so we were locked in.

"Your Uncle Josh was my first date. Way back when."

"Shut up!"

"I'm serious. I was twenty-three and had become fast friends with your mom. It was your fourth birthday party where I first ran into him, literally, ran into him at the front door. Anyway, he was not all that subtly into me and I was certainly intrigued by his goofy smile, but I never expected to see him again."

"But you did?" Chloe asked.

"Yep. Sure enough, when I went to the local animal shelter to rescue a cat, Miss Littlefoot, Josh was behind the counter. Turns out that's where he volunteered on the weekends."

"I'm the one who picked the name Littlefoot!" I proudly announced, despite Hadley and Chloe already knowing.

"You sure were." Hadley's smile was reminiscent.

"So then what?"

"So then he asked me out and I didn't know what to do. I was learning my own boundaries. I said yes then sped home, called your mom and panicked. She assured me it would be fine, so I went."

"Uh-huh, and then?" I leaned in more. Maybe she did know what it was like, the pull to grow up fast whether you were ready or not. To want to date and feel those things, even when it was scary.

"And then, we went to dinner, and he had ordered a whiskey, which was exactly what my dad drank. I hadn't healed from any of that and I immediately feared Josh would be the jerk my dad was when he drank. I tried to bolt, but Josh being Josh noticed something was wrong and got me to talk through it. He handed the drink to the waiter, and we enjoyed our meals and each other's company."

"*Then* you fell in love?"

"Then we had pizza a few times, but ultimately I told him I wasn't ready to date. He was bummed, and honestly so was I. But I was learning my limits."

"I knew you guys always seemed weirdly close." I pointed at her like I had finally figured it out.

"Josh has been there for me through a lot of hard moments. The other night felt like one of them and since I knew calling your mom right away wasn't the move, I called him."

"Well, I'm definitely thankful you called Uncle Josh instead of my mom." I laughed.

"We will be telling her, little lady. Just not this second. That's part of growing up. Knowing when to say yes, when to say no, and when it's okay to change your mind. You thought you wanted certain experiences, and now you're realizing you're not ready. That's normal."

"I guess," I shrugged, rolling a bead between my fingers before setting it back in the bowl.

Hadley's mouth curved into a small smile. "As someone who didn't get to be a normal fourteen-year-old, I'm here to tell you: please, let yourself slow down. Enjoy where you are."

"Yeah, yeah. I get it." I pushed a few beads around with my fingertip, then glanced up at her. "And, Had?"

"Yeah?"

"You are my real aunt. You don't need to marry my uncle for it to be official. We're family."

She smiled, eyes shinier than usual, and picked up her half-braided bracelet. Chloe and I went back to ours, swapping charm bowls – me for a silver star, her for the letter C. We worked quietly, the kind of childhood contentment I'd have rolled my eyes at a few weeks ago settling in without me even noticing.

Now, I couldn't think of anything else I'd rather be doing.

Donuts & Closure

The spare room looked like a craft tornado hit it. There were printer paper sketches of artwork we wanted to find, cardboard paint swatches from Walmart taped to the walls in completely clashing colors, and Chloe sprawled across our unmade bed with torn out pages of *Better Homes & Garden* and *ELLE Decor* magazines surrounding her. We'd spent the last two days planning out how to decorate this space, wanting to turn it into something brighter and funkier. Even though we'd be leaving Thursday, Hadley wanted it to feel like this spare bedroom belonged to me. To us. She said, despite everything, she'd love for us to come back again next summer. With more rules and expectations, of course. It felt huge.

Hadley worked a half day again, which meant we were now piled into her car to run errands like we were three roommates prepping for a home makeover show no one would watch. It was fun to pretend we were our own version of *Trading Spaces*, where the room started off nice and simple and ended so uniquely designed the homeowners weren't sure how to react. Did they love it? Hate it? The at-home-audience never knew for sure.

That's what I wanted. To make the room a moment, to have an impact so strong that whenever Hadley walked in to grab a book from the shelf, she'd be reminded of me. She'd miss me.

I wanted the room to be unforgettable so I was really taking my time browsing the aisles of Bed Bath & Beyond. Chloe clutched a sequined throw pillow like it held emotional power, and we quickly decided it belonged in the cart, beside the random gummy bear bookends I had found. We'd figure out how to tie it together later.

Hadley seemed happy with our decisions so far, even when we dove elbow-deep into a bin of discounted curtain ties, that may or may not have been intended for shower rods.

With the cart half-filled with gold-accented picture frames, a couple canvas quotes that Hadley rolled her eyes at (*Live Laugh Love* got vetoed, but *Follow Your Dreams* stayed), and a lamp with a base shaped like a flamingo, we were ready to move to the floor-to-ceiling wall of shower towels.

When we turned the corner, I froze.

Renzo.

With his mom.

Mrs. Romano looked up from a display of soap dispensers and glass bottles and broke into a bright smile. "Well look who's here!"

Hadley froze behind me. "Terri, Hi!" she said, her voice sounded so extra.

Renzo met my eyes and for half a second, I forgot how to stand correctly and had no idea what to do with my arms. Cross them? Let them swing down casually? Prop them on my hip with attitude? I opted for holding my own hand in a desperate attempt to calm down. He was wearing a World Soccer Club t-shirt and cargo shorts. He looked totally unaffected by my presence, except for the wrinkle between his brows. His reaction was a subtle mix of surprise and completely awkward energy.

A hundred tiny emotional fireworks set off in my stomach. My body was not catching on to the fact that this super cute boy, who a week ago was calling me Hourglass, was definitely *not* interested in me anymore. And his mom was definitely aware of the trouble we had all gotten into, despite her cheer-mom smile.

Hadley sensed whatever was going on in my brain and gut, Chloe too, based on the way she was now at my side, showing me a less-than-interesting hand towel with a silver duck pattern and the words Splish Splash. I focused really hard on it.

Successfully distracted as far as anyone could tell, I was confident Hadley was about to say goodbye and move us along.

Boy was I wrong.

Instead, she leaned down toward me and whispered, not all that quietly, "There's a donut shop next door. Why don't you go talk?"

What! Talk to the boy who's currently more interested in his shoelaces than looking my way?

After breathing in as slowly as I could, dragging out the seconds, I nodded. I knew, now, that part of growing up meant facing the hard parts and admitting when I was wrong. Renzo deserved an explanation and an apology. "Chlo?" I asked, not even needing to finish the sentence.

"Go," she nodded, already turning to distract Mrs. Romano by asking her opinion on how to tie together all of the mis-mash items in our cart. She was elated by the question, stating Laurina never wanted her input.

I caught Renzo's eye again and did the tiny head-tilt thing that meant *follow me*, and he did. I looked back at Hadley who nodded slightly, assuring me she would let his mom know and help hold down the fort. I knew I was grounded, but I was thankful for Hadley's forever big heart. Meanwhile, here's hoping Renzo had a similarly big, forgiving heart.

We didn't say anything as we walked out of BB&B and into the sunlight. The donut shop's bell rang as we pushed inside, and the girl behind the counter didn't bother looking up, even when we asked for two cinnamon sugars and cups of water.

Renzo picked a table by the window. I sat across from him, staring out the window like Britney Spears might walk right in, say *Oops, she did it again* and we'd all laugh at her play on words and move on. Forgive and forget. That obviously didn't happen. What *was* happening was I invited him to sneak off with me and now had literally no idea what to say or do.

Finally, he broke the silence. "So..."

The word lingered between us until the sound evaporated.

"I like you," I said, a little too loudly, because evidently, I have no sense of self preservation. "I did, I mean. Or, well, I mean, I still kinda do."

He looked down at his donut. "You're fourteen."

"Right." I bit the inside of my cheek, embarrassed. "That I am."

He stared at me, but when I had nothing else to add, he continued. "It surprised me, ya know?" He looked out the window, watching a couple walk by, hand in hand. "You don't look fourteen and you weren't really acting fourteen either."

"I have my mom's genetics," I said, as if he knew who my mom was or what she looked like. Great start. "I didn't mean to lie," I said, even though I had. "I just wanted to seem like someone who could belong with you."

"I wouldn't have dismissed you just because you were fourteen," His voice was laced with an obvious hurt. "But it would've changed things."

I stared at him. "I'm sorry. I was being selfish. I was into you the minute I saw you and I knew you'd think I was a baby if you knew my real age."

"I mean, two years isn't twenty, but yeah there's a lot of life that happens between fourteen and sixteen. I feel stupid."

I dropped my head, shoulders slumping in defeat. I knew I disappointed my aunt, but it was only at that moment when I realized my lie had hurt Renzo. He hadn't looked at me earlier not because he lost interest, but because I hurt him.

"Hey, look at me," he said, gently.

I looked up.

"I don't feel stupid for hanging out with you. I meant I should've known you were younger. I should've noticed."

"You weren't supposed to," I said, sliding my water glass closer without picking it up. "I acted older on purpose. I wanted the attention. *Your* attention. I didn't think about the fact that I could be hurting someone by lying."

He nodded slowly. "It's not even that. I just want to make sure I wasn't...pushing. That night, the body shot thing. I now realize why you ran off."

"I got caught up," I said quickly. "I panicked. You didn't do anything wrong. You didn't pressure me or try to change my mind."

We sat in silence after that. Our donuts were half-eaten and our water glasses stayed full, sweating on the table.

"If you knew I was fourteen from the start, would you have paid me any attention?" I asked, folding the corner of my napkin over and over until it was a tight little triangle.

He shrugged. "Honestly, no idea. I was into you for real. You have a killer body—" his eyes widened as he quickly tacked on, "which hopefully isn't inappropriate to say."

"No, it's not." I smiled, a blush creeping up my neck.

"But you're also really funny and outgoing. You got a lot going for you. But, fourteen is young."

"Yeah." I nodded, because what else could I do?

"I'm not really a long-distance guy, anyway," he said after a minute.

I knew he was only saying that to soften the blow. To get out of this without risking the child sitting across from him having a child-like breakdown. I did everything in my power to not let my face show everything I felt.

"Yeah, I get that." I kept my voice even and light.

"It was a fun summer," he said. "You're an unforgettable type of tornado. You know that?"

My throat tightened. Don't cry. I scrambled my brain for something magnetic and significant to say, but all I managed was, "Thanks."

And that was it. No romantic movie ending; this moment wasn't even worthy of an interlude in a pop song. It was just a super cool sixteen-year-old boy, already moved on, and a fourteen-year-old child, who never stood a chance.

Having AIM

Tuesday evening, the house smelled like ground beef and Ortega taco seasoning, and the kitchen counter looked like we had raided a taco truck. Paper bowls were lined up with shredded lettuce, diced tomato, onions that Hadley claimed would "sizzle your sinuses," whatever that meant, and a suspiciously-orange cheddar that came from a bag marked *Tex-Mex Blend.*

Hadley flipped the last of the tortillas in a skillet like she was Martha Stewart, while Chloe and I began assembling our first round. I was halfway through adding sour cream to my taco when I said, as casually as I could, "Renzo gave me his AIM screenname."

Chloe looked up, surprised. I hadn't said much when I'd returned to our shopping cart at BB&B, but my face had made it clear there was no fixing me and Renzo.

"Aim?" Hadley raised an eyebrow without looking away from the pan.

"Instant messenger. The thing I keep telling you to download."

"Oh, right, right. And?"

Chloe tilted her head slightly, the way she did whenever she pretended not to care.

After holding the donut shop napkin with his username on it for the better part of the afternoon, I'd analyzed it to death. The way his handwriting tilted, the little smile he'd drawn in the corner. Eventually, defeatedly, I decided it wasn't an invitation at all, just his way of saving face. He had said the opposite, told me I should use it, but I knew what a lie sounded like.

"And," I shook my head. "I'm not holding my breath on any kind of friendship. He made it pretty clear earlier today that me being fourteen was an issue. Plus, the whole me lying to him thing. The conversation ended nicely and we even hugged, but still. I don't suspect he'd message me back if I reached out."

Hadley turned off the stove and slid the tortillas onto a plate. "How do you feel about that?"

"It is what it is. At least I'll have the memories. Hey, wasn't that stitched on a pillow we saw earlier? *Do it for the memories?*"

Chloe laughed, remembering the cringey bright orange pillow that Hadley had held up. No live, laugh, loving, but doing it for the memories was okay.

"So what kind of memories are we talking about?"

I grinned and focused on building my next taco. "Just memories," I shrugged. "Flirting. A couple of kisses." I paused, the next words slipping out before I could stop them. "One of which had me floating, though maybe that was the alcohol." Heat rushed to my face as it hit me that I'd just said that to my aunt, and not quietly to Chloe.

Hadley gave me a pointed look that landed somewhere between I can be a cool aunt, and I definitely cannot be a cool aunt. "Anything else I should know about?"

I shook my head dramatically. "Nope. Promise. I'm definitely not ready for *any* of that. The kissing was enough to set my whole world spinning."

She smiled, resting her hand gently on mine before she shifted and grabbed the bowl of lettuce. "It's good to know and respect your limits. He's not wrong, though. Fourteen *is* young. But hopefully now you realize there's nothing wrong with that."

I nodded, taking a large bite of my masterly crafted taco. I looked over at Chloe, who was quieter than normal. Halfway through her second taco, she set it down and said, "Must've been nice."

I looked up, not sure what she meant.

"To have closure," she clarified. "With Renzo. To be able to talk to him."

Her voice wasn't bitter, just sad. Dejected.

"Yeah. It didn't end the way I stupidly wished it would, but it helped."

She picked up her taco again and took a small bite, eyes focused just past me. I wondered if she was thinking about Anders and if there would be a chance in the next 36 hours to talk to him before we left.

Knowing better than to press Chloe, who only ever talked when she was ready, I went for a distraction.

"His screenname is BucknBallerz77," I said, deadpan.

Hadley looked up from her plate. "I'm sorry?"

Chloe blinked once before a laugh blew out of her, vibrating her lips. "Buck *n* Ballerz?"

"Yep."

Chloe full-on snorted, setting her taco down like she didn't trust herself to hold it anymore. "Oh my God. That sounds like he's trying to be a MySpace rapper."

"I know," I smirked. "Not to mention he doesn't even do anything rodeo related and plays soccer not basketball. His first pick was KingRenzo69, but apparently his mom vetoed that immediately."

Hadley coughed into her napkin, trying not to choke. "I – wow. Okay, not what I expected."

"Imagine trying to date someone whose legacy begins with Buckn-Ballerz," I said, biting into my taco. "Tragic."

The conversation spiraled after that, Chloe's smile on full display. I was confident she wasn't thinking about Anders anymore. At least not right now. She was instead trying to remember what her first screenname had been. She thought it was DancerDiva102, even though she only took two ballet classes in first grade before she quit because they made her wear white tights. She said they made her legs look totally detached from her otherwise golden skin.

I laughed so hard I inhaled a piece of lettuce and had to do this dramatic, gasping recovery that made Hadley laugh harder.

"Maybe I should change mine from RedHeadMeelz to FlirtynFourteen?"

Chloe laughed.

"Oh, or maybe, ShotsNotTaken, like for the body shot moment," My eyes bounced between Chloe and Hadley, as a laugh bubbled out. "Too soon?"

Hadley mock-gasped. "Amelia."

"Okay, okay. RedHeadMeelz it stays."

"Can we sign you up after dinner, Hadley?" Chloe asked. "So we can talk to you easier once we're back home?"

"That sounds like a great idea. As long as my screenname isn't silly."

"Hmm, how about HorseMasterHadley?" I laughed.

"MintyMare?" Chloe piled on.

"SassySaddles?"

Hadley wiped the tears from her eyes. "Girls, there's no way on God's green earth I'm using any of those."

Chloe and I are bent over in laughter. "Not even GallopingGoddess123?" I forced the words out between my fit of hysterics.

"Especially not the Galloping Goddess." She got up, collecting our plates, and made quick work of cleaning up the mostly empty toppings bowls. "How about HadleyAnn67?"

"Whoa, you're really going out on a limb with that one, Hads." I laughed.

"It's easy to remember. My name and the year I was born."

"If only Renzo thought to use that formula," Chloe raised an eyebrow.

"We should thank him for his—" I tapped my chin. "Unique creativity." I nodded, satisfied with my description. "It brought us twenty minutes of laughter," I added, leaning back in my chair. I wiped taco grease off my fingers and let reality sink in for a second. I was joking about Renzo but he was someone I would miss. Chloe was laughing too, but I knew the back of her mind was swirling with the unknowns surrounding Anders and the complexity she'd be walking into when she went home to a newly divorced set of parents.

I was happy to see Chloe happy in this moment, even if we were grounded, because I'd also heard her crying when she thought I was already asleep. I knew how much everything weighed on her. I was also happy my aunt agreed to set up AIM because it would be great for Chloe to have someone older than me to talk to.

Hadley rinsed off our plates and said she'd sign up later, and Chloe and I couldn't wait, secretly hoping we could convince her to make her screenname something sparkly. We stayed in the kitchen while Hadley wiped down the counters. Chloe found a roll of stickers in Hadley's junk drawer and started peeling off tiny glitter stars, sticking one to the tip of her nose before offering me a smiley face labeled "you tried." Why did Hadley even have these?

"Here you go," Chloe announced, prompting Hadley to turn around and set the Clorox down. Chloe handed her a "you rock" sticker while holding back a giggle. We were leaning into our age, letting ourselves be silly. Hadley proudly stuck it to her forearm.

"I hate that we're leaving in less than two days," I said suddenly.

Hadley faced me. "You girls are more than welcome to come back. But next time, less parties, more horses. Deal?"

"Deal," I said, and meant it.

Chloe looked up from where she had sat on the bench and smiled. I knew what she was thinking – that maybe next summer we'd do this all differently. Or maybe we'd mess up again. But at least we'd do it together. "Deal."

Hadley led us to the far corner of the living room where the desktop computer lived, on top of an old wooden desk. She started it up, ready to download AIM. And no, we didn't win the screenname debate. HadleyAnn67 held strong. But she did let us choose the background theme, so now her chat window had pink sparkles, and her profile said "*~*~*Horse girl, peppermint tea lover, & best aunt eva ~*~*.*" I wanted it to say "Live. Laugh. Neigh." but Hadley deleted it immediately.

Satisfied that we had taught her the basics, added our screennames to her friend list, and designed her main profile, we were ready for bed, but fighting the exhaustion knowing tomorrow was our last day. We didn't want this to end.

Even knowing anyone who wasn't grounded was probably drinking and partying in someone's basement right now. Maybe at Carter's since I highly doubted anything exciting was going on at the barn, based on how Marcus judged Hadley for being "too gentle." I could only assume Anders was locked in his bedroom and the barn was totally off limits. All the same, Chloe and I, in our matching pajamas, were happy exactly where we were. Sitting up in our shared bed, heads rested together, friendship bracelets on display.

The suitcases in the corner basically taunted us, reminding us that once we fell asleep, we'd be waking up to our last day in Montana. I tried my best to not look at them.

Chloe shifted, curling her legs under the blankets. We stared blankly at the little TV across the room, the random DVD screensaver bouncing around aimlessly. I looked around for the remote, but couldn't find it. Silence it was.

Maybe I should ask Chloe how she was feeling. I know she hated getting into it, but I could try. She had a lot on her plate to begin with and I didn't make things any easier by getting us grounded.

"Are you okay not seeing Anders?"

She didn't answer right away. Just twisted the friendship bracelet around her wrist, the one that matched mine.

"Not really," she said finally, pulling the blanket higher over our laps. "But what choice do I have? I mean, it's not like it would've turned into anything."

I didn't respond, because, same. The Renzo thing had been nice and exciting, but it was really just a blip on the radar of my life. Reality had caught up to both of us when Hadley busted through those barn doors. We were too young to be partying the way we were, putting ourselves in the hands of equally immature, but older, teenagers. It could've gone so much worse.

I shifted, tucking my exposed leg under the blanket as I turned toward her. "How are you feeling about going home?"

Chloe sighed, pushing her hair out of her face. "Mixed, I guess. I miss my parents but I have no idea what I'm stepping back into. My mom has sounded unstable on our phone calls lately. She's either really happy, laughing, or taking her anger on my dad out on the fact I haven't done the stupid math workbook she sent with me. Like taking a month off is going to make me forget the Pythagorean theorem. Seriously."

I nodded. "I'm sorry they put so much stress on you."

"It's fine. I imagine there will be plenty of time to do all of the workbooks ever created once mom finds out about our partying. I probably won't see you again until our graduation."

My eyes bulged. "Don't say that!"

"I'm just being honest. It's definitely going to be rough."

"Do you regret it? This month?"

"Not at all. Honestly."

"Same," I smiled.

I didn't push the topic or try to go deeper. I knew there were probably a lot more thoughts swirling in her gut, but she'd open up when she was ready.

She yawned, big and dramatic, like she wanted to make sure I knew the night was over.

"Same, girl. I'm exhausted." I searched for the remote again, flailing my arms and legs around in an attempt to find it. Eventually, I knocked into it with my left shin. Huh, how'd it get down there? I kicked it up toward my hand, grabbed it and turned the television off.

Within a few minutes, I heard Chloe's breathing get deeper, steady. I always envied her ability to fall asleep so fast, even when she was upset or stressed. I closed my eyes and focused on matching my breathing pattern to hers, thinking it would trick my body into sleep. It didn't. Instead, my heart sped up, feeling the crack of losing Renzo, fully aware I never even had him. This must be what teenaged dramatics meant. It felt like a tiny little knife had settled into my heart, and with every inhale it poked a bit, reminding me of the rawness of this entire summer so far. I wanted experience, right? Well. Mission accomplished, I guessed.

Greatest Surprise

We spent yesterday morning doing laundry and packing our bags while Hadley worked. Once she got home, we all walked into town for chocolate chip pancakes from Pancake Patty's and frozen drinks from Java Joe's. She even let us rummage through Book Nook and pick out another book for the flight home.

Now, it was the dreaded morning of. The last 10 AM we'd have in Montana. The last cranberry muffin with butter eaten at Hadley's rustic kitchen table. The last time we'd see Hadley absentmindedly sip peppermint tea while reading whatever book she was into at that moment. Except she wasn't here reading her latest pick, *Bridget Jones's Diary*, which she told us she started reading because Mrs. Romano mentioned it was going to be adapted into a film and she wanted to read the real version so she could judge the movie accordingly. Classic Hadley. She was at work and Chloe and I were moping on the couch, *Full House* on in the background.

We were playing a game called eggshell and yolk, something Uncle Josh used to play with me when I was younger. The concept was simple: when you crack an egg, you get two things, the eggshells and the egg, except when I was four I thought yolk was the funniest word ever, so that's what we said. When Uncle Josh would ask me, he wanted me to share my eggshell, the worst part of my day, and the yolk, the best part. Ten years later, we still went around the room sharing our thoughts at the end of family vacations or big moments.

Chloe was in the middle of sharing that her eggshell wasn't getting caught partying, it was when her mom called and told her about her dad moving out, when we were interrupted by a knock at the door.

Three soft taps.

Hadley wasn't done with work for another two hours, and also, why would she knock on her own door? We were grounded, technically, but what were we supposed to do? It could've been an emergency or a neighbor in need.

I walked over, lifted onto my tippy toes to look through the peephole, and saw a blonde ponytail I definitely recognized. "It's Hadley," I whispered.

"Did she forget her key?" Chloe whispered back.

I shrugged, unlocked the deadbolt, and twisted the door handle to open it. I swung it open, prepared to tease Hadley for getting locked out, when I realized she wasn't alone.

Behind her, smiling the largest smiles I'd ever seen, stood my mom, dad, and uncle. All three wore Hawaiian print shirts, as if they were on their way to an island, not Montana. My eyes dropped momentarily to the three carry-on luggage bags at their feet. What the what.

My brain short-circuited trying to make sense of the scene, like maybe I'd accidentally opened a door to an alternate reality where cross-country family drop ins were totally normal. "What... is happening?" I asked, my jaw stuck unhinged.

My mom stepped forward and hugged me like I'd been missing for three years instead of one month. "We changed the plan," she said into my shoulder. "Figured we'd surprise you and spend the weekend here before flying back together."

My dad gave me a quick squeeze, then turned to Chloe. "Hope you're okay with a longer vacation, Chlo-Money. Flights are booked for Sunday now."

Uncle Josh waved and said, "I brought snacks," like that was the most normal update to share after popping up out of thin air.

Behind me, Chloe's jaw might've actually hit the floor. "Are you serious?" she said, already halfway wrapped into a hug with my mom. "We're staying?"

Hadley laughed. "Thought you deserved a proper send-off, and maybe a little celebration, too."

"We deserve a celebration?" I cocked my head.

I am so confused.

"Celebration... long talk... same thing, kiddo." My dad said, with a triple tap on the top of my head.

Oh. Yeah, that made more sense. I nodded slowly, eyes wide.

"But first, give your uncle a hug, Brat."

I ran into Josh's arms, melting against his embrace. With Uncle Josh here, we'd get through anything. Speaking of... "Hey, Uncle Josh, didn't you want to hug Aunt Hadley?"

Hadley gave me a *watch it* look. I shrugged innocently. He gave me a gross raspberry kiss on my cheek before he waltzed over and wrapped Hadley up in one of his signature bear hugs. I watched them closely, never really seeing them as anything other than Aunt Hadley, my mom's best friend, and Uncle Josh, my mom's brother. I was now picking apart every little piece of them, seeing if there were any decade old residual feelings.

I tilted my glance from Chloe to them, making sure Chloe knew to also overanalyze their welcome hug. Chloe's eyes held the same amusement and conspiracy as mine. We were destined for trouble. Hadley patted Josh's shoulder in the way adults do when they're pretending something doesn't mean more than it does, but I clocked the way she sank ever so slightly against him. Uncle Josh looked like he wanted to twirl her around, but obviously he didn't. It was total old people rom-com material.

Once the hugging chaos settled, and Chloe and I recovered from the shock, Hadley dragged the kitchen bench into the living room to make space. Chloe, Uncle Josh, and I took the couch, my dad landed in the wingback chair like it was his throne, and Hadley and Mom perched side-by-side, arms intertwined, on the bench like they were prepared to start their own morning talk show.

The energy in the room buzzed. Like we were all overcome with excitement despite feeling the undercurrent of the bad decisions Chloe and I made.

My dad announced, "We'll get into all the 'lessons learned and consequences' stuff later." He scooped a handful of trail mix from the snack bowl Josh set out. "Right now, I just want to enjoy your company. You've been missed."

My mom nodded. "Seriously. We've gotten about five percent of the full story. Hadley gave us the spark notes, but we want to hear it all – from you two directly."

Chloe looked startled but smiled. "We will, Mrs. Sanger."

"For the zillionth time, sweetheart, call me Meghan."

"Sorry, Mrs.—" she shook her head and tried again, "Meghan."

I crossed my legs casually, positioning myself to better face Josh. "Where's Stephanie?"

I swore I saw his face twitch, just a little. "She couldn't get off work," he said matter-of-fact. It didn't sound untrue but it also felt off.

I raised an eyebrow. "Bummer."

"Mhm," he said before taking a really long sip of root beer.

Suspicious. But not the hill I wanted to die on today. Not without more proof of what might one day possibly be. Or not be.

And then, because my mom never knew how to let a plan that only existed in my head just sit, she ruined it by turning to Hadley enthusiastically. "So, is Marcus coming? We'd love to finally meet the guy you always talk about."

Hadley froze mid-sip of her iced tea. Did she glance at Josh? I'm pretty sure I was making this up, trying to entertain myself, but also I'm pretty sure she glanced his way.

Regaining composure, she smiled. "I hadn't thought about that but it's a great idea. I'll give him a call and see if he's free. Maybe he can grab pizzas on his way."

My mom clapped with excitement, my dad tipped his glass in the air, saluting the man he's yet to meet, and Uncle Josh nodded absently.

Chloe perked up. "Maybe Anders could tag along?"

I felt my stomach drop. Not because I didn't want Anders to come, but because the second she said his name, my rom-com brain shifted focus. Mention of Anders reminded me of all the things we had done this summer without my parents' knowledge or permission. The drinking, the kissing, the sneaking out. Getting busted. I wanted to go back to thinking about Hadley. And Josh. And why Stephanie hadn't come.

Chloe was now backtracking, saying it was totally fine if Anders couldn't come, she was sure he was grounded like we were. She didn't want to make a bad situation worse. Hadley softly told her she'd at least ask.

Meanwhile, I fell back into my thoughts, mentally scripting a dramatic sunset scene where Uncle Josh brushes Hadley's long hair out of her face and suddenly realizes she's the one. She had always been the one.

"Amelia?"

Busted. "Sorry, daydreaming."

Thirty minutes later, Hadley popped her head into the living room and said, "Pizza delivery is incoming!"

I perked up, expecting an onslaught of drama. Uncle Josh was already here and soon there would be Marcus, Hadley's boyfriend, though they recently fought, with greasy cardboard boxes in hand and possibly a grounded-but-allowed-out teenaged boy at his side. Who would Hadley pay more attention to? Who did she have more inside jokes with?

Chloe sat up straight, brushing her hair quickly with her fingers, just in case Anders walked in. "You look perfect," I whispered.

But when the knock came, it was just Marcus. Solo. Holding three large pizzas with his signature I'm the nice-guy-next-door smile.

"No Anders?" Chloe asked, trying to play it cool but failing, her voice cracking halfway through the sentence.

Marcus glanced at her, expression kind, then dug into his back pocket and pulled out a folded Post-it. "He wanted to come," he said. "Still grounded. Will be for a while. I'm sure similar to you girls," he glanced at Hadley after saying that before he returned his attention to Chloe. "But he asked me to give you this."

Chloe blinked. She reached for it slowly like if she touched it too quickly, it would turn to dust. Inside was his screenname and phone number. She stared at the note like more words would magically appear. Then, she smiled. "Thanks."

"You're welcome. He asked me to tell you he wants to talk when he gets his phone back and that he enjoyed getting to know you. He wants to keep that going."

If she smiled any wider, her lips would crack. She tucked it safely in the back pocket of her black high waisted jean shorts.

We moved to the living room bench-table-couch setup. The air quickly filled with pepperoni and tension. Marcus sat on the edge of the bench, legs wide like he owned the space. Hadley was beside him, not touching, but close enough to show they cared about each other. Josh was next to me on the couch, focused intently on chewing his pizza and not on the fact he was directly across from my aunt's boyfriend. Chloe and I had already demolished one slice each, but I was too busy overanalyzing everyone's body language to go in for round two.

Okay, that's a lie. I could pause real quick to get another slice. I did, then I went back to observing. This was my new favorite tv show, the *Who Does Hadley Really Love* show. She would kill me and double ground me if she knew what I was up to. I'm just a silly kid, I would playfully smile and say, if caught.

Then, out of nowhere, as we're all laughing over a story my dad shared about a fishing trip that went wrong, Marcus leaned forward, setting his plate, crusts uneaten, onto the coffee table. "So you girls *did* end up grounded, right?" He said it casually, but it caught literally all of us off guard. I froze mid-chew. Chloe all but choked on her slice, grabbing her Dr. Pepper to clear her throat.

Hadley shifted slightly. "Of course, Marc. But their parents just got here, so we're saving the bigger conversations for tomorrow morning." She smiled, the kind of hostess smile that says *everything's fine.*

He gave her a look that made me like him a little less. He had been nice all summer and I had admired him and the way he treated Hadley. But ever since they busted us, I saw a different side. Sure, he had every right to be mad at Anders and at us – we were totally in the wrong. But why was he pressing the issue now? I was only fourteen and even I knew when you meet your girlfriend's family for the first time you should try to bond and get on their good side. This wasn't the way. What a rookie.

Hadley's shoulders stiffened. "I'm not downplaying anything, if that's what you're implying. We've all talked, Amelia and Chloe especially. Tonight's just not the night to continue that talk."

Marcus nodded slowly, but his jaw was tight. He reached for his soda, took a swig, then casually dropped his hand to Hadley's knee.

That's when everything shifted. Hadley flinched, not dramatically, but enough that I saw it. Enough that Josh saw it.

I glanced sideways, and Josh's expression didn't change much, but the way he folded his paper plate and tossed it on top of Marcus's plate, like he wasn't invited to have another slice, said everything.

Hadley scratched her thigh, like she hadn't flinched but just got a bolt of an itch. My mom and dad were clueless, but Chloe was just as dialed in as I was. She was used to this type of tension with her parents.

"I think Hadley's done a solid job." Josh said calmly, voice smooth but pointed. "The girls certainly made a few big mistakes, sure, but they're communicating with Hads, learning through it and growing. Meels, here, and Chloe are taking accountability and are being held responsible for their mistakes. That's all we ask for."

"We?" Marcus asked.

"Yeah, we." Josh nodded. "Amelia's family."

"Right, of course." Marcus stared at Uncle Josh with a polite, forced smile and furrowed eyebrows.

Oof.

Hadley half-laughed, the awkward kind like when I'm called on in class and have no idea what the question was let alone the answer. She popped up and grabbed the greasy paper plates. "I'm gonna clear these and preheat the oven for some chocolate chip cookies."

Josh stood up at almost the same moment. "I'll help."

Help with what? The three plates already in Hadley's hand? Hmm.

Marcus didn't move. Chloe and I exchanged a glance so loaded it could've been a whole episode of *Seventh Heaven*.

I leaned over to Chloe and whispered, "This is getting weird, right?"

She nodded fast, her eyes huge. "Did you see the way Josh came to Hadley's defense? He's totally her soulmate."

"No offense to Anders, but Marcus is totally not."

We giggled so hard I almost snorted out root beer.

Late Night Reflection

It was past midnight. The house was quiet except for the faint sound of the living room television on. My parents got a hotel room in town, together or separately I never knew and never dared to ask, but Uncle Josh was crashing on the couch. Marcus left before the cookies were done, using the excuse of needing to keep his eye on his very-grounded son. Nobody minded his departure, though there was a collective eyeroll at his performative kiss to Hadley on his way out.

Chloe was out cold, sleeping the amazing sleep she always managed, the post-it note from Anders proudly on display on the nightstand.

I was still awake. Not reading or watching tv, just thinking.

I slipped out of bed quietly, padded toward the kitchen, and sat at the table. The smell of pizza still lingered in the air and I was happy to find the plate of cookies still out. I grabbed one right as Hadley walked in, tea mug in hand. She had changed into an oversized sleep shirt that said *Horse Hair, Don't Care*. She set her mug on the table and threw her hair up into a messy bun as her gaze lingered on me. "Trouble sleeping?"

I shrugged. "Yeah, I guess."

She sat across from me, grabbing a cookie for herself. "Your Uncle Josh is in the living room but he's out like a light and sleeps deeper than a dead man."

I laughed. One time when I was seven and was sleeping over at his condo, the fire alarm went off in the hallway and he didn't even stir. I had to jump on him to get him to wake.

"Something specific on your mind?"

"Uh, I guess."

She stared patiently.

"Marcus touching your knee," I finally said.

Hadley snorted into her peppermint tea. "Wow, straight to it, huh."

"I saw you flinch."

"I had an itch," she corrected. Then seeing my face, she owned up to the truth. "Okay, maybe I flinched, but it wasn't out of fear, if that's what you're worried about."

I nodded.

"It was from embarrassment. I wanted Marcus to make a great first impression and that clearly wasn't happening. I'm not sure why he's so hellbent on focusing on punishment, since you're not his child to worry about, but it felt embarrassing. So when he placed his never-aggressive-always-gentle hand on my knee, I flinched on instinct."

I toyed with my bracelet string, twisting it around my pinky like stacking rings. "Do you love him?"

Hadley tilted her head. "I respect him. And I like him a whole lot. But love? I don't know." Her shoulders dropped.

"You didn't flinch when Josh hugged you. And you let him help with the dishes."

She smirked. "That's some world-class detective work."

I smiled.

She took another sip. "Josh and I have history, you know that now. But I didn't share that with you to make your imagination run wild.

We were an almost-was that never panned out and it is literally ancient history."

"But Stephanie didn't even come."

"She had work."

"Everyone else got off work, I'm sure she could've if she wanted to."

"I'm sure you're not wrong, Meels, but we need to respect their relationship. There is nothing wrong with Stephanie."

"I know." I sighed. We sat in silence for a few minutes. I looked over Hadley's shoulder into the living room where Uncle Josh was still sound asleep. "Is it dumb that I want you guys to fall in love?" I asked. "Like, *really* fall. Like in the movies."

Hadley set her mug down. "Well movies are just that, movies. They don't show the messy parts. It's sweet that you want that for us, but honestly if it were meant to be, it would've been by now."

"You told me once it's never too late to chase your dreams. In fact there's a canvas sign telling us to chase our dreams currently hanging in the bedroom."

She laughed lightly, her eyes soft. "Chasing my dreams is what brought me to Montana, sweetheart. I'm definitely doing that. But at the end of the day, I want real love, Meels. The authentic, quiet, understands-each-other-without-speaking kind. That's hard to find, but it's worth the wait."

"But isn't that what you have with Josh?" I asked before I could stop myself.

Her pause was long, reflective. "Maybe," she said finally. "If we were brave enough to figure it out. But we're not fourteen like you. That kind of bravery fades with age."

I didn't answer right away. But I reached for her hand, because we had that quiet kind of love, too. Not the dramatic kind that puts on a show, but the kind where someone actually sees you and shows up. No matter what. "I'm glad you were here for us this summer."

Hadley squeezed my fingers. "Me, too."

We sat in mint-scented silence for a few minutes. Eventually, Hadley stood to rinse her mug, and said she was headed to bed and that I should do the same.

I sat a little longer listening to the television that was still on, some late night special airing to my snoring uncle. I spun my bracelet around my pointer finger and let my brain go where it kept seeming to go lately.

Renzo.

His silly screenname. His arm around me, holding me close. That kiss that kind of knocked me sideways and made everything complicated. How he used to call me Hourglass like it was my actual name, and how it made me laugh even though I pretended to be annoyed.

I guessed he counted as my first love. It wasn't love, but it was *something*. Sure, it didn't last. Obviously. But it mattered.

And maybe that's the whole point. Not everything has to be forever to leave a mark. I'd probably never talk to Renzo again, and Hadley would probably, eventually, break up with Marcus. But the moments still counted. All the good and the bad, they left impressions.

There would be more mistakes, more boys, more kisses I regretted or didn't regret. I was only fourteen, so yeah, this was barely the beginning. I already knew not every crush I had would be like Renzo. Some would be kinder. Some louder. Some would expect too much.

But maybe one day, I'd meet my own Josh and maybe I would be brave. Like, actually brave. Brave enough to make it last, to jump without overthinking it. To trust it's okay to want the real kind of love. The scary kind.

I finally stood up, turned off the kitchen light, and tip-toed back to bed. Chloe mumbled something in her sleep when I first climbed in, probably dreaming out a conversation with Anders.

I didn't know what was coming next. Maybe next year I'd be allowed to have a cellphone, and I'd be texting Chloe about some cute boy from math class that told me a dumb joke and made me laugh. Maybe Hadley would be at her desk in the living room, peppermint tea in hand, asking me for life updates through AOL IM. Who knew.

But for now, I'm here. I'm fourteen. I'm me. And weirdly? I'm okay with that.

Epilogue
First Week of High School

I always thought high school was supposed to be a fresh start. Like, finally the big leagues of education. No longer a nerdy little middle schooler with themed socks laid out by your mom the night before. But so far, my big fresh start smelled like overripe bananas and social anxiety.

My locker was next to a kid who didn't believe in deodorant and spoke only in *Magic: The Gathering* metaphors. My homeroom teacher wore bowties and called everyone "champ." Even the girls. I cried twice in the girl's bathroom – once because a junior named Tiffany was meaner than Laurina ever managed to be, and once about a broken mechanical pencil. Don't even ask me why. So yeah, great start.

Chloe made jean skorts her entire personality and started wearing her long black hair down, instead of that ballerina bun she loved last year. Anders messaged her on AOL last week so now she basically floats through the hallways, waiting on anyone to ask her about her long-distance almost-boyfriend. Spoiler alert, nobody ever asked.

I hadn't heard from Renzo. His AIM away messages were always about playing soccer, practicing soccer, watching soccer, or made reference to being part of the "bad boyz 4 life." Maybe he wasn't all that cool after all.

In English, the only class Chloe and I had together, Mr. Gaines gave us an in-class assignment: "Write a personal reflection on your summer. What was your pivotal moment?"

I stared at my notebook for ten full minutes. I didn't want to write about drinking or lying or kissing someone who wouldn't remember me this time next year. But eventually, the words showed up anyway.

> *This summer, I lied more than I meant to, and yes, I meant to lie at least a little. I kissed someone I shouldn't have. I went to parties meant for older kids. I got grounded and scared and dramatic. I wished on dandelions. I laughed so hard I choked on lettuce. I floated down a river in Montana with my aunt and my best friend. I learned how to be fourteen. Nothing more, nothing less. My pivotal moment? I learned how to be myself.*

I handed it in without rereading it.

Later, Chloe and I walked to lunch, dodging hallway drama to the best of our ability. I adjusted the hem of my shirt for the eighth time, and somewhere between the vending machine and the weird smell near the gym, I realized something. The Montana version of me still existed. Deep down, I was still messy, impulsive, and desperate for attention. I wasn't actively pursuing wild experiences, but a piece of me still wanted to grow up, despite my aunt's reminder to slow down.

I smiled at a boy who shuffled past me. No clue if he saw me. Maybe next time he would.

Maybe high school wasn't a clean slate. Maybe it was just the next page in my story.

We stepped into the cafeteria and saw it was pizza day.

So, yeah.

Best day ever. (Until tomorrow).

Thank you for supporting indie authors and the stories they share.

Acknowledgements

Thank you isn't really enough to express how grateful I feel, but it's a start, so here we go.

My husband: Thank you for loving me with your entire heart and for allowing me to love you just as deeply in return. With you, everything feels magnified. I cannot wait to see what our future holds.

Corrine, Kyle, and Connor: You are quite possibly the best set of children anyone could ever wish for. Thank you for keeping life interesting and for always being down for a night of Grotto's pizza and scary movies.

My parents: You always reminded me I was capable of even my wildest of dreams. Thank you for blindly believing in me, even during my most stubborn years.

Gina: You are the most amazing sister ever. I am so proud of who we grew up to become and am grateful for our forever-strengthening friendship. Shout out to her company, @eatwellcollective, designed for anyone who needs help healing their relationships with food and body.

Who runs the world? GIRLS: In alphabetical order, as it would be impossible to place you in any other order. Amanda, Carli, Jessica: I have the most overwhelming love and appreciation for our friendships.

Significant teachers (who may or may not remember me by my maiden name, Consalvo): Rose Sottovia, my second-grade teacher (1996-1997), Lori Freeman, my high school English teacher (2006-2007), and Susan Magee, my English professor at CHC (2011-2012). You all played a significant part in developing my love for writing. You may not have realized you were placing a positive imprint on me, but please know that you did.

Kate Angelella at Engelella Editorial: I am beyond appreciative of your other-worldly editing skills and incredible insight. In reading your reviews, I saw a caution that warned if I work with you, I will become addicted to knowing what you think about my writing. Spoiler alert – it's true! I cannot wait to work with you again on future projects.

Madison at Love Lee Creative: Your brain is magic. I'm so glad I got to know you and work with you. Thank you for taking my chaotic thoughts and turning them into the most beautiful cover art I've ever seen.

Last, but certainly not least, to everyone who read early versions, and/or the final published novel: Thank you. Your support truly means the world. Stick around, there's more to come!

About the Author

Dana Harp grew up in central New Jersey where a fun Friday night was walking across the street from the only movie theater in town to the only Applebee's in town.

She moved to Pennsylvania after graduating from Chestnut Hill College with bachelor's degree in English and communications. She continued her education by earning her master's level certification in project management from Rochester Institute of Technology and her PMP certification from the Project Management Institute. She currently works in global operations for oncology clinical research; a career she would not trade for the world.

She lives a private life on the bay in Delaware with her husband, their dogs, and her three bonus children. If the sun is out, you can find them on their boat fishing for flounder or tuna, crabbing, or out raking the clam beds (Dana often takes the easy way out for this one and will tan while reading instead).

It was Dana's childhood dream to become a published author. *Growing Up Hadley* actually began as a 10-page short story she wrote at age 19. Now, she's proudly released *Slowing Down Amelia* – the second book in *The Moments That Make Us* series. While both books share the same world, each one stands alone with its own powerful story.

She will always remember that dreams never die, they just lay dormant until you're ready to make the leap. Thank you for reading and making the leap worthwhile.